QUEEN OF THE TILES

ALSO BY HANNA ALKAF

The Weight of Our Sky

The Girl and the Ghost

QUEEN

OF THE

TILES

HANNA ALKAF

SALAAM
READS

NEW YORK LONDON TORONTO SYDNEY NEW DELHI

An imprint of Simon & Schuster Children's Publishing Division
1230 Avenue of the Americas, New York, New York 10020

For information about special discounts for bulk purchases, please contact
Simon & Schuster Special Sales at 1-866-506-1949 or business@simonandschuster.com.
The Simon & Schuster Speakers Bureau can bring authors to your live event.
For more information or to book an event, contact the Simon & Schuster Speakers
Bureau at 1-866-248-3049 or visit our website at www.simonspeakers.com.
Interior design by Hilary Zarycky
The text for this book was set in Adobe Garamond Pro.
Manufactured in the United States of America
First Edition
2 4 6 8 10 9 7 5 3 1

Library of Congress Cataloging-in-Publication Data
Names: Hanna Alkaf, author.
Title: Queen of the tiles / Hanna Alkaf.
Description: First edition. | New York : Salaam Reads, [2022] | Audience: Ages 12 up. | Audience: Grades 7-9. | Summary: Fifteen-year-old Najwa Bakri is forced to investigate the mysterious death of her best friend and Scrabble Queen, Trina, a year after the fact when her Instagram comes back to life with cryptic posts and messages.
Identifiers: LCCN 2021045663 (print) | LCCN 2021045664 (ebook)
| ISBN 9781534494558 (hardcover) | ISBN 9781534494572 (ebook)
Subjects: LCSH: Muslims—Malaysia--Fiction. | CYAC: Scrabble (Game)—Fiction. | Contests—Fiction. | Grief—Fiction. | Friendship—Fiction. | Malaysia—Fiction. | LCGFT: Detective and mystery fiction.
Classification: LCC PZ7.1.H36377 Qu 2022 (print) | LCC PZ7.1.H36377 (ebook) | DDC [Fic]—dc23
LC record available at https://lccn.loc.gov/2021045663
LC ebook record available at https://lccn.loc.gov/2021045664

This one's for the word nerds.

(And for Malik and Maryam, of course. I'd never forget you two.)

AUTHOR'S NOTE

People talk about the stages of grief as if they're levels to clear in a video game, and once you hit the Final Boss Level and defeat the monster therein, you're free.

The truth is that there is no linear progression to grief. If it is a game, it is one that twists and turns and darts back and forth through many layers; one day it's easy, one day it isn't, and one day it attacks you out of nowhere just when you think you've moved on.

This is a book about Scrabble, and about murder, and about complicated relationships. It is also, in the end, about the many ways we cope with loss, and about beautiful, hideous grief. I trust you to know if you can handle that today.

And if you can't, there's always tomorrow.

For those who love to play Scrabble, having a good dictionary is key. The definitions used in this novel [largely—if not] derive from the Collins Scrabble Dictionary https://blog.collinsdictionary.com/scrabble/scrabble-word-finder/, a useful resource.

PROLEGOMENON

seventeen points

noun

prefatory remarks; specifically, a formal discussion serving to introduce and interpret an extended work

When Trina Low walks by, the world holds its breath.

Everything seems to stop as she saunters past: the click of tile on tile, the murmur of conversation, the occasional slap of a hand on a timer. Trina treats every entrance like a show, and she expects you to drop what you're doing and watch. And for some reason, everyone does.

She calls herself the Queen of the Tiles, a glamorous beacon in a sea of garden variety word nerds. Her tens of thousands of followers on Instagram love the image of Trina, in her tightest tops and shortest skirts, hovering in intense concentration over the board, the light gleaming faintly off what she calls her unicorn hair: tumbling waves of pale teal and pink and lavender that hang down between her shoulder blades in soft curls, a worn friendship bracelet in matching colors always tied around her delicate wrist.

Like most of us, you probably judged Trina the first time you saw her, had her pegged for some empty-headed fool who just wanted to mess with some Scrabble geeks. But it's all an act. She lures you in, and somewhere between the clothes, the hair and the perfume, the cooing voice and the soft giggles, you emerge on the other side of the game dizzy, confused, and the loser, usually by more than two hundred points. "She distracted me!" you say, angry and embarrassed. "She doesn't play fair!" "She just got lucky." Except, one glance at the board shows the work of a pro: a string of bingos (JOUSTED, OBVIATE, UNDERDOG, and the obscure CEILIDHS, among others) sparkling like well-placed jewels against the shorter words that she whips out of her vast arsenal with practiced ease.

Trina Low wears her gleaming, aggressive prettiness like armor and wields her formidable vocabulary with devastating precision. If you find yourself lost in the starry depths of her eyes or contemplating the gentle curve of her rear instead of focusing on her razor-sharp gameplay, you only have yourself to blame.

She takes her time making her way to the empty seat that awaits her at table four, swaying her hips as she walks between the rows of tables in her tight black jeans and high, high heels. As you watch, you see even the most hardcore players, the ones who barely look up from their word lists and anagram apps to notice what time of day it is, break out into a light sweat as she breezes past. Guys, girls, and everything in between, it doesn't matter. Trina gets to all of us.

Well, maybe not all of us.

At table four, Josh Tan sits in his seat, his arms crossed, glowering at Trina as she approaches. She doesn't seem to notice. "Hi, Joshy!" she says, leaning down to drop a kiss on his cheek. "Long time no see."

She ignores his sharp intake of breath at her touch, slides into the chair across from him, and flashes him that signature Trina smile, that crooked, dimpled little grin that hints at secrets and scandals, the one that lands her thousands of Instagram (and a handful of real-life) stalkers.

"You're late."

She rolls her eyes. "By what, three minutes? Relax lah, bro. Now smile!" She holds her rhinestone-encrusted phone up at just the right angle and tilts her head just so, hits the button, then inspects the photo.

"Seriously, Joshy?"

Josh coughs, a harsh, hacking sound that echoes through the hall. "My name is Josh, Trina. Not Joshy. Just Josh. Surely even you can manage words with a single syllable. And I'm not your bro. I'm not your *anything*."

She ignores him. "I've known you for what, five years now, Joshy? Always so grumpy. You couldn't just smile a little bit? Show off those pearly whites we know must be in there somewhere? If you just tried a liiiiittle bit harder, you could look positively . . ." She pauses, as though looking for the right word, before settling for: "Mediocre."

"Don't tell me to smile."

Trina's smile never leaves her face, but if you were watching closely, you might see it freeze around the edges, and a dangerous glint appears in her eyes. "Why not? Men tell me to do it all the time."

"Whatever. Can we start now please? This is a tournament for goodness' sake, could you not drum up the least bit of respe—"

"One sec." Trina holds up a finger, the nail perfectly painted shocking pink, a tiny gold crown in the center. Her eyes are focused on the little screen as she selects the perfect filter, taps out the perfect caption. "You wait ah. Hold it . . . and . . . done!" She sets the phone down and smiles brightly at him. "The Queen is ready. Let's go."

The game begins.

Every player knows that words can be twisted to suit your purpose, if the board allows it, and Trina knows this better than most. She is fantastic; she ignites fantasies. She is spectacular; she attracts spectacle. As games end, people draw closer to see the two of them duke it out over the board, which reads like a spelling bee word list: UVEA, ATEMOYA, ZEATIN, KUBIE, ETALON. Josh likes to think this attention is because he and Trina are locked in an epic battle for the lead in a tight championship, that it's because he finally has a shot at beating the Queen of the Tiles herself.

The only person he's really fooling is himself. Because, of course, all the attention is on Trina and Trina alone.

Which means that all eyes are on them when table four's

timer begins to beep loudly and insistently; a lot of people watch when Josh leaps to his feet, his fist in the air, whooping with joy; a lot of witnesses see Trina fall forward as if in slow motion, strangely graceful, her forehead hitting the fully loaded board almost exactly in its center, displacing tiles from their snug berths and scattering them across the table and onto the floor.

As bystanders begin to take in what's going on, begin to understand the meaning behind the arms that hang oddly by her sides, the eyes that now stare vacantly upon the ensuing chaos and commotion, the saliva that leaves a faintly glistening trail as it slides from her open mouth; as they slowly realize that Trina isn't just unconscious, that she is, in fact, dead; as phones are quickly whipped out of pockets and people begin taking pictures and videos, mouths agape; as the low buzz of chatter swells to a wave; as Trina's best friend, Najwa, crumples to her knees by the table, pale and disbelieving, and a girl named Yasmin begins to wail, Josh slowly lowers his arms and leans toward the officials who have begun to congregate in flustered, nervous droves around table four.

"So . . . this means I still win, right?"

CHAPTER ONE

Friday, November 25, 2022
One Year Later

INERTIA

seven points

noun

feeling of unwillingness to do anything

Most people play casual games of Scrabble in their living rooms, squabbling good-naturedly for points over sets their parents bought them in the hopes that it would be "educational."

No, actually, this is a lie. Most people probably barely even think of Scrabble at all, and the sets they do get wind up gathering dust in the very backs of shelves and cupboards, forsaken in favor of games like Snakes & Ladders or Monopoly or Clue or Twister. You know. *Fun* games.

The tournament circuit is a different world. Here, people play Scrabble as a game of probabilities and cunning strategies, a math problem to be solved. Here, we carry around reams of paper crammed so full of words it looks like they're teeming with ants; we recite anagrams with such rapid speed that each syllable hits you with the force of a bullet; we can tell you the most probable combination of letters you'll get on a rack (it's AEEINRT, for the record) with which you can score a bingo— that is, to use up all seven letters at once and earn an additional fifty-point bonus. Here, we never *stop* thinking about Scrabble.

For most of my peers, words are little more than point-amassing units, each tile merely a stepping stone for building high-scoring pathways to victory. For me, the words aren't just points: They're the whole point. I collect them, hoard them like a dragon hoards its treasure, reveling in their strange, alien meanings, the feel of them in my mouth. The words are how I process the world. People like Josh say I waste precious brain space clinging to their definitions. "There are one hundred eighty thousand possible combinations of letters you need to know," he told me once. "Caring about what they mean is beside the point." But how can you not? Take AEEINRT, for instance. Picture each letter in your head—the reassuringly symmetrical A, the graceful curve of the R—and rearrange them in your head, over and over again. Most people will settle for RETINAE or TRAINEE, but why go for such clumsy, obvious choices when you have the delicate wonder of ARENITE, a sedimentary clastic rock? That gives you the equally lovely CLASTIC—those bookending hard Cs so satisfying as they roll off the tongue—which means composed of fragments, and to FRAGMENT means to break into pieces, and that's what I'm doing right now, aren't I? Sitting here in the driveway of a generic three-star hotel, falling apart.

"What are you so afraid of, Najwa?" my mother asks. She's trying for a gentle tone, but the note of impatience that she can't keep from sneaking in kills that vibe. My mother has a fondness for things that endure: Birkenstock sandals, melamine dishes, old and usually racist actors who never seem to die. Tough things. Unbreakable things. She likes them low on maintenance, high on durability.

This is not me: One year later and I'm still a mess. Tiny things send me into panic spirals. I lose things. I forget things. I walk from one place to another and then have to walk back because I can't remember why I ended up there in the first place. It's as if Trina's death cracked me open, and now pieces of me keep escaping, scattering themselves everywhere. It's funny—well, maybe not to anyone but me—to ENDURE also means to suffer something patiently, and my mother is definitely suffering. My therapist has told her to respect my grieving process, but Mama's patience, like the cheap cotton T-shirts I buy from fast fashion retailers that she hates ("So low quality!"), wears thin fast.

I fiddle with the phone in my hands.

Me: She's so tired of me
Alina: So am I. Doesn't mean we don't love you, mangkuk.

Alina and I have been sending each other WhatsApp messages for the past few hours. She may only be fourteen to my sixteen, but my little sister knows to be on hand when I'm about to do something big, something that could potentially send me careening off-course.

Mama clicks her tongue now as she sits at the wheel of the idling car, waiting for me to reply, to pull myself together, to get my things and get out—or preferably all three at once, I'm guessing. It's been more than four hours since we left our home in Kuala Lumpur to get to this shining, anonymous box of a hotel in Johor Bahru where the tournament is taking place this weekend; this is more time than we've spent with just each other since I was about ten, and neither of us knew quite how to handle it. She tolerated my music for approximately twenty-three minutes (a playlist heavy on K-pop, indie rock, and Taylor Swift) before making me switch to her favorite radio station (playing "easy listening hits," which seems to translate to "absolutely no songs from the past ten years") for as long as it took to get out of range. Then when the music gave way to nothing but static, she made me plug in her iPhone so we could listen to some sheikh reciting Quranic verses. *Verily, in hardship there is relief.*

"It's a lot to take in, okay?" I fiddle with the friendship bracelet tied around my wrist, then pull the sleeves of my black top down low so only the tips of my fingers peek out of the edges. I'm always cold these days. "It's been a year. I'm just nervous."

"Nervous? Buat apa nak nervous?" Mama glances up at the rearview mirror and adjusts her deep blue headscarf. In her youth, she was a beauty queen; we have sepia-tinted pictures of her poised and smiling on stage, her hair lacquered to terrifying heights, her tight kebaya skimming her curves. Now she adheres to a strict regime of creams and potions designed to scare off any wrinkle foolhardy enough to try making its presence known. "There's no reason to be. You know this game inside out. You've been playing Scrabble most of your life, thanks to your father and me." (My mother likes to take credit for my word-wrangling prowess, such as it may be, because she and my dad bought me my very first set. "It will help improve your English," she told me on my eighth birthday, when the present I tore open so eagerly held my first Scrabble set instead of the long-desired Rock Star Barbie I'd begged for with the spangled clothes and the hot pink plastic guitar, and I had to bite my tongue to keep from saying something I'd regret.)

Mama continues, not waiting for my reply. As usual. "You're good at it. And you'll be with all your friends."

"What friends? I only had one."

Mama stiffens. Like most of the Malaysian parents I know, she doesn't like it when I bring up "sensitive" topics. She *especially* doesn't like it when I bring up Trina, which means I instantly feel like I need to yell it in her face: *Yes, that one, Trina, you know, my best friend in the whole world, the one I saw die right there in front of my eyes, at this very hotel in fact. You remember.* Mama never did like Trina. Oh, she never said so outright—she was much too big on etiquette, on keeping up appearances, on maintaining face for that sort of thing—but there was a telltale sniff any time her name came up, as if just the sound of it gave her allergies, and I'd catch her discreetly eyeballing Trina's outfits with distaste whenever she was in sight. Trina came with too many "toos" for my mother to stomach: skirts too short, tops too tight, tongue too sharp, gaze too knowing.

"Yes, well. That was a long time ago. Maybe this is what you need to get some closure."

CLOSURE, I think. A feeling that a traumatic experience has been resolved, but also just the act of closing something—a door, an institution, this conversation that is making my mother ridiculously uncomfortable. Only how can anything be resolved when we never figured out what caused Trina's death in the first place? No explanations, no conclusions, only a door forever ajar, letting a million what-ifs drift in as they please.

"Dr. Anusya says it's time for you to move on, get back to the things you love," Mama reminds me now. "And you love Scrabble."

It's true. I do. There was a time, after it all happened, when even the sight of a tile was enough to set off a tidal wave of anxiety sweeping through my body. But we've worked our way up to this point so gently, so carefully, from casual games in Dr. Anusya's plush office to local Scrabble club meetups to small competitions and now this, the Word Warrior Weekend that takes place every November during the school holidays: part elite tournament, part sleepover, all awkward teenage hormones and chaste, chaperoned social events in between. Scrabble is the one thing in which my brain hasn't failed me, and each remembered word is a life raft on days when I feel like I'm drowning. Nobody's dictating my pace here; nobody's forcing me to move on. I want to do this. I need to do this. So why is uncertainty gnawing away at the frayed edges of my nerves? "Maybe I'm just not ready yet," I say, and I hate how small my voice sounds.

As if Alina somehow knows how I'm feeling, my phone buzzes again.

You've got this, Kakak.

My mother checks her watch surreptitiously; I don't think I'm supposed to notice, but I do. "Come on, sayang. Berapa lama lagi nak hidup macam ni? It's time to get out of this cave you've built around yourself and get back to being . . . you." This time, the gentleness rings true, and my immediate instinct is to want to cry. Nothing undoes me quite like people being nice to me. She's right, and I hate that she's right, but I can't keep living like this.

"Yeah, okay," I say. I sling my backpack over one shoulder, check the front pocket for my signed permission slip, grab the duffel that holds enough clothes for the weekend. "I'll see you on Sunday."

"Have fun," she says. "Call me to check in." She gives me one last look, a slight frown on her face. "And fix your tudung. Senget tu."

I sigh. Of course her final words to me would be to fix my crooked headscarf. What else did I expect? "I will." The moment is over. I don't offer a hug or kiss, and she stares straight ahead because she doesn't expect either one; we're just not that type of family.

"See you," I say as I struggle to haul myself and my baggage, seen and unseen, out of the car. Grief is a heavy thing; it weighs you down, turns all your limbs to lead. There have been so many times in the past year when I've wanted to stop, wherever I was—in the cereal aisle at the supermarket, in the middle of doing jumping jacks during PE, in the middle of a shower—when I've had to fight the urge to just lie down, just rest, feel the coolness of the floor beneath my skin. Bet my mother would have hated that.

"Bye," she says.

I slam the door shut as if closing it tight enough will trap all my fears and worries and memories in there, as if shedding them means I, too, can become a thing that endures.

CHAPTER TWO

ANAMNESIS

eleven points

noun

ability to recall past events

step forward. The doors glide open. I step back. The doors glide shut.

I do this a few more times. I know the doorman in his sleek gray uniform with the gold trim is staring at me, and he's probably not the only one. I just can't make my feet go any farther, can't make them take that next step beyond the big glass doors and into my past. So I do this dance, feeling the weight of my duffel bag press against my shoulder, feeling the blast of too-cold air-conditioning brush against my face, feeling the surge of long-lost memories crash into my brain, as cars come and go and people mill past me.

I pull up my phone and open up my DMs on Instagram.

I don't know if I can do this without you.

Then I put it away again and stare at the doors before me. I'm not expecting a reply.

Do you know what happens when there's a sudden, unexplained death in a public space like a hotel? They call in the police, who drive up in trucks known as Black Marias even though they aren't actually black, but a deep, dark blue. They treat it like a crime scene. By extension, therefore, they treat you like a suspect—at least, until they have no reason to. Until you give them a reason not to.

Oh, they were very careful not to tell us that. We were fifteen-year-olds, after all. We'd just watched our friend die. We were a bunch of scared, confused minors they somehow still needed to extract information from. They tiptoed so carefully around us it was like being in the middle of a performance of *Swan Lake*. But we knew anyway.

Not that I was much help. A couple of hours after it happened, a very patient young sergeant took us each into one of the hotel's small meeting rooms. I watched familiar faces go in and out, one by one—though my brain, fueled by anxiety and running at a bazillion kilometers an hour, only really managed to register a trembling Yasmin and a stone-faced Mark—the sinking feeling in my stomach deepening with each one, waiting for that discreet tap on my shoulder, the polite request to "please follow me."

The room was cold. The sergeant was warm. The questions were endless: *Where were you when the incident happened? Can you tell me in your own words what you saw? Were you close to the victim? Was there anything off about her leading up to the game? Was she upset? Was she agitated? Did she complain of not feeling well?* I stammered and I stumbled, not understanding, not knowing what to say. It took me a while to even register that "the victim" meant Trina, and when I realized it, I started crying all over again. I was still crying when my mother burst into the room, shirt rumpled from the long drive down from Kuala Lumpur, hijab all askew. I remember taking in the sight of that hijab, the one clue to how absolutely agitated my usually poised mama was in that moment, and feeling my heart crack a little further.

"What is the meaning of this?" my mother had said, all of five feet one point five inches and yet somehow staring down the suddenly groveling sergeant. "Why are you harassing my daughter like this?"

"I'm just asking her some basic questions, puan. . . ."

"Questions? What questions? What right do you have?" She squinted up at him and I swear I saw him go slightly gray. "She is only fifteen years old! A fifteen-year-old who has just gone through major trauma! Can you even ask a fifteen-year-old questions like this without an adult present?"

"Oh, can puan, can," the sergeant says quickly. "It's perfectly legal, trust me."

"Trust you?" Mama folded her arms, her expression stormy. "Not bloody likely. Typical incompetence. Come, Najwa, we are going."

"We are not done here, puan!" the sergeant spluttered, and for a second I almost felt sorry for him. Bet he thought this would be a nice, easy gig, all done by teatime.

"You can give her time to regain her composure, and when she has, I will bring her back and sit with her while she answers your questions." She stared at him, daring him to disagree. "Will that do?"

The sergeant's shoulders sagged in defeat. "Fine, puan. That will do."

"Thank you."

She marched me out of the room then, one hand gripping my shoulder so tight that I could feel her nails digging into my flesh, just one more clue at how rattled she really was. We sat in a nearby café together in silence as she watched me swirl a spoon in a cup of vanilla ice cream until it melted entirely. When she brought me back, I'd stopped feeling the urge to cry at every mention of Trina's name—or at least, I could hide it enough to fool the casual observer—but I could remember nothing from that day, nothing at all up until I saw my best friend's face hit that board and felt the ground shift beneath my feet. What I got back came only weeks later, and in bits and pieces.

And here they are, still coming one year later. It's as if I'm following crumbs someone else has left behind for me, as if, by Hansel-and-Greteling my way through these barren woods I'll eventually find my way home.

I take a deep breath.

And finally, I step inside.

Immediately, I'm disoriented. There are simultaneously too many people in this lobby and not enough; I have all the noise-induced headaches and anxieties and none of the benefits of being able to melt into a crowd and enjoy that sweet, sweet anonymity. The local Scrabble scene is passionate but small; even after a year away, there are few faces here that I don't recognize. Some are converged in tight little groups, catching up on whatever they've been doing since the last tournament. Some are with parents who take the time to help them sign in, settle in, linger over their good-byes like they'll actually miss their kids. Some are hanging out on their own. But most are doing what they do best: playing some form of Scrabble. Around the biggest coffee table available, a few kids are huddled over a board playing Clabbers, a version of Scrabble where any string of letters is valid as long as it can be rearranged into a word. It's not my favorite—it's eye-wateringly confusing to look at a board and understand that ARFM is FARM and TIEX is EXIT, and it's just more of a headache than necessary to figure out that EDLINTU is DILUENT. I wonder if any of them realizes that to CLABBER means to cover something in mud. Ironic.

I hear Mark before I see him, hear that laugh I've heard so often, and I know when I turn around that his head will be thrown back, eyes squeezed shut, mouth wide open. So many people I know have timid laughs, tee-hee-hees, polite little things that don't want to take up too much space. Mark laughs with his entire body. He laughs like he *means* it. It's a sound that brings up the kind of montage of sun-washed memories you see in movies, with some kind of peppy soundtrack in the background: Trina and Mark and me, their perpetual third wheel, laughing our way through late-night McDonald's drive-through runs, tournament downtime, marathon *Lord of the Rings* viewings, word study sessions. Trina's dream Scrabble word was SYZYGY, an impossible, unplayable thing that requires you to have the Z, both Ys, and one of the two blanks. It means the perfect alignment of three celestial bodies. That's what it felt like sometimes, with us: three totally different planets, spinning in perfect harmony at the exact same time.

Mark laughs again and I quickly look away. The last time I saw him, his girlfriend had just died. Now I hear through the social media grapevine—I unfollowed ages ago, unable to deal with any more reminders of the way life used to be with Trina in it—that Mark's been parading a different girl around KL every other week. Some grief, eh? The juxtaposition between the carefree guy in front of me and the tear-stained one in my memories is jarring.

Be honest with yourself, Najwa. It's all jarring.

The truth is without Trina, I am untethered. We probably looked like a strange, unlikely pair to most: I am short where she was tall, plump where she was luscious and curved, quiet where she was loud, sour where she was sweet. My hair, when it isn't hidden away by my hijab, is shoulder-length and black, and that's all you can really say for it; it doesn't have the bounce and luster that Trina's had. My eyes are standard-issue brown; Trina hid hers behind a series of colored lenses that she chose according to how she felt that day, like ocular mood rings. It's not that I'm particularly ugly, I'm just ordinary. And that's okay. I've never wanted to stand out.

So I don't begrudge anyone their skepticism; we just didn't look right together, like Scrabble words that seem like they're made up, that shouldn't exist but do: APATITE, FANTOM, GREWSOME, PEEPUL. But the truth is that we fit, the way pieces of a puzzle can never be exactly alike because they're meant to complete each other. The truth is without her here to tie me down, I feel like I may crumble and blow away, nothing but dust mites borne on the wind.

Me: It's been five minutes and I already have regrets.
Alina: Stop it. Kill the ants.

The ants aren't real ants—they're capital A-N-T ANTs, or automatic negative thoughts, and every once in a while, they swarm all over me, nipping away at my insides. Every time I start to spiral—*I know something bad will happen*, or *This will never work*, or *I could have done more*—Dr. Anusya says I'm supposed to stop myself, squash the ants, clean up my mess.

Some times are easier than others. Some ants are bigger than others.

The registration line is long, but it moves fairly quickly, and I only have to wait for about fifteen minutes before it's my turn—which is good, because I can feel people starting to look my way, starting to clock my return to the scene, starting to talk. "Najwa," I hear in low tones that I try my hardest to ignore. "That's Najwa."

I sign in with a woman in an electric blue tee that clings to her body, the words DON'T PANIC! FORTY IS ONLY 11 IN SCRABBLE stretched tight and white across her boobs, "forty" spelled out in individual tiles. "Najwa . . . Bakri?" she says, running her finger down a long list of names. I nod. She makes a note and I hand over my permission slip, Mama's signature with its elegant swoops and curls scrawled along the bottom, the paper rumpled and deeply creased from the many times I folded and unfolded and stuffed it back into my pocket until I finally decided that winning would be the best way—the most *me* way—to honor Trina's memory. "So you know how it works, yes?" she asks, then plows on without waiting for my answer. "It's seven games today, starting at twelve p.m., then eleven games tomorrow, then six games on Sunday. Modified Swiss draw, King of the Hill in the last rounds. That means you'll be paired with opponents who have roughly the same ranking as you, based on your win-loss record in the tournament. First round is random; last rounds, the top-ranked players after two days will play against each other, so first against second, third against fourth, etcetera. You got all that?"

I nod. I'm annoyed she feels the need to explain all of this. I'm not a newbie. I'm Najwa Bakri. Sure, I've been away for a year and my memory is a sieve, but she doesn't know that.

She doesn't know I'm here to win, either. But she'll soon find out. They all will.

"Alrighty! Enjoy!" she says brightly, handing me a folder that includes assorted tournament info, a badge printed with my name in capital letters, and coupons for the coffeehouse just off the lobby. The tag pinned to her top says her name is HAYATI. This is also—surprise, surprise—spelled out in tiles.

"Thanks," I say, pinning my badge to my chest. "When will I know who my roommate is?"

"We'll post the list in a few minutes," she says. "Right on those bulletin boards over there."

"Cool."

I grab my things and stand off to one side, trying to stuff my folder into my bag. I'm preoccupied, but not too preoccupied to hear my own name.

"Isn't that Najwa Bakri?" I hear a girl behind me whisper.

"Yeah," her friend says. "I can't believe she came back." I bow my head, pretending to be engrossed in my phone, pretending I don't hear a word.

"What do you mean?"

"Well, with Trina gone . . . I mean, why would she come here after all that? And after all this time?"

"Maybe she just wants to play again." A pause. "She's good. Good enough to be the new queen, even."

There's a sniff. "She's not *that* good."

I look down and realize I'm clenching my fists so hard that my nails are digging into my palms, leaving half-moon indents in the flesh. *Just wait,* I think. *Just wait and see.*

CHAPTER THREE

POTHER

eleven points

noun

fuss or commotion

verb

make or be troubled or upset

After I'm done with registration, I just stand there for a minute, uncertain of where to go. When she was alive, I was Trina's shadow, always following behind; now that she's gone, with nothing solid to anchor myself to, I disappear. All around me, kids are acting like kids are supposed to; the sleek, modern benches and armchairs scattered all over the lobby are full of them, talking, laughing, shrieking at the sight of friends they haven't seen in months.

In the absence of anywhere else to go, I slide into an empty seat next to a girl named Emily, who smiles tentatively at me. I know Emily, although to be fair, this isn't some grand feat of memory on my part. Everyone knows Emily. Emily was caught up in a cheating scandal a couple of years ago and that's the kind of thing that clings to you like the smell of rotten durian.

You don't mention it—or at least I don't, I'm a good Malay girl, remember? So polite, so careful, so guarded—but you're always a little more observant, a little more careful, when you sit down at the board with Emily.

Across from us are—and here I crane my neck slightly to get a better look at their name tags, because I may be great with words, but names are one of those things that slip right through the cracks of my fractured memory—Shuba, who has written "(they/them)" in block letters under their name with black Sharpie, and Ben, who has "Singapore!" above his in barely legible writing. Singapore Ben is so named, as I recall, to set him apart from the lower-ranked KL Ben. Shuba has a mane of shiny dark curls, perfectly winged eyeliner, and lips painted a bright, look-at-me red that pops against their dark skin; Singapore Ben has floppy boy-band hair, skinny jeans with a discreet designer label, and too much cologne. His mother regularly drives him across the causeway for these tournaments. It's weird to remember these random things and still not be able to tell you what I ate for breakfast two days ago.

"Hey, Naj," Ben says easily, nodding in my direction. *The last time I saw you,* I think, *I beat you by 217 points.* Remembering feels good. "We're just playing Anagrams since we've got time before this whole thing starts. You want to join us? Seven letters and up only. What you do is, you call out the letters of a word in alphabetical order and then—"

"I know the rules," I interrupt. I can feel how tight my smile is, how forced. "Don't worry about me. I'll just hang out and watch." If one more person acts like I can't play anymore just because I've been gone for a while, I think I may scream.

Once they get back to their game and nobody is looking at me anymore, I grab my notebook, with its worn, cracked green cover and a black pen jammed into the rose-gold spirals looping over the top, and open up a new page. The notebook is like an extension of my memory, like buying more RAM to supercharge an overworked laptop. I take it with me everywhere, making a note of anything I don't want to forget. The last thing I want to do for this grand comeback is call attention to how broken I actually am. Carefully I write them down:

Ben: Singaporean, mommy's boy, overly familiar
Shuba: they/them, wildly glamorous, says exactly what they think
Emily: nervous, ladylike, that whole cheating thing

Then, job done, I put it away, sit back, and breathe it in. This is what I have missed: the words, yes, but also just being around people who are as passionate about the words as I am, who see the invisible threads on which you can hang individual letters and create magic. I wonder idly whether I should join in the game, in the name of "interacting with my peers in a healthy manner," which is something Dr. Anusya says I should do more. It just seems like so much work.

"My go, then," Shuba says. "AEFLNOPT." Their voice is raspy, low but sure, and they rattle off the sequence in alphabetical order faster than it takes most people to spell the word itself.

There's a pause. Then, from Ben, "PANTOFLE."

Shuba nods. *PANTOFLE,* I think. A high-heeled slipper, like the heels that were Trina's footwear of choice. Trina loved playing Anagrams, the way she loved any game she knew she could win.

I close my eyes. *Stop it, Najwa. Kill the ants. You're supposed to be enjoying this.* I touch the friendship bracelet on my wrist, soft yarn in alternating strands of pink and purple and turquoise and teal, woven together in a delicate pattern. Trina made us each one of these at the height of the friendship bracelet craze at our school, tongue poking out of one side of her mouth as it always did when she was concentrating, her brow furrowed as she worked. "There!" she cried triumphantly when she was done, freeing the completed bracelet from where she'd kept it clamped tightly in place between the jaws of her metal pencil case. "One for you, one for me." She tied it around my wrist, and I did the same for her. "Never take it off," she told me seriously, clasping my hand in hers, lacing her fingers through mine. "Promise me."

"Promise," I said. And true to my word, I haven't taken it off since, except to shower. Even though nobody can see it beneath the long sleeves I always wear, the softness of the braided strings against my skin is strangely comforting, as light and warm as Trina's touch on my arm. I tap out another DM on my phone:

I'm only doing this for you.

It's Ben's move. "EIIMNRT," he says. Then, to me: "How're you feeling, Najwa? You doing . . . okay?" His voice drips with earnest concern.

"I'm good," I lie.

A split second later, I hear "INTERIM" in Emily's crisp tones, just as Shuba says, "MINTIER." Emily's parents are divorced, and she inherited her English father's accent, rather than her Ipoh-born mother's Chinese lilt. She taps her fingers quickly on her knees; her smile is laced with anxiety. Emily never stops moving.

"Sorry, Shubs, I think Em got that one." Ben smiles, pushing his glasses up from where they've slipped down his nose. Much of what you need to know about Singapore Ben is contained in the fact that he is precisely the type of person who condenses people into single-syllable nicknames without their consent. "Nice job, Em. And I didn't even think you were listening." A flicker of irritation crosses Shuba's usually impassive face.

"I'm always listening, Benjamin," says Emily.

INTERIM, I think. *An interval, a stopgap, this rut I've been stuck in ever since Trina died.*

"So what do we think?" Shuba says.

"About what?" Emily picks absentmindedly at a scab on her elbow, and bits of skin flake away, floating slowly down to the carpet.

"About who the next ruler will be, of course." Shuba sits back, arms crossed. "Now that the Queen is no longer here to occupy her throne . . ."

Emily glances at me, discomfort shining from every line on her furrowed brow. "Maybe we shouldn't . . ."

"Oh, Najwa doesn't mind. Do you, Najwa? We're just talking, that's all."

"I don't mind," I say. I'm getting quite good at lying.

There is a sudden buzzing. "Sorry," Ben says apologetically as he quickly fishes his phone out of his pocket. "It's probably just my mom." We say nothing. Everyone knows Singapore Ben's mom is That Tournament Parent; she comes with him to every competition, forcing him to eat, massaging his shoulders between games, making snide remarks about his competitors. She hands him strong-smelling little jars of a dark liquid labeled Essence of Chicken, which she says helps with focus and concentration. Once, in the middle of a game with me, she came right up to us and draped a sweater over his skinny shoulders. "Sorry ya," she said, simpering at me and ignoring the pained expression on her son's face. "So cold in here. I don't want my Benny to get sick."

Emily clears her throat. "AABDNRU," she announces, enunciating each letter like she's a post–Henry Higgins Eliza Doolittle.

Without missing a beat, Shuba says, "BANDURA." They look at me as if they're appraising a painting for sale, as if the clues to my worth are hidden somewhere on the surface of my skin. "I'm telling you now, I'm damn well going to make sure I'm in the running for that top spot," they say, the lightness of their tone belying the whisper of steel I can hear on the edge of their words. "Not as Queen, of course. Something more gender neutral."

"The Monarch of the Tiles?" Ben chimes in.

He's rewarded with one of their expansive smiles. "Perfect."

"This all seems rather crass," Emily murmurs.

"Alright there, Miss Priss." Shuba smirks in her direction. "As if you don't want to win. As if that isn't the perfect way to stick it to all the people who still think you're out here palming tiles and peeking into bags."

Emily flushes a deep red. "I never did."

"Relax." Shuba begins gathering up their hair, tying it back with the scrunchy around their wrist. "I didn't say I believe the rumors. But what a perfect way to get everyone to shut up, don't you think?"

A BANDURA is a type of LUTE, which can either mean a musical instrument or to seal with cement and clay, like I've done to my own heart. Feelings, I've found in the past few months, are simply not worth the energy. But listening to all this now, I can feel hot flames ignite deep in the pit of my belly, reaching up to lick my chest. *None of you are worthy.*

This is why I'm here. This is why I had to come. I can't bear to see Trina's legacy picked over like this, her memory relegated to anecdotes about the tournament's tragic past.

She protected me while she was alive, and now that she's gone it's my turn to protect her.

"Excuse me, Miss Najwa?" I look up to see two kids standing next to me. They look like they're about thirteen, brimming with self-importance and shining with efficiency. "We were wondering if we could talk to you."

"Please," I say, "start by not calling me 'miss.'"

"Okay, Kak Najwa."

"AEDINOR," Shuba says. "Who are you?" they ask the kids directly.

The two of them tell us their names, but I just can't hold on to this information; they keep slipping through the cracks of my brain and so in my head I christen them Tweedledee and Tweedledum and desperately hope I never say so out loud. Tweedledee has a notebook in her hand, long braids, and the familiar lilt of a Sabahan accent; Tweedledum is an Indian boy with gelled spikes in his hair, too much body spray, and a camera trained right on my face.

"We wanted to ask you some questions, Kak Najwa," says Tweedledee.

"About what?" I ask. "Also, just Najwa. Please."

"About Trina Low," supplies Tweedledum helpfully as Tweedledee rifles through her notebook. "Not too many," she says cheerily. "Just . . . four pages or so . . ."

"ANEROID," Emily says.

ANEROID: relating to a barometer that measures air pressure. The main symptom of a sudden drop in air pressure is dizziness, and dizzy is how I feel because even though she's been in my head this whole time, there's something about hearing her name spoken out loud, the way it hangs in the air, the way it creeps under my skin.

"Trina?" It comes out as a croak, and I clear my throat. "What do you want to know about Trina? And . . . and why?"

"We're making a documentary," Tweedledum explains. "Think along the lines of the poignancy of, like, *Amy*, you know, the Amy Winehouse documentary? Or, like . . . like . . ."

"*Life Itself*," says Tweedledee, her voice muffled by the sound of the pen she's stuck in her mouth while she peers at her notes.

"Yes! A moving portrait of the Queen of the Tiles, an ode to her memory, but also . . ."

"An investigation of the chilling circumstances of her unexpected death," Tweedledee adds, her smile just a little too jaunty for my liking.

"CEEFIMORT," Emily says. "And that sounds terribly . . . morbid and unnecessary."

The Tweedles just keep talking, and I'm having trouble breathing. "So we thought as her best friend . . ."

"You'd have some amazing insights . . ."

"We want to strike the right tone, you know, nostalgic, emotional . . ."

"There's real potential for going viral here . . ."

Breathe, Najwa, breathe.

"FOCIMETER," Shuba says, jiggling their knees up and down, up and down.

A focimeter is what they use to make sure you've got the right prescription in your glasses, so you can, you know, actually see. Which I can't right now, because angry tears are making everything soft and fuzzy around the edges.

I'm surrounded by vultures, picking at Trina's remains until nothing is left.

"Are you okay?" Tweedledee leans in to peer closely at my face. "You look kind of pale."

"I'm fine," I manage to croak out. "I'm just fine." Except I'm not, because I can feel the telltale signs: cold sweat, racing heartbeat, trouble breathing. The ants swarm until my brain is covered in them, thick and black with no way out.

I'm about to have a panic attack.

No, not *about to have*. Having. I'm having a panic attack.

I bend low in my chair, trying my best to suck in air, trying not to drown on solid ground.

I didn't used to be this person. Dr. Anusya says all of it— the panic attacks, the anxiety, the weird memory gaps—they're all "symptoms of the incident," as if Trina's death is a disease I just can't shake, like a bad case of the measles. "Think of it as an amygdala hijacking," she said in her soft, sure voice. "The amygdala is the part of the brain that responds to fear, and Trina's death has heightened your baseline stress level so that every little thing makes your body think it has to go into full-on flight-or-fight mode."

"So when will it stop?" I asked her.

"When your brain decides there's nothing to fear," she said, her deep voice gentle. "When it feels like it's safe."

"Are you okay?" Emily's voice is high with panic. "Do you need anything? Wait, I think I have something that can help. . . ." I hear the familiar rattling of pills against plastic as she rummages around her voluminous bag. Emily has great faith in the power of supplements, from curing indigestion to improving your brainpower, and is always happy to share both her knowledge and her pills. In the background, I hear Tweedledee whisper, "Make sure you get this on camera!"

"It's a panic attack," a familiar voice says, and Yasmin appears, crouching by my chair, cool hands on my arm. "Can you look at me? Focus on me, Najwa."

I force my eyes to lock onto Yasmin's.

"Deep breaths."

I struggle with this the first couple of times, but eventually I manage. Just like I practiced in Dr. Anusya's office: breathe in for three seconds, hold for one, breathe out for six, hold for one, and repeat at least ten times, until I wrestle back control.

"Okay. Can you center yourself? Practice mindfulness?"

Every time someone says this—hell, every time I have to say it— I feel like I'm laying a wreath at the rose-scented altar of Gwyneth Paltrow's GOOP empire. But it works, as it always does. I fixate on the little things: the weight of the pink hijab on my head, the way my jeans feel on my legs, Yasmin's cool fingers brushing against my hot skin. I think about other words for panic: alarm, confusion, consternation, dismay, dread, agitation, hysteria, horror. I think about how horror also describes things that center on or depict terrifying, macabre events, like the sudden, inexplicable death of your best friend. I twist the soft, faded yarn of the friendship bracelet around my fingers as though its pastel strands are the only things tethering my soul to my body.

Eventually, I start feeling my body calm down. Sure, I feel like a piece of paper that someone crumpled and then dropped into a puddle: pale, damp, used. But I'm here. I'm still here.

"Better?" Yasmin is still peering at me intently, her expression all warm concern.

"Better," I croak. "Thanks."

"No problem, lovely."

Yasmin straightens up and beams at everyone else. "How are you guys? Isn't it great to be back?"

Have you ever been to one of those kiddie parties where the adult in charge has Planned Games and Prepared Prizes and is intent on making sure Everyone Has a Good Time? Yasmin has big Children's Birthday Party Organizer energy: fluffy hair, fluffy personality; equal parts energy and anxiety all wrapped up in an elaborate desire-to-please and topped with a big ol' bow of cheerful. Everyone, I find, has a word that suits them perfectly, describes exactly who they are. If Yasmin were a word, she would be COMPLAISANT: eager to please, obliging. She isn't someone I'd normally gravitate toward, but she was one of Trina's oldest friends, one of those grew-up-together, splashed-naked-together-in-the-paddling-pool type friends that you can outgrow but never truly leave behind, so we became pals by proximity. And frankly, I'm grateful for her presence now, that comforting familiarity yet another anchor that grounds me solidly in the here and now.

"So excited to be here," Emily murmurs, though she keeps shooting worried glances in my direction as if I'll evaporate at any moment.

"Just great," Ben says brightly. "How are you, Min?"

"I'm about to kick all your butts," Shuba drawls, not bothering to wait for Yasmin's reply to Ben, or even look at any of us as they scroll through their phone, a bored look on their face.

"Excuse me, I rather think I have a decent shot at this, really," says Emily.

I sit back and let their chatter wash over me. The Tweedles have melted back into the crowd. The cement blockades around my heart lie in ruins, shattered, exposing the tender flesh beneath.

The vultures are at it again, acting as if Trina's death was the gift they'd all been waiting for.

There was only one Queen of the Tiles. And I'll be damned if anyone else decides they're going to take her place or hitch their dreams of glory to her memory. I'll be damned if I let them use her that way.

So I guess that means I'll just have to win.

CHAPTER FOUR

AMBIT

nine points

noun

an area in which something acts or operates or has power or control

The hashtag popped up right after Trina died—#TheTruthAboutTrina—along with the many, many theories, both credible and conspiracy, surrounding the circumstances of her death. And even though the police had declared no evidence of foul play, the hashtag persisted. Trina's death was the subject of much feverish speculation. Depending on the time of day, the way the stars were aligned, whichever planet was in retrograde, the culprit could be anyone from Mark—he was a popular bet; it's always the boyfriend, isn't it?—to Josh, to Emily. And then, of course, the Internet favorite: me.

I've seen the comments. *Best friend looking kind of shady, no? Aku rasa mesti ada kaitan tu, orang pompuan kalau bab jeles ni . . . This girl looks like trouble. How much u wanna bet it's the bff lmao.*

I'd never taken them seriously, but they had driven Trina's

parents to distraction. "Why are they doing this?" her mother had sobbed to me over the phone two weeks after her death. "Why can't they just leave it alone?" There was a time when she called me every other day, sometimes to ask a question about Trina, sometimes to recall some recently unearthed memory, and sometimes to say nothing at all.

It's ironic, really, how much she seemed to care that Trina was dead when she cared so little when Trina was actually alive. Trina's parents are high-powered lawyers who work in the same firm and who had wanted a child right up until she was born, at which point they realized how much work it took to raise a little girl and decided the easiest solution was to hire other people to do it instead. Not to say they weren't nice people, but they usually operated under the assumption that if they provided ground rules, maids, chauffeurs, and enough spending money to keep a young sultan happy, this would make a decent substitute for actually being around. I'd taken plenty of rides in the sleek silver Mercedes-Benz driven by a kindly old man called Pakcik Zakaria and spent many pleasant days at their high-rise apartment being fed, watered, and generally waited on hand and foot by Maria, a gentle Filipino lady who had taken care of Trina since she was a week old. Maria kept a scrapbook in which she painstakingly pasted photos of Trina throughout the years, noting her accomplishments and milestones in barely readable cursive—first steps; first word ("bikit" for "biscuit," her favorite snack and also the name of the fluffy white Persian cat they used to own); the date her first tooth fell out; every first day of school, from age six to sixteen. By contrast, on her fifteenth birthday last year, her mother brought home a cake that said HAPPY 14TH BIRTHDAY TRINA in bright red letters. "Aiya, I could've sworn . . . ," she began, and we had to laugh it off as one of those aww-shucks mistakes right out of American sitcoms, all while shoving forkfuls of cake into our mouths.

Trina craved the messy, chaotic life I lived, crammed into a tiny house with my family, our neuroses forever colliding and spilling over for all to see; I yearned for her independence, her freedom, and the blissful silence of her gleaming, chrome-filled apartment. But life, like Scrabble, is like that—you get the rack you get, and you just have to figure out how to make do.

The rumors never went away, but the fervor surrounding them did die down eventually, and the phone calls died with them. These days when Mrs. Low sees me she always looks faintly embarrassed, as if the stench of her grief still clings to her, as if she wants to forget those calls ever happened. And I get it. Sometimes, I just want to forget too.

It's almost twelve p.m.

It's almost time to begin.

As I walk toward table seven, there is a fluttering in my stomach, a hammering in my rib cage. *I'm nervous,* I realize with a shock.

I've never been nervous to play Scrabble before.

The decision to come here wasn't one any of us had taken

lightly. Mama and Papa both spent the days leading up to it saying some variation of "Are you sure?" Even Alina got in on the act as she sat cross-legged on my bed and watched me pack with my usual organized approach, which is to perform a sniff test on various pants and T-shirts and sweaters and then, in the absence of offending odors, toss them into my duffel bag.

"Are you absolutely positive you're ready for this, Kakak?" She rubbed her nose, an unconscious gesture she's done ever since she was little, a habit that hints at her own discomfort. Alina and I have the same nose, a nose we got from our father: round, slightly too big for our faces, a nose that Papa says we have to grow into. It irritates my mother because in every other respect, Alina inherited her face—fine-boned, pale-skinned, full-lipped. She seems to think plunking Papa's nose in the middle of her features sullies them somehow. She doesn't seem to have the same qualms about me inheriting the same nose, but maybe that's because I also took everything else from Papa: my slightly stocky build; the brown complexion my grandmother used to lovingly call hitam manis—a sweet darkness, as though that made the comparisons to Alina easier to swallow. ("Tak payah lah," she'd say gently, trying to dissuade me from going outside to play in the sunshine with the rest of my cousins, "nanti gelap, takde orang nak kahwin awak," as if I cared about anyone wanting to marry me, as if I wanted to get married at all.)

"I wish you'd stop doing that," I said lightly, trying to hide my irritation. "I'm the kakak, you're the adik. I'm the big sister here, not you."

I tried to say it like I believed it, but the truth is that for the past few months, it felt like we'd switched roles. When I had my first panic attack, the morning of Trina's memorial service, I thought I was going to die. Afterward I refused to leave the house for a month, terrified that it would happen again. Alina sat with me in the living room with the curtains drawn and we watched every episode of *Gilmore Girls* from beginning to end, munching on murukku and rempeyek that my mother bought along with the groceries from the wet market every Sunday morning and writing a definitive ranking of who on this show was The Worst. (We disagreed on a lot of things, but number one was, of course, Rory. Always Rory.) Since then, she's treated me as if I was something fragile, something that needs protecting. It's something I am equal parts grateful and annoyed about.

"It's just that there's no need for this, you know. Like, pushing yourself to do this." She crossed her arms and regarded me steadily. Alina is capable of the world's most unsettling gazes, and she deploys them with devastating regularity. "Why would you want to go back?"

I remember staring at her, wondering how much I should say, how much of my true motivation I should reveal. I visualized telling her that I wanted to go back and win it all, continue Trina's legacy, honor our friendship. I imagined the way she'd wrinkle her nose, try to find the words to tell me how she thought this might not be healthy or rational, how becoming Queen wouldn't make any difference.

I didn't think I could bear hearing it.

So instead, I said, "It's like . . . remember when you first learned to ride your bike?"

Her eyes narrowed. "What does that have to do with—"

"Just hear me out."

"Fine." She sat back with a sigh. "Continue."

"When you first figured out how to actually do it, you were zooming around everywhere. Remember? You were so confident. You got to that point where you didn't even have to think about it, you were just enjoying it all. And then we got to your first hill."

Alina nodded slowly. "The one like two streets away from us. Near Auntie Nana's house. The road slopes up . . ."

"Right, and that was hard for you, and you got so tired and so sweaty. But you did it! Except when you got to the top and looked down . . ."

"I got scared."

"You got scared." I sat down and picked up my old Totoro plushie, patting the faded round curve of its belly. "We stayed up there for ages, me and you, and I kept telling you it was going to be okay, you could do it, that if you were careful and stayed alert you'd make it to the bottom just fine."

"You told me I'd feel like I was flying."

"I did." She grabbed Totoro from me and buried her face in his soft head. "I couldn't push you. You had to decide to do it yourself. But once you made that decision . . ."

She glanced at me. "I flew," she said quietly.

I nodded. "You flew." I got up and began to pick through

my pile of T-shirts. "I've spent the last few months working my way up the hill," I told her. "It took me longer than I thought. And I'm tired. And Trina . . . she's still dead. But I'm alive. And I'd like to feel free again. I'd like to feel what it is to fly."

The thing about flying is that the scariest part isn't soaring through the air. It's the moment that comes right before. It's making the decision to let yourself fall. It's surrendering yourself to gravity, knowing there is no turning back. Now as I stand here, taking in the scene around me, I find myself asking the same questions: *Are you sure you're ready for this, Najwa? Are you sure you want to fly?*

Carefully I slide into my seat. I grab my phone and send another DM:

> **First game. I'd ask you to wish me luck, but we both know that won't work. Still. Doing this for you.**

Then I set it aside and take a minute to tether myself to this moment. The smoothness of the tiles, the ridges on the board that make sure nothing slips out of place, the hard plastic of the chair beneath me—I close my eyes and center myself. *This game is yours. It belongs to you.*

When I open my eyes, my opponent is sitting across the table, staring at me with a baffled expression on his face. "H-Hi?" he says hesitantly.

"Hello."

"It's an honor," he says, and the admission surprises a small smile out of me. *They still know you. They still see you.*

"Are you ready to play?" I ask him.

"Yes."

And we begin.

It's the first game, so we draw tiles to determine play—he gets an F, I draw the O, so he gets to go first. He smiles when he sees me flip my tile onto the board. I can see the light bulb flash in his head. *She hasn't played in a year. I have a chance.* He's memorized the statistics, knows that the player who goes first wins 54 percent of the time, all things being equal.

But are we really equals here?

I don't know yet. But for the first time in a long time, I'm excited to find out.

I hit the clock to start his timer, and his twenty-five minutes begins. His first play is QUAY for thirty-two, a respectable enough move—it may be worth ten points, but the Q is nothing but dead weight. Best to get rid of it early on, in hopes of building a better rack, one more conducive to creating a bingo and padding out your score with those sweet, sweet extra fifty points.

I stare at my rack as my time starts ticking. DGOAESI. No bingos, and nothing particularly helpful on the board. I contemplate DIGS, lined up beneath QUAY so it also forms QI, UG, and AS, or SEADOG or GEOIDS, both of which would allow me to hook the S onto QUAY to form QUAYS, and make use of a handy double-letter and double-word score. The problem with that is that neither of them makes up for using the much-coveted S. The S and the blank are the best tiles you can draw in the game, and someone once told me that you shouldn't use your S unless it scores at least eight more points than your next-highest-scoring play, and you shouldn't use the blank unless it scores at least twenty-five points more than your next-highest-scoring play. The most any of these plays yields is thirty-six.

You can do better than that.

Then I see it. Grabbing my tiles, I slide them into place, one by one: first A, then G, E, S. QUAYAGES, a system of quays, straddling both a double-letter score for the A and that highly coveted triple-word score. Sixty-six points. I smack the clock, look up, and smile.

"Your move."

It goes on like this for a while. I fall into a steady, comforting rhythm. The motions are familiar and soothing; the rules are a language I speak fluently; the ants stay silent. Scrabble is a game of words, but its shape is defined by the mathematical precision of numbers: the fifteen-by-fifteen cell board, the one hundred tiles rattling around the bag, the point values printed in the right-hand corner of each one, the colored squares that denote double- or triple-word or letter scores. My opponent disappoints me; the first word turns out to be the only fleeting glimpse of strategy I get to see. Afterward he plays like it's his first time, producing limp, uninspired moves as he fishes for letters to make that one word that will yield big points, trying to close the board so that I won't get to the bonuses. I don't let him. The biggest difference between regular players and the elite is fearlessness. Why be scared of those spaces? The beauty of the game lies in openness; the best players find ways to dance across the board like ballerinas.

And oh, how I love this dance. The words flow from my fingertips—INCONNU, BAFFLEGAB, SYNOEKETE, ATIGI. After a while, I don't even bother looking up; I just stare at the board and think of all the different paths the tiles can open up to me. He takes forever to think of his next move, the hands of the clock tick tick ticking away, and in that time I've already plotted my attack. The final move merely adds insult to injury, and I almost feel bad about it; he misses an opportunity to block, allowing me to fork the board and create two separate quadrants where I can score big. There is no stopping me. I place my final tiles confidently, reveling in the satisfying click they make: HAZIER, through a floating E already on the board, with my Z nestled in a double-letter score and the R sliding into place firmly, finally, on a triple word. Eighty-four points. By this time a small crowd has built up around us, people quietly watching as we make our moves, and I bask in the attention that I would never crave otherwise.

"Congratulations," my opponent says. His face is gray.

"Thanks," I say. "Good game." I only say it to make him feel better. I have beaten him by 342 points. He walks away, melting into the crowd, and I bend down to gather my things. All around me there is a rustling, a swell of chatter now that the match is over. "She's the one to beat," I hear someone whisper.

"I guess we may be looking at the next Queen of the Tiles," someone else says. He laughs like it's a joke, but for just one moment, I let myself think it: *I'm back. And I'm going to do this. I'm really going to do this, for Trina. I'm the next Queen of the Tiles.*

It's the start of something, a loosening of the vise clutching my lungs in a tight grip, a breath long held and now set free. Time races past. I am me again, more me than I have ever been. I have six more games, and I win them all.

CHAPTER FIVE

WIDDERSHINS

nineteen points

adverb

in a direction contrary to the sun's course, considered as unlucky;
anticlockwise

Me: You'll never guess who my roommate is

Me: Go on

Me: Just guess

Alina: Gimme a hint

Me: It's someone who hates my guts

Alina: . . .

Alina: That's not a hint

Alina: hint. noun. a HELPFUL suggestion. a clue.

Alina: I thought you were the word person here

Alina: It actually needs to be HELPFUL

Alina: That could be any number of people

Me: . . .

Me: I hate you

I'm finally in my assigned room with my assigned roommate, and it's at this point that I decide that this whole tournament is cursed, because apparently, I'm spending this entire weekend sleeping in the same room as Puteri.

How do I describe Puteri? I once won a Scrabble game by 102 points playing NONPAREIL on my second-to-last move, using a NO already on the board to place that final bingo with a flourish. It was one of those moves with a set of circumstances so incredibly specific that it's almost impossible to ever replicate it, which makes sense, because NONPAREIL means excellence, a thing or person without equal. Puteri is what some people might describe as nonpareil, like one of those stone sculptures of goddesses they display in museums: beautiful and about as close to perfect as you can get, but also stiff, cold, hard, and plastered all over with DO NOT TOUCH signs. She also just happens to be Mark's ex-girlfriend. In fact, the rumor is that Mark cheated on Puteri with Trina before breaking up with her.

I never asked Trina if this was true, because I wasn't sure I wanted to know the answer.

To be fair, I don't really know how Puteri feels about me. But I've based my whole Scrabble career on reading people's tells, the tiny things that give them away, and judging from the pained look she gave me when I came into the room and the lukewarm "hi" she threw my way, my guess is she's about as excited about this as I am, which, on the Oh God Please No scale, ranks somewhere between "sitting through yet another viewing of *Frozen II* with my little cousins" (tedious but manageable) and "wisdom tooth extraction" (pain and suffering).

Since switching isn't an option—I checked—I guess we're stuck here in this box of a room, with two narrow twin beds and not nearly enough space between them.

"So, uh. How have you been?" I regret it as soon as the words leave my mouth. *What are you doing??* NUMSKULL, DUNDERHEAD, DIMWIT; there are dozens of high-scoring synonyms for "fool," and right now one of them might as well be Najwa.

"Peachy keen, thanks," Puteri says, not bothering to look my way as she unpacks her shiny, expensive-looking leather holdall and slips her shiny, expensive-looking clothes into drawers and onto the three hangers that dangle forlornly in our shared closet. She doesn't ask me if I need one. Maybe it's obvious that my travel style is less "carefully selected and displayed outfits" and more "rummage around depths of bag for wrinkled, not-too-obviously-stained T-shirt and yesterday's jeans."

"Cool." Why can't I stop talking? "Are you excited for the tournament?" Shut up, Najwa, SHUT UP. I touch my bracelet like a talisman. *Please, deliver me from my own mouth.*

She's draping her telekung carefully over the wooden back of the chair in front of the writing desk, and I can't help comparing its smooth teal sheen and intricate lace borders to the plain white cotton one buried somewhere beneath my clothes. Even Puteri's prayer clothes are perfect.

Her eyes flick my way for the briefest of seconds. "Sure," she says. "Can't wait."

"I saw Mark earlier," I offer, even as my brain tries to strangle my mouth into submission. "It's . . . been a while."

Puteri's hands still ever so slightly over the folds of the peacock blue tunic she's slipping onto a hanger. "Did you, now?" she says, her tone carefully casual. "I hope you had a pleasant reunion."

I cough. "We didn't really talk. Just kind of . . . saw him from a distance . . ."

She finally looks right at me for the first time, and when she speaks, it's in a voice edged with ice. "That's probably the best way to interact with Mark, don't you think? Take it from me."

Well. That was awkward.

I fall silent as I take off my scarf, grab my phone, and lie back on my bed. Before I can stop myself, I'm on Instagram. Specifically, I'm on Trina's Instagram. It's a habit I can't seem to break. I can already hear my sister's voice telling me to stop, but I've been practicing ignoring her lately. Most of the time it doesn't work. This time it does.

I scroll through her carefully curated images the way I do every day, several times a day. Mrs. Low wanted to shut it down weeks after Trina's death. At least two of those phone calls that came through in the old days had been to ask for my help. "What do I do ah?" she'd say. I could hear her crying as she scrolled past image after image of her daughter's perfect face.

"How do I get rid of it? I want to delete the whole thing." I tried to show her the links for memorializing a deceased person's page, or requesting for it to be removed altogether, but it was hard to get through the call without remembering that it was Trina who used to be her parents' tech support, and I was nothing but a poor substitute. Despite Mrs. Low's best efforts, the Instagram account remains, there for me to turn to whenever I need it.

Mama and Alina both think this reliance on a stale social media feed is an "unhealthy coping mechanism." I'm not even sure why I do it; I know I could never forget Trina smiling wide, throwing fistfuls of shiny tiles up in the air; Trina bent over a Scrabble board, her face scrunched up into an adorable frown; Trina in glasses she didn't need, flipping through the pages of a dictionary; Trina, perfectly made-up, perfectly lit, perfectly posed in every shot. I took most of these, straining to get the perfect angle, catch the perfect light, make sure the picture met her high standards. I took every shot multiple times, just to be sure. This isn't the Trina I know, not really—it's the shined up, highly polished version, served on a platter for the masses to consume. But it's better than nothing.

I slip into my DMs and tap out another message:

This is all your fault.

There is no response. There hasn't been for the past year. How can there be? I'm sending messages to a Trina-shaped void, nothing more than a username and a face I used to know. And Mama and Alina thought the scrolling was unhealthy. Wait till they find out I've spent the past year sending messages to nobody.

A delicate cough interrupts my thoughts, and I look up to see Puteri staring straight at me.

"What?" I say. It comes out more defensively than I intended, mostly because I feel like I've been caught doing something I shouldn't be doing.

"I said I'm going to Starbucks." She hesitates for a minute. "Do you . . . want anything?"

I guess we've decided to play this the polite way. "No, thanks."

"Okay." She pauses for a minute before heading out, the door closing with a firm click behind her. My sigh of relief rushes to fill the space she left behind. I grab my notebook and, to the bottom of my name list, I add:

Puteri: still perfect, slight possibility that she hates you a little less than she used to

Then I turn my attention back to Instagram, back to this perfectly posed and shot world, back to a universe where Trina Low still exists.

CHAPTER SIX

CATALYST

thirteen points

noun

substance that speeds up a reaction without itself changing

The weekend of "Stupendous Scrabbulous Fun!!!" the tournament promises in garish technicolor on its promo materials includes evening and nighttime activities to "allow players to chill out, socialize, and forget the stresses of the competition!!!!" I don't trust people who use multiple exclamation points in such cavalier fashion. I staunchly avoided this morning's opening ceremony with its upbeat speeches and endless icebreakers, and there's no way you'll find me within yelling distance of the scavenger hunt they've apparently put together for this evening ("Exciting Prizes to be Won!!! Come Have Fun with Ur Friends!!!!"). But I can't put off dinner—I haven't eaten anything since breakfast and I'm starving—so with many deep sighs, I haul myself off my bed, change, pray, drape and pin a fresh headscarf, and shuffle down to the hotel restaurant.

Me: i don't think i can do this

Alina: just think about how annoying it would be to hear Mama say "I told you so"

Well. Never let it be said that my sister isn't a great motivator.

I'm late—the schedule told us to be seated by eight thirty p.m., and it's almost nine now—and the restaurant is full by the time I get there. This was by design: I'm looking forward to pulling up a chair somewhere in the back of the room and stuffing my face in peace. Alas, Yasmin has other ideas. "NAJWA!" I hear her shriek over the steady hum of conversation. "OVER HERE! I SAVED YOU A SEAT!"

I try to figure out if ignoring her is an option, but she just keeps screaming my name and waving her arms and the way people are staring is making me anxious. So I nod in her direction and start making my way over. I notice the Tweedles perk up when they see me the way I imagine predatory animals do when they spot prey, and make sure to give them a wide berth. Yasmin has, of course, chosen seats right in the middle of the room, so I have to squeeze past what seems like miles of other diners, muttering a litany of "sorry, sorry, excuse me, sorry" under my breath, accidentally bopping the backs of heads with my canvas tote, grimacing at the harsh scrape of chair against floor when people are forced to move to let me pass.

When I finally get to the table, Yasmin gives me a big

squeeze during which I try to keep my arms as much to myself as possible. Then she pats the chair next to her. "Sit here, love, you're right on time."

The thing about Yasmin is that her affection seems over the top, until you realize she's an equal opportunity term of endearment deployer and will literally honey-sweetie-sayang-love just about anyone.

"Thanks," I say. I hadn't realized this was a formal thing, but there's a square card on the table that lists the menu (mushroom soup, roast chicken, cream caramel pudding, and a small note that says "please ask your waiter about our vegetarian options") and off in one corner, I can see a sound system being set up, so clearly there's a speech or two coming our way. What's worse, I look around and our table of ten has faces I recognize: Mark, busy pecking away at his phone; Shuba and Ben discussing last night's Manchester United–Arsenal game; Puteri next to Ben, arms folded and lips pursed; Emily, picking nervously at a hole in the hem of the otherwise pristine white tablecloth, her usual array of supplements lined up before her like sentinels in their plastic cases; a couple of other kids I sort-of-maybe-not-really recognize and whose names I'll probably never remember.

The final seat is empty. Yasmin nudges me and nods toward it. "For Trina," she says solemnly. The light glints off the unshed tears in her eyes. "To show we haven't forgotten her." She leans close, gripping my arm and whispering in my ear: "I miss her every day. Every single day."

The way she manages to inject such absolute sincerity into

her voice somehow simultaneously impresses me and makes me squirm. My grief puts me on one side of an invisible fence, apart from everyone else; it is isolating, immobilizing. Yasmin is on the other side of the fence busking her sorrow loudly to the world: Her grief is ostentatious, all-encompassing, in your face. I would literally give my right arm right now to be in my room, nestled in bed with some piping hot Maggi cup noodles—curry flavor, obviously—and a playlist of oddly soothing YouTube videos of people playing with slime on loop.

Get a grip, Najwa.

"Yup," I say. I can tell from the look that flashes on Yasmin's face for the briefest of seconds that she considers my response entirely inadequate, but before I can say anything more, she settles back into her usual expression of benign cheerfulness.

The speeches begin. They're the usual welcome, and nice-to-see-you, and haven't-we-done-such-a-wonderful-job-organizing-this-for-you platitudes, stiff as cardboard and about as interesting. Each one conspicuously avoids mentioning the sudden death of the tournament's star participant a year ago, but nobody in the room has forgotten it, and I can feel eyes boring holes in the back of my head as I sit there, Yasmin gripping my arm as if I may slide off my chair at any moment. And I hate this attention, hate being the subject of this scrutiny, but I feel like in some way, I have to deal with it. Because I'm the reason Trina got into Scrabble in the first place. I'm the whole reason the Queen of the Tiles ever existed.

• • •

Trina was a creature who fed on superlatives: first, most, best. It would have been easy to hate her for it, and maybe I did at first, just a little. But that was before I really understood her. So when she went from making fun of me for playing Scrabble to beating me at it, it was hardly a surprise. That's just how she was; she saw something she wanted and she went for it with a laser-sharp intensity that could border on the obsessive. All or nothing, perfection or perish. I started collecting Funko Pops and the next week she had a full collection lined up on her shelves and staring at us with their oversized heads and large staring eyes, all courtesy of Daddy's credit card, absentee parenting, and guilty conscience. I mentioned saving up for my very own pair of the Doc Martens I'd seen on so many glossy, sunlit influencer Instagram feeds; a few days later she turned up with the deep red, eight-eyed pair of my dreams on her dainty little feet.

So it was with Scrabble: I started playing and she howled with laughter, making fun of me every chance she got—"God, Najjy, you're turning into the BIGGEST DORK"—and then one day, suddenly she was right there with me, winning games, hearts, and entire tournaments with apparent ease.

At our first official game against each other, we shook hands formally across the table, laughing as we did. "You still going to be my friend after I beat you?" she asked me, her head tilted to one side, winking a big, exaggerated wink as if to say *Of course you will, Najjy, we're always going to be friends.*

"Absolutely not," I told her, laughing to show her that I was in on the joke, to show everyone that I didn't really mean it, of course I didn't. Why would I? I had nothing to fear. I'd been playing Scrabble since I was a kid. It was clear I was going to win.

You'd think I, of all people, would know not to underestimate Trina Low. But I fell into the same trap so many others did. I severely underestimated her vocabulary, the way she maneuvered the board, the way she made plays that forced my own. Given a rack like BIMOOX and a blank, most people would have played BOX or OX—MOXIE, if there was a spare E on the board—and waited for better letters in the next turn. Trina saw two unconnected Cs on the board with seven spaces between them and played COXCOMBIC with the M nestled on a triple-letter score. Seventy-nine points. A COXCOMB is a jester's red-striped hat, but there's another, obsolete meaning: a fool. And that's what she played me for, reading me as if I was an open book, anticipating what I'd do as though she knew me better than I knew myself.

She won by forty-two points.

"Still friends, Najjy?" she asked afterward. In her eyes, in the lift and swell of her voice, I detected a hint of worry.

"Still friends," I said, and we went out for fries and milkshakes as if nothing had ever happened, as if the world hadn't shifted and realigned itself once again in Trina's favor, as it always did.

"Najwa?"

I shake myself out of the grip of my memories and back to the here and now, where Yasmin is smiling widely, expectantly at me.

"What?"

"I said I'm just so glad to be back here," Yasmin says, as bored-looking waiters begin passing out hard dinner rolls and lumps of cold butter. "And I'm glad you're here too, sweetie." She reaches out to squeeze my knee as I tear off a piece of bread and pop it into my mouth, trying hard not to think about how much this annoys me, how little I want to be touched. "Only I do think it's slightly crass to still be competing, after all that happened . . . We could have turned this into a memorial weekend, just spent time playing together and honoring her memory . . ."

"Speak for yourself," Puteri says quietly from across the table.

"Yeah," Shuba chimes in, arms folded across their chest. "I'm here to win, not mope."

Yasmin glares at them. "That is incredibly disrespectful."

Shuba shrugs. "I'll say it's in her honor if that makes you feel any better."

Vultures, I think. *Vultures, ready to swoop.*

"It does seem like it might be best if we all just got on with it," Emily ventures timidly. "You know. Get back to some semblance of normalcy? I, for one, quite missed all this wonderful buzz and camaraderie. . . ."

Mark, I notice, says nothing at all as he sits scrolling through his phone and ignoring the conversation.

"Camaraderie my foot," Yasmin sniffs. "Some community this is turning out to be. What a bunch of selfish—"

"Hey now," Ben jumps in. "There's no need for that. We

all miss her, but we're here because we love the game, and I'm pretty sure all of us would be lying if we said we didn't want to win." He makes an attempt at a jovial grin, the kind of grin that tries to nudge you into grinning back. The kind of grin that tries too hard. "Even you must have that competitive streak in you somewhere, Min."

"It's Yasmin," she snaps at him, and we all jump, because seeing Yasmin angry is a bit like seeing a bunny bare fangs. But Ben should have known better; nobody ever called Yasmin that but Trina.

"Sorry," he mumbles, shifting awkwardly.

"I cannot believe the nerve of you people." There's a glint in her eyes I've never seen before, the kind of spark that you see when you strike a flint. "None of you are worthy of the kind of success she had. None. And if you think I'm going to let you just take everything she built for herself . . ."

"And what do you propose to do?" Shuba asks. "Stop any of us from winning? Because the only way you can do that, sayang, is by beating us all."

Yasmin stares straight at them. "Watch me."

Shuba snorts. "Delusional," they mutter under their breath. "She's delusional."

"Right." This is getting to be too much for me, and I'm literally just here for the food. Time for a subject change. "I think we can all agree that the past year has been tough—though tougher for some than others—and just being back here, being together . . . that feels good, you know?" I clear my throat, suddenly intensely aware of the eyes on me. "I'm just . . . really looking forward to playing some Scrabble. Everyone ready for the tournament?" I'm not that invested in their answers, but I want to be done talking about me, and one thing that Trina taught me is that people are always perfectly happy to carry on a conversation when they get to talk about themselves. And it works, as it always does. People start talking animatedly about word lists and new mnemonics, and the table groans as Josh— sitting at the next table, but alas, close (and loud) enough to hear—launches into a detailed explanation of his new training regime. Yasmin subsides into silence, her face a thunderstorm. As I watch her, I feel a twinge in my chest, a flicker of recognition. We're both here for the same thing, I realize. The same person. And for maybe the first time ever, I feel a sense of kinship with Yasmin that I didn't think was possible.

My job done, nobody notices when I take out my phone and start scrolling, looking, as usual, for Trina's profile. I promised Alina I'd stop doing that, but you know, she isn't here, is she? And I am, and this night is already proving unbearable, and I just want to see Trina's face right now.

Only it doesn't take me long to find it at all, because it's right there at the top of my feed where it has no business being, that familiar profile photo of Trina in pale pink heart-shaped sunglasses, smiling and happy in the Kuala Lumpur sunshine. I know that picture. I took that picture.

Dead girls don't post social media updates.

I don't even pause. My finger trembles as I scroll down

to see the image, to read the caption that comes with it, but I couldn't stop it even if I tried.

A Scrabble board. Jumbled tiles nestled in those familiar ridges. ICEDRGIE. And the caption, in all caps: *LONG LIVE THE QUEEN*. My brain, usually so quick to find the patterns, to string the letters together, to crack the code, feels swollen and heavy. I suddenly realize how sweaty I am, how hard it is to breathe. I can feel the ants nibbling away at the periphery of my brain. *Calm down, Najwa. You don't need this right now.*

"Najwa?" Yasmin is peering at my pale, sweaty face. The waiters have presented us with the next course, a watery bowl of what the menu says is mushroom soup, and mine sits congealing and untouched before me. "You okay, hon? What's the matter? Is it another panic attack?"

I can't speak. I just shove my phone in her face. I hear her gasp, and as she begins to tell the others in frantic whispers what the hell is going on, I can sense the mood at the table change palpably.

But I don't care. I need to focus.

I close my eyes, one finger caressing the tight weave of my friendship bracelet. In my head, the Scrabble tiles move slowly into place. DEICE RIG, which is what it feels like I'm doing, thawing out the frozen mechanism of my brain, trying to get it to work the way it should. Another: ICE DIRGE, appropriate enough: a funeral lament for a body now long stiff and cold. The tiles shift again, and I can almost see it, I'm almost there, I'm so close . . .

"REGICIDE," someone says, and I snap my head around to look at whose voice that is.

It's Josh.

I nod. "Regicide," I say softly.

"What?" Ben is looking back and forth between us like he's at Wimbledon.

"The letters. That's what they spell."

There is a pause. I see Emily moving her lips silently. "Twelve points," she says.

"That's not bad," Shuba says thoughtfully, taking a small sip of their soup. "Especially when you account for the bingo bonus, assuming these are all tiles from one rack . . ."

"Eight tiles, though," Ben points out. "Means there's at least one already on the board, possibly even two or three. Like what if they hooked it on ID, y'know? They'd only have used six tiles. No bingo then."

Are they serious right now? "Stop," I snap. "Don't you know what this means?"

"Najwa." Puteri leans back and regards me coolly. "You must realize by now that nobody knows or cares what these words mean but you."

I ignore her. "REGICIDE means the killing of a monarch. Like a king. Or . . . or a queen."

"The Queen of the Tiles," Yasmin whispers.

Josh snorts. "That stupid nickname. I can't believe people are still using it. You'd think now that she's dead people would—"

"You're missing the point," I snap. "It's REGICIDE. It's

not the *death* of a queen. It's the *killing* of a queen." I can't believe I have to say this aloud, but I take a deep breath and do it anyway. "It's murder."

Around us, the noise has gotten even louder; when I listen, I can hear fragments like "Trina" and "Instagram" and I know that everyone else has seen what I just saw, is figuring out what I just did. I catch a glimpse of Mark's face across the table, his eyes glued to the phone in his hand, his wide mouth a hard, thin line, every trace of laughter gone.

"Who do you think did it?" Emily says softly.

"The murder or the message?" Puteri murmurs. I'm not sure anyone hears her but me.

"Impossible to know," Ben says, leaning back and crossing his legs. "But I'm sure it's just a prank. Someone who knew there's a competition this weekend and wanted to create some drama."

"It's so tasteless lah," Shuba says, wrinkling their nose. Their thick curly hair has started to escape the scrunchie holding it in place, and they begin the process of tying it back all over again. I take a deep breath to try and recenter myself, and catch a faint whiff of coconut oil. "Why would someone do that? It's been ages, anyway. Why would they—"

"A year," I interrupt them, closing my eyes. "It'll be exactly a year. On Sunday."

There is silence at our table.

"A coincidence, I'm sure," Yasmin says, though the jollity in her voice sounds forced. "It's just a prank, like Ben said!

Now let's just ignore it and focus on having an amazing tournament. And celebrating Najwa's comeback!" She leans over to give me an awkward side-hug. "It's been too long, sweetie. We missed you. Didn't we?"

She hits the others with the full force of her Birthday Party Organizer vibes, and they all mutter their agreement.

"See?" Her smile is so bright it actually makes my head hurt. "Nothing to worry about, hon. Just enjoy this weekend. Okay?"

"Okay," I say. They're right. I know they're right. It's just a prank. Dead girls don't post social media updates, right? But as I look around the dim hall, at the strange, familiar faces of my friends bent over their cell phones, illuminated by the bright light of their screens, there's only one face I can see clearly, one face looking straight at me, intense and unblinking, instead of at the image that just turned our whole world upside down.

Josh.

I can't stop the feeling of cold dread that settles into the pit of my stomach, the feeling that tells me *this was a mistake, Najwa. This whole weekend was a mistake.*

SUBSTRATUM

fourteen points

noun

that which underlies something, as a layer of earth lying under another

awake in the eerie stillness of dawn, panting and drenched with sweat, thanks to a series of WhatsApp messages from my mother:

Good morning 🌞 ☺ 😊 how is competition so far. Winning? Otherwise cannot come home ha ha ha
Jk
alina told me that means just kidding
eat a good breakfast
Call u l8ter

And then, just as I'm reading the third message, the classic:

Why never reply

I'm not sure what punctuation ever did to my mother, but apparently they're no longer on speaking terms.

I groan and roll over, shoving my phone back under my pillow. I barely slept last night, and what sleep I had was taken up by strange, vivid dreams that I can't seem to remember, but that seem to cling to me even now, like barnacles on a shipwreck. Dr. Anusya says before I go to sleep I'm meant to think of at least three good things that happened during the day, "so it sets your brain up for positive dreams and more restful sleep." So what three things did I think about last night before I fell asleep?

1. Trina;
2. Who could have possibly hacked into Trina's Instagram account;
3. Why they'd play the most tasteless prank of the century on all of us

My mind won't stop whirring. I think about Ben's strangled laugh as he'd tried to play off last night's Instagram incident—"It's just someone's terrible idea of a joke lah, Najwa, relax." I think about Yasmin's openmouthed shock, Emily's dainty exclamations of dismay, Shuba's contemplative mutterings as they formulated possible explanations, the looks on the faces of the two younger players who were desperately excited at this unexpected turn of events but far too polite to show it. I think about the tiny flicker of something—but what?—I saw cross Mark's face before he rearranged it into a perfectly blank expression.

Most of all, I think about Josh. I think about the intensity of his gaze, how he was the only person at the table not looking at their phone. I think about how quickly he came up with the answer I was looking for, how easily REGICIDE fell off his tongue. If they were there, then whoever posted the image would have been the only person in the room who didn't have to be on their phone, right? They wouldn't have needed to. They could look around the room, enjoy seeing the chaos they'd created.

Like Josh.

Stop it, Najwa. You're reaching.

I roll back onto my side as the sun slowly begins to rise over the cusp of the world, wondering if I should just skip breakfast and go back to sleep, when I glance over to the bed next to me and realize where Puteri should be is just an empty space.

I sit up and look closer, squinting in the dim light, trying to make out a silhouette that isn't there. . . .

"You missed it."

I whirl around, my heart pounding so hard I think it may combust. Puteri is standing at the foot of my bed, staring straight at me, clad in her telekung, the long, loose prayer garments making her look exactly like a ghost.

"What?" is all I can bring myself to croak out.

"You missed Subuh." She nods to the digital clock on my bedside table. The glowing red digits show 7:02 a.m. "You're going to have to make it up later." She turns around and begins to take off her telekung, folding it neatly, smoothing out the nonexistent wrinkles as she goes. She's already dressed for the day: skinny jeans, royal blue top. Despite the early hour and the lingering dredges of panic still clinging to my belly, it doesn't escape my notice that Puteri looks like she belongs in a commercial for something like shampoo or toothpaste or sanitary pads—pretty in that wholesome, clean, good-girl way, like she rolled out of bed with perfectly styled hair and glossed lips and smelling daisy fresh from head to toe. I'm suddenly very aware of the toxic fumes escaping my mouth and clamp my lips firmly shut.

"I tried to wake you," she continues as she sits down and begins combing invisible tangles out of her long, straight hair. "But you refused to open your eyes. And you were tossing and turning a lot." Her eyes catch mine in the mirror. "Night-mares?"

"I don't remember," I say honestly. "Maybe."

"Maybe you're just nervous for this weekend." She leans toward the mirror to inspect a spot on her chin, frowning slightly. "It's been a long time."

"I did just fine yesterday," I point out. "And I don't get nervous when I play." This, too, is the truth. I may have felt a little shaky before I began playing yesterday, but everything fades away when I'm at the board. Scrabble doesn't make me nervous. It's the people that I find challenging.

"Must be another reason for those nightmares, then." This time her glance lingers. "Trina, maybe?"

It's weird to hear her name come from that mouth, and I feel a strange twist in the pit of my stomach. "Mmm," I say. It's the equivalent of a conversational full stop, an oral Gandalf:

You shall not pass. And I know from the look on her face that she gets it. But that doesn't stop her muttering something just before she heads out the door, something she probably doesn't want me to hear, but I hear anyway.

"She's certainly mine."

In the blessed silence Puteri leaves in her wake, I take deep, shaky breaths and try and rein in my racing thoughts, my tattered emotions. Then I turn my attention to Trina's Instagram.

Every post has thousands of likes and comments, most of the newer ones a string of bland condolences and well wishes: *RIP beautiful. u will always be our QUEEN.* Line after line of hearts in every color of the rainbow, interspersed with crying face emojis. *I can't believe you're gone. Kenapa lah tuhan ambik yg muda2 ni dulu. I don't even know you but I miss you so much.* And then, because not even death can stop spammers, comments shilling weight loss supplements and colored contact lenses. In one of my very first small tournaments—open to the public, mixed age groups, very casual—my opponent, an older lady with graying hair in a tight bun who reeked of cigarette smoke played EXEQUY. I must have had a puzzled look on my face, because she leaned close, almost choking me with the smell, and whispered hoarsely: "Funeral rites, my dear. It's got to do with funeral rites. It's a real word, don't waste a challenge on it." After the game, I looked it up just to be sure, and there it was, just as she said: EXEQUY. Funeral rites, a ceremony, a procession, a funeral ode. I suppose it's only logical that social media darlings, then, must beget social media exequies.

I pause. My thumb hovers over that jarring new post, a year after her death: LONG LIVE THE QUEEN. The comments are divided into two camps: There are the ones who assume the whole thing's a prank, who are spitting mad about the desecration of Trina's memory: *What does this mean? Orang mati pun boleh main insta ke. Who is doing this? This is so SICK. Gila ke apa. Leave the dead alone!*

Then there are the others. The ones who believe. *I knew it all along. See? There was something fishy about the whole thing. Kenapa polis tak siasat ni betul-betul?? Kesian nau keluarga dia. Come on lah, cannot be that a strong, healthy girl just can so suddenly drop dead like that. Where there's smoke, there's fire.*

For a moment, I find myself wavering. Where there's smoke, there's fire . . .

Stop it, Najwa. It's a silly trick. A prank. That's all it is.

Still . . . I pick up my notebook and on a fresh page write *REGICIDE* in block letters. *Just in case,* I think. The tricky thing about memories, after all, is that you don't really know which of them is important until you need it.

Then I pick up my phone and bring up my list of favorite contacts. I scroll past the listings for Mama, Papa, hovering ever so slightly above Trina's name before moving past it to Alina. I need a sisterly kick in the pants to bring me back to reality before today's games. But before I can make the call, I hear it: a familiar swooshing sound, one I haven't heard in a long, long time. One that makes my blood freeze in my veins.

It's the sound of a direct message coming into my Instagram inbox.

For a second my mind goes blank. My socials are all set to private; nobody can DM me except friends. Friends like . . .

Like Trina.

My hands start to shake uncontrollably.

There's no greeting, no preamble. It's a reply to my last message, the one I posted late last night:

Why is this happening?

And there it is, an answer to my question:

Because it needs to.

WHO ARE YOU????

I'm typing so furiously I feel like I may break my screen.

ANSWER ME, I say.
WHY ARE YOU DOING THIS??? I say.

And I wait, and I wait, and I wait.

But there is no response.

"It's a prank," Alina says almost aggressively. "It can't be anything else but."

"I know," I say. If we all say it often enough, maybe it'll dull this strange fluttering in my chest. My hands are still shaking, but I don't tell her that, just like I don't tell her about the DMs.

"Kakak." Alina's voice softens, and I hate this, hate how our roles have reversed, how she has to be the one to take care of me, and most of all how much I need her to do it. "She's dead. You know that."

There it is, that flare of anger blazing from the depths of my belly. "Of course I know that. I'm not *that* far gone."

"I never said you were." She's immediately contrite. "I just mean . . . don't give idiots more importance than they deserve."

"Sometimes you talk like a fortune cookie."

"That doesn't mean I'm not right, mangkuk."

I snort. "Have some respect for your elders."

"Have some respect for yourself first." I hear her rummaging around, the familiar dull clink of pencils rattling together. "I have to go. I have tuition today. One whole hour with Mr. Foo. Mama is on the warpath about my sejarah grades. Why do I have to care about history anyway? It's stuff that *already happened*."

"Because you have to know where you've been to know where you're going," I say, rubbing my eyes. I'm exhausted.

"Deep." There's a slight pause. "Are you going to be okay?"

I take a breath. "Sure," I lie. "Just on my way down to breakfast. Talk to you later."

The first people I see hanging around the entrance to the coffee shop where the food is being served are the Tweedles.

"Kak Najwa!" they cry in unison.

"Hey," I mumble. I'm trying to get past, but they're in my way.

"Can we ask you some questions?" one of them says perkily.

"Yeah, can we ask you some questions?" the other says.

"It's about Trina."

"And those Instagram posts."

"It won't take more than a couple of minutes."

"We're very efficient."

"Please?"

It's a little bit like watching an intense badminton game, listening to these two go back and forth like this. "No," I say abruptly, swatting away the creeping ants. "No, thank you," I add, as if they're doing me some kind of favor. I don't want to be impolite, after all, but I can already feel anxiety tapping on my shoulder, and the last thing I want to do is give it a way in.

"Oh, but please," Tweedledee says. "You'd be such an important voice."

"So necessary." Tweedledum nods. "And the hits we'd get! Have you seen the first video in our series?" He taps quickly on his phone and shoves it in my face. "See?"

I glance at the video, which has Josh wearing a grim expression in the thumbnail and is titled *Trina Low: One Year Later— The Last Person She Ever Spoke To.*

"*Him?*" I spit out. "Of all the people you could talk to, you chose *him?*"

"He was very willing," Tweedledum says defensively, taking his phone back.

"*Really??*" I frown. "I find that hard to believe." Josh does nothing unless it suits him.

"Well." Tweedledum rubs his nose. "Maybe more like . . . he wasn't actively *un*willing."

"And he was the last person she ever spoke to," Tweedledee chimes in.

"Yeah, I got it. Saw the title and everything." I think I may throw up. "Count me out. I'm going to eat now."

The Tweedles exchange glances. "We'll come back to you once you've had your breakfast," Tweedledee says.

"Don't bother," I toss over my shoulder as I head for the nasi lemak. I can't deal with *anyone* on an empty stomach, much less bargain-bin Sherlock and Watson.

I try my best to concentrate on my food, shoveling spoonfuls into my mouth and barely tasting them. But now that I've seen the Tweedles, now that I know what they're up to, they're impossible to miss. I keep looking up and seeing them, whispering together in the corner, talking to other competitors, and always, always looking at me with smug, knowing eyes, as if they see me, really see me. And I don't like it. I don't like it at all.

CHAPTER EIGHT

ATARAXIA

fifteen points

noun

calmness or peace of mind

head for the tournament hall at 8:15 a.m., fifteen minutes before the first games are due to begin. I have eleven games to get through today, and I want to be ready. I want to win. I want to make sure nobody else gets their grubby hands on Trina's title, that nobody else gets to call themselves the Queen of the Tiles ever again.

I stand in the doorway and take it all in. I don't know about everyone else, but I always remember the words I lose on. Well, that's not entirely true—I remember most words anyway. But the words that were my downfall tend to stick, like bad smells or wayward ghosts, whispering their definitions constantly in my ear. In 2014, Emily beat me by clearing the last six letters on her rack to spell ATARACTIC, and annoyingly, she did that by hooking onto a word I'd placed on the board myself, TAR, which made sense, because now I was stuck as she swanned ahead to victory. ATARACTIC:

an ability to calm or tranquilize. I haven't forgotten it since.

I remember it now as I breathe in the lightly perfumed hotel air and survey the familiar sight of the tournament hall: the rows of tables set up with timers and shiny Scrabble boards, the unopened green velvet bags filled with infinite possibilities of tile combinations. My pulse steadies, my mind clears, something loosens in my chest and breathing works again. I know the relief is temporary, but grief, I'm learning, is a burden you carry your whole life, and a smart person would welcome any breaks they can get.

Unbidden, the ghosts of comments past worms their way into my consciousness. *Best friend looking kind of shady, no?* And for a second, I waver. What will they think? How will they react? Will they see this as me eager to take advantage of my best friend's death and gleefully grabbing her spot? My stomach flips at the thought, and I shake my head to try and snap out of it. *What does it matter, Najwa? You never cared what they thought before; why should you start now?*

"Over here, sweetie!"

I know that voice.

I stride over to where Yasmin is sitting cross-legged on the carpeted floor, open laptop balanced on her lap, phone in one hand, slight frown on her face. I'm not sure what I expected her to say, but "How much do you think it costs to hire a hacker?" isn't it.

"Excuse me?"

"A hacker." She squints at her laptop. "I have a cousin who

says he can do it, but . . . well, I don't want to say he's a liar exactly, but he always stole my dessert when we were kids and he just doesn't seem all that trustworthy lah to tell you the truth. But maybe that's what you want from a hacker? They're doing inherently untrustworthy things, after all. . . ." Her voice trails off as she ponders this and I try to catch up.

Apa kejadah? "Yasmin, what are y—"

"Oooh, or there's this." She shoves her phone in my face. "This site says if you pay them twenty-nine ninety-nine, they can hack into any social media account for you. You just have to give them the handle."

"Ringgit?"

"Dollars," she says, scrolling busily. "American."

Catching up, I decide, is a lost cause. "Yasmin," I say firmly. "What in the world are you doing?"

She has the audacity to look at me like I'm the one being ridiculous. "What does it look like, hon? Trying to find a way to get into Trina's Instagram account and stop those . . . those nasty messages." She jabs at the screen. "Do you think this guy would do? He posted on this message board that he can hack his way into anything."

"I don't think you should put too much trust in someone who misspells 'anything.'" I lean against the wall next to her and sigh. I guess Yasmin had the same idea I did, only, being Yasmin, she's gone about five steps ahead of me and taken a couple of wrong turns for good measure. So much for ATARACTIC. "Why are you doing this?"

"Why?" Yasmin is the only person I know who actually bristles. Before meeting her, I thought it was just a word writers used to seem, I don't know, poetic or literary or something. "Because she is OUR FRIEND, and her name is being USED to create DRAMA." She's also the only person I know who can speak in capitals, in italics, in bold and underlined, the full accoutrement of word processing capabilities.

"Was." I reach into my pocket for the pack of gum I keep there and pop one into my mouth. "She was our friend. And now she's dead."

"And nobody seems to care." She suddenly seems to deflate, all the bluster leaving her body until all that's left is sadness. "I've been working hard all year, you know. The title deserves to go to someone who cared about her. Someone who isn't doing it just . . . for glamour and glory."

"Someone like you," I say.

"Or you," she counters. "The Trina we mourn . . . it's the same one."

I nod. I know what she means. Of all the faces Trina presented to the world, the one she saved for us was the one we knew and loved best. I think of Yasmin training so hard for this moment, and feel my heart soften. Our grief may have different symptoms, but deep down it's the same disease after all.

There's a ping from the laptop, and Yasmin squeals. "Ooh! This guy says he can give me a discount! Only twenty dollars!"

So much for that. "It was just a prank, Yasmin, someone's gross idea of a joke. And when Trina was alive, she was the one who created the drama, remember?" I shrug. "For all we know, she might actually have enjoyed all of this."

Yasmin stares at me, openmouthed. "That is a DESPICABLE thing to say." She begins gathering up her things, her mouth a hard, thin line. "I should've known. My mother always told me if you want something done, you have to do it *yourself*."

I guess the moment's over. "Look, just don't spend that twenty-nine ninety-nine," I tell her. "That's almost 127 ringgit for what's basically a scam."

"Thank you," she says primly. "But I think I can handle this on my own." And she sweeps off.

I stay there for a while, leaning against the padded hotel wall, trying to figure out what it is about death that makes people think we need to paint over all the cracks. "Don't speak ill of the dead," they say, as if the dead care. For the record, I don't speak ill of Trina, but I guess I don't feel the need to pretend that she was anything other than what she was—what I loved her for being—and I'm certain that posthumous sainthood wasn't really Trina's style. Then again, worshipping Trina was definitely Yasmin's, and I'm not sure I want to find out what happens if you get in the way of that.

Frankly, I'm not even sure how Yasmin came to be part of the Scrabble scene at all. She just turned up one day, tagging along behind Trina like the tail of a kite, smiling and nodding and so very eager to please.

"You play a lot of Scrabble?" I asked her that first day.

"Oh, not too much," she answered, smoothing her unruly

curls back into a ponytail holder that barely held them back, enthusiasm radiating out of every pore. "But dearest Trina does seem to enjoy it, and I'm so excited to be part of her world, you know? It wasn't so long ago that we were always together, and now that she's switched schools and does this whole Scrabble thing, I barely see her at all! Kan, T?" She leaned forward and squeezed Trina's arm in a gesture both familiar and somehow almost possessive.

"Sure," Trina said, shooting her a quick smile. As I watched, I thought I saw her move her arm ever so slightly out of Yasmin's grip, and a slight wavering of Yasmin's ever-present smile. But I couldn't be sure.

From then on, she was always just . . . there. Not after school on weekdays, but on more weekends than I was comfortable with. It's not that I disliked Yasmin. There were even perks to having her around: she was always willing to do you a favor, had a love of baking treats that she was more than happy to share, and always carried a bag full of the most random things, "just in case"—Band-Aids, a comb, a handful of hair elastics, pins, Tiger Balm, tape, a tiny pair of scissors. It was like being friends with Mary Poppins.

No, I didn't dislike Yasmin. What I disliked was the awkwardness of adding a new ingredient to a tried-and-tested formula. What I disliked was having to take the time to explain a million inside jokes; having to rethink our usual configuration of pillows, perfectly arranged for movie night; not being able to eat at our favorite hangouts because Yasmin had an aversion to the food there. What I disliked was not being able to say exactly what I wanted because I didn't trust Yasmin the way I trusted Trina, because I didn't know Yasmin the way I knew Trina. What I disliked was having to take this room the two of us had created for ourselves, with all of our neuroses and our baggage, and expand it to fit three. Around Yasmin, it felt like I was all angles and edges, not quite fitting in or fitting out, just fitting awkwardly in this space that was meant to be mine.

I asked Trina about it and she shrugged. "Min's having some trouble letting go," she said. "There's too much shared history there to cut her loose. You know how it is with these childhood friends."

I didn't know, actually. But I imagined that childhood friends were a lot like childhood toys: some grow with you, some you keep around for sentimental reasons, and some belong in the past.

A deafening crackle shatters the quiet of the hall, then the high-pitched whine of feedback as someone starts up the microphone. "Testing," a voice says tentatively. "Testing. Is it on? Ya? Okay, ladies and gentlemen, day two of the tournament is about to begin. If you could please make your way to your tables . . . Thank you. Thanks."

I peel myself away from the wall and take a deep breath.

Time to get this show on the road.

No tournament I've been to has ever managed to strike the right balance between arctic temperatures and tropical sauna, and I rub my hands together as I head to my seat, trying to limber up fingers made cold and stiff by the freezing blasts of air-conditioning.

My first table today is table sixteen, and my first opponent is a soft-spoken boy with glasses and an old-fashioned courteousness that is both disarming and disorienting—or perhaps I am simply unused to polite boys. He stands when I approach, sits only when I have, asks if there is anything I need before we begin, and offers me the bag for the first draw.

"Shall we?" he asks.

"We shall," I say, reaching in for my tile. I am charmed, as if he's a curiosity in a museum, a relic from times long past.

Somehow, this display of manners puts me at ease. I beat him, as if I always knew that I would—my absolute favorite play being when I place ZEATIN on the board through a floating E (in JEERED) and a floating T (in CRETIN)—but I am almost sorry about it.

"You're a wonderful player," he tells me admiringly as he bows slightly in place of a handshake—oh so respectful, all the way to the end. "This board is beautiful."

"Thank you," I tell him. "Good luck for your next games."

As the small crowd that's gathered around to watch us begins to disperse, I hear someone whisper, "Amazing, isn't she?" and I feel like I'm flying. ZEATIN is cytokinin derived from corn, and cytokinin is a group of hormones in plants that promote cell division and slow down aging, and none of it matters, but knowing these things makes me feel . . . I don't know.

Powerful. Strong. Unstoppable. *You're doing this for Trina,* I remind myself. *You're protecting her legacy.*

And then, almost immediately: *But that doesn't mean you can't enjoy the process.*

He's my first win of the day, but he isn't the only one, and nobody is more surprised by this than me. I've been talking a big game to myself, and yesterday's wins buoyed me, but I still didn't expect this. I didn't expect to keep winning.

I win my second match, and my third, and my fourth.

Since my game ends early, I walk around, scoping out the competition. You can tell who's making waves by the crowds around the table; the bigger the crowd, the bigger the fish in this pond. Josh is a big fish, which is no surprise; Shuba also seems to be accumulating more people with every round. I pause to watch them play for a second and am struck by their graceful movements, the way they place each tile on the board. "Seventy-two," they say in that husky voice. "Your move." As I turn to leave, I hear someone whisper, "Shuba's got a real shot at the whole thing."

I feel a wrenching in my chest. *Not if I can help it.*

CHAPTER NINE

OBNUBILATE
fourteen points
verb
to darken, cloud over

> Alina: how's it going?
> Me: What a question. I'm winning, obviously
> Alina: Don't get too cocky

I don't answer. The comment annoys me, and Alina knows it. I'm not cocky when it comes to Scrabble—I just know how good I am. There's a difference.

They've laid out long tables in the hallway covered with packs of food: fried noodles and nasi lemak in plastic containers, packets of curry puffs and wilted sandwiches, bottles of lukewarm water, boxed sugarcane juice and chrysanthemum tea. I grab a pack of egg sandwiches and some water and head off to find the quietest corner I can, dodging the little knots of people chattering loudly, and most of it is about Scrabble, but every once in a while, I catch people glancing in my direction or a whisper of Trina's name, and I feel a strange pit begin to open up in the depths of my stomach, breaking into the buzz of my wins.

No, Najwa. Don't let them take this from you.

I go out to the hotel's tiny excuse for a garden and find a bench, and even though it's sweltering out here, it's quiet enough to feel like I can at least hear my own thoughts. I take out my sandwich, a generous name for what is essentially two slices of soggy bread glued together by a thin layer of egg and mayonnaise and one meager slice of cucumber. And then, because I can't seem to stop myself, I open YouTube on my phone and search until I find what I'm looking for.

The Last Person She Ever Spoke To, uploaded one day ago by The TrinaProject.

Josh's face scowls up at me from the thumbnail as my finger hovers uncertainly over the play button. Should I watch this? Do I really want to?

I take a deep breath. Then I start the video.

The first few seconds pass by in a blur. There's some dramatic music, then a photo of Trina, smiling in the sunshine, swirls into view, then as the music swells, fades slightly to form a background to the title (*Trina Low: One Year Later*, and in smaller letters just below, *A Documentary*). Then everything fades to black. White text begins to appear on the screen, letter by letter.

Trina Low had it all. She was beautiful, funny, and one of the best Scrabble players on the local youth scene. But one day in 2021, during an intense endgame, Trina simply fell across the table . . . dead at just sixteen years old.

Josh Tan was the last person she ever spoke to.

Cut to several artistic shots from a typical Scrabble tournament: the bustling crowd at registration; a close-up of a timer ticking down; two players across the table from each other, heads bent, frowning over the board; another close-up of a hand arranging fresh tiles on an empty rack: GRUUPAY.

AUGURY, I think. Foretelling of the future. An omen. I feel it then, a thin sliver of panic reaching up to wrap a wispy tendril around my chest.

"I see even in death, Trina Low manages to monopolize the popular narrative." Josh's face swims onto the screen, his brow furrowed. "My favorite memory of her? I do not have one. I opted to keep our interactions outside of games minimal. It was vastly preferable to the alternative."

"But you knew her?" a voice asks off camera, and I recognize Tweedledee's Sabahan lilt.

"Of course I knew her," he snaps irritably. "Who didn't? Trina Low made it a point to be known. It was a feature, not a bug. But Trina and I simply did not care for each other. I felt that she was superficial, vapid, and inane. She felt that I was rigid, uptight, and boring, and never missed an opportunity to tell me so, except in terms far less polite." He pauses to cough, his chest heaving, before continuing. "We were not destined to be friends."

"How many times had you faced each other in tournaments before this?"

"More than I care to count, over at least four years."

"And what would you say she was like, as a player?"

His scowl deepens; I hadn't thought it was possible. "Mercurial. Disrespectful." There is a pause, and then, through gritted teeth: "Brilliant."

I swallow, my throat suddenly dry. Somehow, I never thought he'd say it.

"Can you tell us what happened on the day of the . . . incident?"

Josh sighs. "Very well. I will attempt to recount the facts as I remember them, though you must understand that such a significant amount of time has passed that it may impair my recall ability. . . ."

"Of course," Tweedledee quickly supplies.

"Well then. My game against Trina was due to begin at exactly nine a.m.; however, as per usual, Trina was late." He sniffs disapprovingly. "She would possibly have been more punctual if she had spent less time on her *entrance*, but that's neither here nor there. We began our game at 9:07 a.m., after she had taken a selfie of us and posted it online—without my consent, might I add."

I remember that picture—Trina's sunny smile, Josh's dark frown. It has the dubious distinction of being the last photo posted to Trina's Instagram account.

At least, until yesterday.

"Then what?"

"We began playing, and from the first move it was clear that I was going to have one of those games where everything was just going to fall into place for me. Every rack I drew was a winner. High-scoring words at every turn. And I was playing with a clarity and focus that was unparalleled, even for me. Even when some kind of commotion broke out in the hall somewhere, I could not be moved. And I think Trina recognized this fact as well, because I had never seen her so agitated. Fidgeting, sweating. I had the great Trina Low *nervous*." He smiles with satisfaction at the memory, and I suddenly feel an overwhelming urge to punch him.

"Trina doesn't get nervous," I say aloud, as if he can hear me, and it takes me a beat to realize I'm talking about her as if she's still here.

"And then what?"

He shrugs. "And then nothing. We were in the endgame. She ran out of time—I remember the buzzer being very loud, making me jump. And then she fell onto the board. Sent tiles scattering everywhere." He pauses and wrinkles his nose in distaste. "It was a tremendous mess."

I don't know whether he's referring to the fallen tiles, Trina's death, or the ensuing commotion. Maybe all of the above.

"Was she acting any differently?"

Josh shakes his head irritably. "This presumes I knew her well enough to know what range of behavior would have been normal for Trina Low, which I did not. However, I will say that based on what I knew of her as a player, she made some silly mistakes. Quite uncharacteristic for her. For instance, she played WING once when she could have played WINGBACK with an open K I'd left on the board. But as I say, I made her nervous—I put it down to that."

"Did you notice anything else about her?" I can practically hear Tweedledee trying to dig more out of this, get something they can work with.

He lets out a long sigh. "Unlike most of you, I am a serious competitive player. I focus on the game."

"Okay. Well." There's some shuffling of papers and whispering just off camera, and I hear Tweedledee say softly: "*You ask him.*"

Tweedledum's voice booms out, making me jump. "There's a story that gets told about you. About what you said at the end."

"And what was that?" Josh isn't looking at the camera; he's looking right at them with the most intense expression, as if daring them to mention the words.

It's Tweedledee's voice that comes through, cool and assured: "The story goes that as Trina lay there dead, you asked officials, quote, does this mean I still win, unquote. Is that true?"

"Close enough." The slightest of pauses. "I simply wanted clarification. In any competition, winners and losers must be made clear, no matter how . . . distasteful the circumstances."

"You don't think it comes off as . . . cold? Even cruel?"

"No," Josh says matter-of-factly. "She was dead, and the information about the rankings was most relevant to me at the time."

"So you must have been pretty annoyed when they decided to just cancel everything, huh?" Tweedledee pipes up. "No winners when there's a dead body involved."

Josh frowns. "We had made it to the end of the game, and I was the clear victor. So yes, I was somewhat irritated at the unwillingness of the committee to simply award the win accordingly."

Tweedledum clears his throat. "Still, you have to understand that there was a dead girl . . ."

"Dead or not, I won. And Trina Low was not a nice person."

"Most of us aren't," Tweedledee says. "That doesn't mean she deserved to die."

"Maybe. It certainly means I am not obligated to express some false sentimentality about it."

CALLOSITY, I think. I played it in a game once, hooking it onto a SIT that was already on the board, my heart pounding with the exhilaration of a word well played. An abnormal hardness and thickness of the skin, used both literally, as in the calloused soles of overworked feet, or figuratively, as in Josh's callous soul.

"Are we done here?"

"Is there anything else you remember from that day, anything that might change how people view this story?"

There is the slightest of pauses and Josh blinks rapidly at the camera twice, owl-eyed, before he replies. "No."

"Okay, ya, I think we're done."

The video fades to a group photo. I remember this one. It's

the customary shot they take at the start of this tournament every year. WEEKEND WARRIORS 2021, a banner pinned to the wall reads. Then it zooms in, past rows and rows of smiling faces, until it finds Trina, eyes squeezed shut, mouth open in a joyful squeal, flashing double peace signs, and me next to her, a little more subdued, but happy nonetheless. And then I see Josh, two rows away, just off to the left. Only he isn't looking at the camera. Instead, he's shooting a look of pure, venomous hatred . . . right at Trina.

Fade to black. *End of Part One,* the text says. *Stay Tuned for Part Two.*

My sandwich lies in my lap, forgotten. It's hot out here, but I suddenly find myself shivering and can't stop.

"Najwa?"

The glare from the afternoon sun makes it hard to recognize the figure standing before me for a second, but I'd know that deep voice anywhere.

"Hi, Mark."

If people are words, then Mark is ADUMBRATE: to overshadow, which he did to me often as far as Trina was concerned; to conceal partially, which is what I felt like he was always doing. There is something decidedly slippery about him, like a fish you can't quite grip between your fingers.

We played against each other for the first time in a tournament two years ago. He was a newbie, but everybody knew his name: Mark Thomas, the boy who'd given up a burgeoning career as a swimming prodigy to hang out with the word nerds. He had the same warm smile he gives away so easily now, the same smooth, creamy dark skin and broad shoulders, a tendency to make small talk when he should have been quiet. The tournament press and social media teams played up his backstory and ate up his ridiculous good looks, which, let's be honest, sent a wave of resentment crashing through some of the others. (I'll give you a clue: starts with J, ends with OSH, fourteen points total.) Because the truth is that Mark wasn't that good. He still isn't. He's decent, but in these parts decent isn't enough to elevate you in the ranks. Faced with a bingo-friendly rack like EHORRST—SHORTER, I think, or RHETORS, a teacher of rhetoric, or even ROTHERS, a nail used to fasten the rudder irons of ships—he squinted at the board for an age before panic-playing SHORT on a double-word score, placing the S under SMART on the board for a total of just twenty-four points. A total rookie move.

He coughs and gestures to the bench. "May I . . . ?"

I make space for him beside me, and he sits down, careful to maintain a safe distance. Mark is always very aware of my Muslimness and by extension, his own non-Muslimness. "How are you doing?"

"I'm fine," I say. I've been saying it a lot lately and the lie slips off my tongue with practiced ease; the interview with Josh has left me drained, as if I, too, am a version of ADUMBRATE: an adumbration, a faint image or outline of my real self.

"Fine." He laughs, and it's the first time I've heard one so utterly devoid of humor. "You sure look fine." I've experienced Mark in both friend mode and boyfriend mode, and this is neither; this is some new evolution I haven't experienced before. I'm not sure I like it. No, actually, I'm sure: I don't like it.

"Scintillating as this conversation is, I'm not really here to be insulted. I've got games to win." I stand, dusting my butt off with two hard swipes. "Hard for you to imagine, I know," I add. It's a mean thing to say, but hey, it's the truth. The kindest thing you can say about his gameplay is that he's very enthusiastic about it. In that first game, he played PAIRS when he should have played REPAIRS, SUDDEN where he should have played SUDDENLY, and the worst of all, the terrible YO when he had the opportunity to play YODEL. From what I've seen and heard of Mark's games in this tournament, little has changed since.

"Sit down, Najwa." There is something about his tone that brooks no argument. I sit.

"I want to talk to you about that Instagram post."

I sigh. "Not this again. Yasmin already tried this with me too. Look, it's just someone's idea of a really, really terrible prank, and I honestly think if we just ignore it . . ."

"That's not what I'm talking about," Mark interrupts me. We are sitting in a patch of sunlight, and his dark skin glistens with sweat. I always forget how handsome he is when I haven't seen him for a while, and then forget to breathe when I catch a glimpse. He got all the best features from his Chinese mother and his Indian father; when he and Trina walked into a room together, it was too much, like trying to look directly at the heart of a star. You had to look away.

"Then what?" In the distance, thunder rumbles ominously. Hujan panas, older people call it, hot rain, rain that falls in defiance of the sun that still shines high in the sky.

ADUMBRATE, I think: *a foreshadowing.*

"I'm talking about the fact that it's right."

I can't believe this. "You think Trina was *murdered?*"

"Yes. No! I don't know." He wipes the sweat off his brow and looks me straight in the eye. "Look, I just . . . I've been having this nagging feeling for a long time now that something just doesn't add up. There was nobody more full of life than Trina. People like that . . . they don't just drop dead."

I can feel my heart pounding in my temples, a headache demanding to be let in and take over. "People drop dead all the time, actually. It's an inconvenient fact of life."

"Not people like Trina." He says it so definitely, and I marvel at what it must be like to be so sure of yourself. "I know it sounds ridiculous. Maybe it's nothing. But I just think . . . what if something really did happen to her? Don't we owe it to her to find out? Nobody knew her like us, right?" His smile is soft, and coaxing, and sad. "Nobody knew her better. If anybody can figure this out, it's you and me. Together. We were friends once, after all. Weren't we?"

I don't know, I think. *Were we?* I think back to two years ago, when we first met. "You have a tell," I'd told him after that first game. I'd beaten him handily, by ninety-eight points.

"A what?"

"An unconscious action, thought to betray an attempted deception," I recited, as if on command. "Everyone has one. That guy over there—" I nodded toward a boy in a rugby shirt and wrinkled khakis. "He quirks his lip just a tiny bit to the right when he gets a bingo rack. And that girl sitting by the vending machines, she clenches her left fist when she gets a blank, like a teeny tiny fist pump."

He stared at me. "How do you even know all of that?"

I shrugged. "I spend a lot of time looking at people. Some tells are more subtle than others. Not yours, though. I always know when you're about to do something stupid."

His wide grin only slightly masked the surprise in his eyes; he couldn't believe I would be so straightforward. It struck me then that like Trina, he wasn't used to this kind of honesty. Maybe when you're born beautiful, people always bend over backward to tell you what they think you want to hear.

"So what's my tell?"

To TELL also means to communicate information, but there was no way I was doing that. "The point of knowing someone's tell," I said, "is to keep it to yourself. How can you use it to your advantage otherwise?"

This time he laughed, and I noticed that his eyes shut when he was amused, crinkling until they buttoned themselves up into tight slits. "What can I say? I'm new, I haven't gotten all the stupid out of my system yet."

I felt it then, a familiar tug. Trina and I met on the very first day of secondary school, during recess. She was alone because she was new and didn't know anybody. I was alone because I knew everybody and liked very few of them. She sat there in the courtyard, placidly watching everyone watch her, and I could tell from the gleam in her eye that she was thinking a lot of things about all the girls around her, and I realized I wanted to know what those thoughts were. And I remember thinking that this was odd for me, because I don't usually care at all what people think.

And now here was this boy, with the same magnetic pull, the same way of making me want to know more about what was happening in that brain of his. There was something about his candor, his endearing enthusiasm for just playing the game, that made me want to reach out and hug him. I shook away the feeling, putting it down to too many matches against intense players, the Joshes of the world, who act like nothing exists beyond the board.

"I miss being your friend, Najwa," Mark says quietly, bringing me abruptly out of my memories.

I close my eyes, as if doing that will block out the flood of memories his words unleash. He's using that Mark Thomas charm on me, and I resent it, and him, and the fact that it feels like it might work.

"What are you thinking?"

I don't tell him I'm thinking about tells.

"It's your nose," I told him that first time, surprising myself with my own honesty. "You wrinkle it just a teensy bit just before you put down a word you're not totally confident in, every time."

"Really?" He raised a hand to half cover his face, almost embarrassed, then looked at me quizzically. "Wait, so you've been staring at my face this whole time?"

I felt the tips of my ears turn hot and suddenly was extra thankful for the hijab that hid them from his sight. "So you'll work on that, right?"

"On what? It's not like I can fix my face." He laughed again, and the sound swept me along and made me smile too.

"Well, then you're just going to keep losing," I told him.

He shrugged. "Call it a learning curve," he said. "I can only get better from here, right?" He paused then and looked directly at me. "Thank you for telling me," he said, his voice suddenly quieter, more serious.

"No problem," I managed over the tingling of a thousand new goose bumps. "Why wouldn't I?"

The smile this time was knowing. "I may be new, but I've been around long enough to know that not everybody tells their opponents things that will make them better players." He glanced around, then leaned toward me conspiratorially. "Don't worry," he whispered. "I won't tell them how nice you really are."

"They wouldn't believe you," I told him, fighting to regain control of my burning cheeks and my churning stomach.

"Oh?" He arched one eyebrow. "So you're only nice to me?"

I'd said nothing. To TELL is also to decide or determine

something with certainty, and I didn't want to confirm what he already knew.

But it's certainty I'm looking for now, so as Mark speaks, I watch his nose, looking for a sign that he means what he says. It never moves, not even when he says he missed being my friend. And still I wonder: Is Mark telling the truth, or did he just get a lot better at lying?

"Say something," he says, drawing me out of my memories.

"Why?" I say softly. "Why didn't you say something sooner?"

"Why now?" He sighs. "I know, it's been so long, right? Why even drag it all back up? It's just . . . look, Trina was worrying about something that weekend, okay? It was really weighing on her mind. She kept telling me that she had something she needed to take care of, and that it was better to do it in person, even if she was afraid of the outcome. And now these posts, these clues are coming out, and if there's even the slightest possibility . . ."

"Stop." I can't listen to any more of this. "I meant why as in, why do you even care? Honestly, Mark. You don't even miss her. Why bring all this back up?"

"I don't miss her?" He stares at me, incredulous. "You think I don't miss her?"

"Well, you sure haven't been acting like a broken-hearted boyfriend," I say. My grief adds a sharp, snide edge to my voice; it slices through the pressure building painfully in my chest, and for an all-too-brief moment relief rushes in, followed almost immediately by regret. It doesn't matter. It's not just me that the words cut into. I can see it in his face.

The sound of thunder breaks the silence between us. The storm is closing in—you can tell from how close the thunder is, how oppressive the afternoon humidity gets. My skin is damp beneath the layers of cloth that cover it; I am fully covered yet I'm not sure I've ever felt more exposed.

It takes a minute for him to speak; before he does, he takes a deep breath.

"Look. I'm not here to pick a fight with you. It's just . . . I have so many questions. And I think you're the only person here who can help me find some answers. So what do you say?" In his eyes, I see so many things: hope and anxiety and anger and fear and something else, something I can't quite place or don't want to name, all mixed up together.

I don't want this. I don't want to feel this again, not now.

I stand up and take a deep breath. "I say stay away from me." And then lightning rips a hole in the sky, and the rain begins to fall.

CHAPTER TEN

MUMPSIMUS

seventeen points

noun

opinion held obstinately

There are ten minutes until my next game, and my thoughts will not quiet down. The ants come marching in, rows and rows of them, making my brain itch: *Is Mark right? Should I be more worried? What if this wasn't really a prank at all? What do I do? What do I do now?*

No. Stop it, Najwa. Kill the ants.

I imagine a fist squashing each ant one by one, flattening them beneath strong, capable fingers, mashing them into nothing. Then I sit down and close my eyes, spreading my fingertips out across the tiles, which the last players at table two have already arranged in four squares, five tiles wide by five tiles deep, as is custom to make sure none of the hundred are missing. I block out Mark's face even as it keeps trying to insinuate itself into my consciousness. *Deep breaths, Najwa. You need to do this. For Trina, remember? The game is yours. The game is yours. The game is . . .*

A familiar ding interrupts my thoughts. Who could be messaging me at this time? I fish my phone out of my pocket to put it on silent mode. The last thing I need right now is a distraction.

But I get one anyway. Because there it is, a new DM from trina.queenofthetiles. Just one line.

Are you ready to play?

For a second, my vision blurs. I start to type a reply, but before I can finish, an urgent buzzing interrupts my attempts. One after another, they come in: WhatsApp messages from Mark, from Yasmin, from Alina, all saying some version of the same thing:

Check Instagram. Check Instagram now.

I take in a shaky, shallow breath.

Sure enough, there's the familiar profile picture at the top of the page, ringed with the orange-pink gradient that indicates a new Instagram Story. This time there are eight letters: MROANIJF. There's a caption too, in all-white text.

They hide among us.

What does that even mean?

No matter. *Focus, Najwa.*

I frown at the tiles on the screen, willing them to move, to reveal their secrets to me. The first few that swirl into my vision don't make sense—INFORM, FORM, FIRMAN, AMINO—all too simple, too basic. *You need to use all the tiles, Najwa.* I stare and stare at the familiar shapes, until suddenly one word swims into focus.

JANIFORM.

JANIFORM comes from the Roman god Janus. Like Janus, it means to have two faces, which means . . . which means Trina was deceived. Betrayed.

There's a sudden roaring in my ears.

I know what it means. I always know. But what kind of betrayal? The kind that resulted in murder? Or something else? And by who?

Who could have betrayed Trina? Who could be posting these clues?

I look up and see people darting glances my way. The whispers layer and blend together until they barely make sense, except for the words that float to the top and drift lazily through the air before wending their way into my ears: *Trina*, and *murder*, and *Mark*.

And one more.

Najwa.

Because of course, to BETRAY means to be disloyal, to break someone's faith in you, and you can't break what you don't have. Betrayal implies intimacy. Betrayal means that whoever did this to Trina had her trust. My fingers tremble as I reach into my back pocket for my notebook, and my writing is barely legible, but there it is, right below REGICIDE: JANIFORM.

They hide among us.

Immediately I remember Josh's steady gaze on the night of

the first message, and something akin to fear runs a cold finger slowly up my spine.

"Hello." My opponent slips into the seat across from me. She has two braids running down her back and a pink fanny pack, which she unzips and rummages around in before emerging with a pack of gum. "You want?" Her accent is unmistakably Filipino; I'm almost positive I've played her before.

"No, thank you," I manage to croak out.

She shrugs. "Okay." The sound of her frantic chewing makes me grit my teeth. "You okay? You look like you've seen a ghost."

I have, I think. "I'm fine. Let's play."

I am not fine. I want to hide in the safety of this game forever, not having to look up, not having to acknowledge everyone's eyes boring holes in my back, not having to think about Trina, or Mark, or Josh, not having to hear those low voices talking about me and whether I'm capable of murder or betrayal. What do they care about whether it's true? Remember Emily? Rumors stick, and with every minute that passes I can feel my reputation, my place here in the only world that makes me feel like me, circling the drain, ready to disappear. The ants squirm all over my brain, marching round and round in circles—*you can't do this you're an imposter why are you even here you should have just stayed home Trina was murdered and you're nothing without her nothing nothing nothing*—and no matter what I do, I can't shake them loose. I stare and stare at racks of letters and see nothing, and when I'm not staring at my rack, I'm staring out into the crowd, largely silent save for the clicking of tiles, the smacking of hands on timers. *One of you is the betrayer. One of you is responsible for this.* I squander plays on easily detected phonies—OUTRISE when I should play STOURIE, RETONES when I should play ESTRONE. I don't challenge QUIS, a word that I know isn't valid in Scrabble, even if Merriam-Webster says it's a European woodcock. I open a triple-word score lane when I know my opponent holds the ten-point Z. And worst of all, I go two minutes overtime, adding an unnecessary twenty points to my opponent's final score. This is not a dance; it's a freefall. I lose, 412–275.

"Good game," Fanny Pack says.

"You too," I say. Only one of us is telling the truth.

The day continues, because time is selfish and thinks nothing of the suffering of others. And I try my best to make it through. I try to concentrate on breathing, on mindfulness. I try and I try, and nothing works. At my very first big-time out-of-state tournament in Melaka, I covered myself in glory by using my opponent's first move, CAR—ten points—to play my first move, ESCARPMENT, M on a double-letter score, T on a triple word. Fifty-seven points. It proved startlingly apt: An ESCARPMENT is a steep slope usually formed by erosion, and my one move eroded my opponent's confidence so much that for him, it was all downhill from there. I won easily, and by one of those margins you don't even like mentioning, because it just seems mean.

Well, joke's on me, because that second clue proves to be

my very own ESCARPMENT. My descent is swift and igno-
minious. The tiles, usually so pliable in my hands, so willing to
rearrange themselves into different combinations in my head,
remain stubbornly still. Bad racks lead to bad decisions lead to
bad plays. And I lose, again and again. I hear the whispers in
the crowd around me: "She's lost her touch." "Maybe she's not
so much of a threat after all." "My cousin could beat this chick,
and she's six."

By the time we reach the eleventh and final game of the
day, I have won five and lost five. And my mood isn't helped
when I run my finger down the tournament director's list and
realize who my next opponent is.

Table seventeen. Najwa Bakri vs. Josh Tan.

He's already sitting there waiting for me, and I take a
good look at Josh as I walk toward him, from his mop of hair
to his trademark checkered shirt to the dirty white sneakers
on his feet. I take in the expression of furious concentration
on his face, the deep furrows of his brow, the tongue-clicks of
irritation. As I get closer, I hear him mutter to himself under his
breath. "Why'd I play REPAIRS instead of PEREIRAS? So *stupid*, Josh." If Josh were a word, he would be ADAMANTINE,
I think: firm, unbending, utterly unyielding. There's a reason
Wolverine's claws are made from adamantium; much like them,
Josh's rigidity can often cut those around him to the quick.

The first time I played against him, fresh on the tournament circuit and owl-eyed with excitement, I started off by
smiling brightly and saying "Hi! I'm Najwa!" He glowered at

me and barked "No coffeehousing. Just play." And that's how I learned that coffeehousing, or trying to distract your opponent with small talk, is one of those unspoken rules of tournament play that everyone just *knows* but doesn't appear in any rule book. It's also how I learned about Josh. Precise, mathematical, calculating Josh, who plays the way he carries on a conversation: intense, relentless, and with zero tolerance for what he views as time-wasting nonsense, who works the board as if he's destined to win and knows it. I'd never seen anyone read the board the way he could: He may not have known as many words as I did, but he saw the board in a web of possibilities and probabilities I never could grasp. I bingoed with REALISE early on in the game; Josh took one look and, barely twenty seconds later, laid down ENTASIS right below it, forming a parallel: a perfect row of seven two-letter words: RE, EN, AT, LA, IS, SI, ES. After each move, he meticulously noted down each word we played, counting off tiles under his breath, anticipating everything: my next move, his next move, the number of tiles left, what they were, what I might get, what he might get. In the endgame he drew the last letter N left to play, played through a floating U on the board, and finished with a bingo: FUNGIBLE.

"Lucky break," I told him afterward, "drawing that N right when you needed it."

"Lucky?" He looked at me as if I'd called him a dirty word. "I knew I was going to get it. My calculations are rarely wrong." And then he walked off abruptly, without so much as a good-bye.

Josh doesn't just play by the rules; he *lives* by them, adhering to them with a strict devotion bordering on the obsessive. Trina, on the other hand, regarded rules the way she regarded her parents: there to be obeyed or manipulated when it was to her benefit, and otherwise ignored. I remember his words from the video: *We were never destined to be friends.*

An understatement, to be honest.

"Josh," I say with a nod as I take my place.

"Najwa," he says, putting away his phone, less a greeting than an acknowledgment of my existence. His voice is raspier than usual, and he clears his throat noisily before he speaks again. "Shall we begin?"

Something about his brusqueness, the ease with which he brushes me aside, flips a switch somewhere inside me. "Nah," I say. "We have a little time. Let's chat."

"I don't *chat*."

"You did to the camera," I can't resist replying. "Saw your little interview. Scintillating stuff."

"What I choose to do or not do is none of your business."

"Trina is my business." I look directly at him, expecting him to squirm under my gaze, but he just looks back, clear-eyed and unfazed. "My question is why? Why talk about all of that now?"

He shrugs, reaching into his bag for a bright orange packet of lozenges. "They asked," he says, popping one into his mouth.

"And you just answered? Just like that?" I swallow, my throat suddenly dry. "If I ask questions, will you answer me?"

He regards me with narrowed eyes. "It depends," he says.

"On what?"

"On what the questions are." Josh grabs the bag that lies crumpled beside the board and begins shoving the tiles into it. "Enough now. It's time to play."

"Fine."

We finish bagging the tiles in silence, and Josh shakes it a couple of times for good measure before we each draw one to determine who goes first. "M," Josh says, flipping his tile over.

I open my palm to show him the tile nestled in the center. "A."

He exhales sharply. Josh hates when the odds are against him, even slightly. "Fine. Your move."

We slip the tiles back in and I hold the bag at eye level, flashing him my open hand first to show that I'm hiding nothing; there have been instances where bags have been held too low, allowing less scrupulous players to peek surreptitiously at tiles before selecting the best ones, or palming blanks to use on a later turn. One by one, I place seven on my rack: T, E, A, S, N, E, I. The words begin to swim into focus. *TEASE,* I think. *SATEEN. TISANE. TENESI.* And then I see it. ETESIAN, a Mediterranean summer wind. I place the E on a double-letter score and let the rest follow, careful not to give away that triple-word lane. Eight points, double up for sixteen, add fifty for using all my tiles . . .

"Sixty-six," I say, slapping the timer. "Your turn." Maybe this day isn't a lost cause for me after all.

Josh says nothing, just lays down ZARF, the Z and A lined over the A and N in ETESIAN, with the ten-point tile resting, crucially, on a double-letter score. "Forty-nine," he says, hitting the timer.

Games with Josh aren't sit-back-and-relax games; they're sit-up-and-pay-attention games. You can't get comfortable. So we keep going, back and forth, back and forth, trading increasingly complex letter combinations, and I hate to admit it but oh, do I love this, this thrill of playing against a worthy opponent, of knowing everything you put out can be matched or exceeded. It almost makes me forget about Trina.

Almost.

And then it happens. With tiles in his hands, ready to place on the board, Josh pauses ever so slightly, blinking as though to clear something from his eyes before laying them down: M, A, L, T, I, E, S. MALTIES.

MALTIES?

MALTIES doesn't exist in the Scrabble dictionary, but it's also the combination of letters most likely to yield an eight-letter word—there are thirty-eight different words you can put together, as long as your opponent is kind enough to place one of the right tiles on the board for you. If I put down a B, for example, Josh could make BALMIEST, or TIMBALES, or LAMBIEST. It's all strategy, I realize. Josh is playing a phony, counting on my challenging his made-up word so he can take it back, wait for the letter he needs to appear, and then bingo, giving him a huge lead, a lead impossible to beat in the moves we have left. And to my growing horror, I realize that I've managed the board horribly and that there are at least two—no, three—legit spots in which he can place it.

I cannot let Josh bloody Tan win.

I can feel his eyes on me as the clock ticks down, wondering when I'm going to raise my hand, call out for a challenge. He knows I can't miss this. I scan my tiles, trying to figure out what to do, how to cut him off. I need to win this. Trina needs me to win this.

Come on, Najwa. You're missing it.

I scowl as I scan the board, my fingers nimbly arranging and rearranging my tiles, my mind whirring through all the possibilities it can see.

Think, Najwa, think. You're usually so wary of tells. . . . The voice at the back of my head is insistent. I close my eyes as if I'm pondering my next move and replay that last sequence in my head. Josh put down MALTIES, and . . .

No. That's not it.

You've almost got it, Najwa.

My eyes fly open.

Josh paused and blinked twice before he put down MALTIES. Before he played a phony. Just like he paused and blinked during his interview. *Is there anything else you remember from that day that might change how people view this story?* I remember the way his eyes sought mine when we got that first clue, how quickly he found REGICIDE, the weight of his gaze, never faltering, and shiver.

"It's your move," he says impatiently, drumming his fingers on the table.

Hold on, Najwa. Don't get ahead of yourself. If this is really a tell, then I need to be sure. I can't go assuming someone is shady based on some blinks, a pretty common Scrabble tactic, and a hunch.

And so I ignore the obvious move—adding a T to MALTIES to make MALTIEST, turning his phony into a legit word and playing TRENAIL to bingo—and instead, raise my hand and call it out, loud and clear: "Challenge."

The TD comes to tell us what we already know—the word is invalid—and Josh takes back his tiles, sliding them onto his rack one by one.

"I don't know what I was thinking," he says.

I do, I think. Slowly, deliberately, I place RAIL on the board in a prime scoring spot. If I'm right, if that is in fact Josh's tell and he deliberately played that phony as a strategy, then he can't ignore the opening I've given him.

And he doesn't. With a smirk and a flourish, he lays down LAMISTER through my floating R, just as I expected him to do, and bingos out of the game, leaving me with three tiles and a tornado of thoughts swirling through my head.

He doesn't bother to wait for my congratulations as he starts arranging the tiles for the next players. But I don't care. My heart is racing; my mouth is dry. Josh Tan has a tell—but more importantly, he has a secret, one that has to do with Trina and the day that she died. And I'm going to find out what it is.

Afterward I walk up to where Mark stands, watching the crowd as they mingle, discussing games and moves at what seems like top volume.

"I'm in," I tell him. "I'm all in."

CHAPTER ELEVEN

CACOETHES

sixteen points

noun

uncontrollable urge or desire, especially for something harmful

B y the time we met again at our second tournament, we were friends, Mark and I, sitting side by side—halal gap included, of course—on the plush red carpet of the posh new convention center where it was being held, knees up against our chests, passing a pack of chips—crinkle cut, sour cream and cheddar—back and forth. It was another tournament that Trina was missing, the second in a row. The first was due to sickness; the second, purely because she just didn't feel like it. Sometimes, Trina said, Scrabble was just too *boring*.

"Your dad came this time," I observed, taking a bite of a chip and somehow sending a shower of crumbs cascading down my black T-shirt.

"Can't take you anywhere," Mark said to me, shaking his head as he grabbed a handful of chips from the bag. "Yeah, he's having the time of his life standing around looking important with his arms crossed and his face all disapproving."

"If he doesn't approve, then why is he here?" I took a swig from the plastic bottle of mineral water they gave us all at the start of the day. It was room temperature and disgusting; I remember wondering who I needed to kill for something ice cold and sweet.

Mark shrugged. "To see what I gave up swimming for."

"So what did you give up swimming for?" Mark was improving, slowly but surely, mostly through immersion and osmosis since he refused to study like everyone else. But by this time, all of us had heard about Mark's jock past, the medals and trophies, the accolades, the glory. It was hard to imagine giving all of that up for . . . this.

He didn't answer right away, stretching his long legs out and rubbing his neck. But I knew he would. Mark likes to take his time, choosing his words carefully in a way he can't seem to master when he plays Scrabble.

"My dad thought he had me all figured out," he said eventually. "He thought he knew who I was before I ever did, and he put me in a box and expected me to grow to fill it and not even mind that it was there. Do you know what I mean?"

I nod. "But you minded," I said.

"I minded." He leaned back against the wall and reached for another chip. "I guess I just wanted to see what would happen if I destroyed the box."

I dusted the crumbs off my T-shirt. "Well. How do you like it out here in box-free land?"

He smiled at me then, the corners of his eyes crinkling up. "It's okay. You meet some interesting people."

I smiled back.

"What are you thinking about?"

I blink owlishly in the light, forgetting for a second where I am. Then I remember: It's eight p.m., and I'm sitting awkwardly across from Mark in the corner booth of an American-style diner about ten minutes' walk from the hotel, avoiding another stilted tournament dinner in favor of discussing murder with my dead best friend's ex-boyfriend. "American-style" means it boasts a menu of greasy burgers loaded with various toppings—the more, the better—in ridiculously large portions, with a list of all the sides you'd expect, most of them fried. It also has sticky vinyl seats and a playlist heavy on the Elvis. The awkwardness, however, is all mine. Being friends was a habit Mark and I unlearned when Trina came along; being alone with him now is as strange as shrugging on a borrowed coat. Something just doesn't fit right.

The waitress comes over to take our order. She's dressed in a cherry-red knee-length dress, a white apron, and a dour expression. Light glints off the tiny cross nestled in the hollow of her neck. Her red lipstick has begun to bleed gently onto her teeth. "WhatcanIgetyou," she fires off in rapid monotone.

"I'll have a vanilla milkshake," I tell her.

"Make that two," Mark says. "And an order of curly fries."

"Themilkshakeyouwanttoupsizeornot."

"Huh?"

"Upsize." She sighs and gestures vaguely with her hands. "You know. Make bigger. Youwantornot."

"Oh. No, thanks. Mark?" I raise an eyebrow at him and he shakes his head. "Yeah, we're good. Thanks."

"Fifteenminutes."

For a while after she's gone all we do is sit in silence, and I find myself contemplating the curve of Mark's head, and how familiar this all feels, how almost comforting, even with all that's happened between us.

"So how do we do this?" The question drags me out of my memories. Mark takes one of the shakers and tips a small pile of salt onto the table, then grabs a toothpick and begins to draw shapes idly in the white grains: spirals, triangles, crooked little squares. "I've never played detective before."

"And you think I have?"

"No. But you're a lot smarter than I am." He looks up at me and grins, and for a moment my heart constricts.

Stop it, Najwa. It's such a bloody cliché, the stuff YA novels are made of, the hopeless crush on the best friend's boyfriend. *You're over it. You've been over it for months now.*

"That's a low bar," I say, and he laughs, and I hate how absurdly pleased the sound makes me feel. "But shouldn't the first question be why are we doing this? Why not concentrate on figuring out who's posting the clues in the first place?

Yasmin's already started doing that, why not join forces, like . . . I dunno, like the Avengers? The Planeteers? Some kind of Scooby gang?"

"Because we need to figure out who killed Trina."

"*If* anyone killed Trina," I shoot back. "What makes you so sure, anyway?" For some reason, I'm still having trouble opening up to Mark and admitting how unsure I am, how much my encounter with Josh earlier has thrown me off, how perilously close I am to teetering from "there's something weird going on here but surely it's not *murder*" straight into "someone *definitely* killed Trina and we have to figure out who it was" territory.

"I mean, that's one part of the mystery," Mark says. "But I told you, she was worried about something. Scared, even. You can't just take that out of the equation, right? That has to mean something."

"Yeah, but what was she worried about?"

"I don't know."

I sigh. "Did she let you in on anything else? She had to have said something. Given you some kind of hint?"

He looks away, shamefaced. "She started telling me about it on the phone the day before the tournament, and then her dad walked in and she had to cut it short. She said she'd tell me when she saw me. And then when she did, we . . . Well, we were in the middle of one of our . . . uh . . . episodes."

He means they were in the "off" phase of their on-again, off-again relationship. Trina and Mark had more highs and lows than Mariah Carey's entire vocal range.

"Okay. But what makes you think what she was saying was true?" I lean back and contemplate the white plaster ceiling. "Trina wasn't always known for her honesty."

"I just know." He shakes his head. "You know as well as I do that Trina wasn't afraid of anything or anyone. We can't just ignore that." He tosses a sideways glance in my direction. "Did she not say anything to you?" There is an obvious note of incredulity in his voice, a tone that implies *But how is that even possible?*

I stay silent. Because I didn't know it was possible, if I'm being honest. And for some reason, I don't want to say it out loud, confirm that there were things that Trina kept from me. From *me*. How could she? Why would she?

"Why would she hide things from you?" Mark says, an eerie echo of my own thoughts. "Me, I get. But you? It just doesn't fit. The only way it makes any sense at all is if it was something too small to bother with, or . . ."

"Or so big it killed her," I whisper.

We lapse into an uneasy, restless silence, the kind that makes your skin itch.

"Maybe we should tell the police," I say finally.

He scoffs. "Nobody ever takes teenagers seriously. What makes you think they will now? Who's going to investigate a possible murder a full year after it's happened? *Especially* without evidence. *Especially* when the victim wasn't, like, a politician or a celebrity or caught up in some scandal."

I let out a breath. "Fine. Say we decide to Sherlock our way through this together. You just said it—we have no evidence, just a feeling that something was wrong. And feelings are so . . . so *fickle*. I can barely hang on to those long enough to commit to a new pair of shoes."

"That's what I thought." He takes a deep breath and shoves something across the table at me. "Until I got this."

I'm almost too afraid to look, but I force myself to pick it up. It takes me a second to realize what it is—half of a photograph, crumpled and then smoothed over, ripped nearly exactly down the middle. It's Mark, his head thrown back, laughing. On the back, someone has written two words in bold, black Sharpie: *I KNOW.*

"This was from last year's bulletin board." Mark's voice shakes slightly; I pretend I don't hear it. I know how much it sucks to be vulnerable. "You know, the one they put up to welcome us every year. They plaster photos from the year before all over it. This was a photo of me and Trina at the farewell dinner. Someone must have taken it off that board last year . . . I found it this morning. They'd slipped it under my room door."

"What does this mean?" I say, tracing the letters with trembling fingers. *I KNOW.* "And where's the other half?"

"It could mean so many things." He sighs. "Do they know something about what happened to Trina? Do they know who's posting these things on Instagram? Do they know something about me? I'm not sure what it is, but it feels like if we don't at least try to figure it out . . . something else may happen. Something bad." He levels an intent gaze at me. "And you believe it too, deep down. Otherwise you wouldn't be here."

I think about the Josh-shaped mass of doubt that's taken residence in my chest and nod slowly.

"Tell me," Mark says.

"It's probably nothing," I say, as if it's a warning. "Just a feeling."

"I know what your hunches are like," he tells me. "I've played against you before. Tell me."

"It's Josh," I say. And as I tell him my suspicions, I can feel myself unclenching, as if my body is remembering what it's like to fill this space across the table from Mark Thomas, remembering what it's like for us to be friends.

"It makes sense," he says, breaking his toothpick in half and running a finger gently over the splintered ends as he speaks. "Remember what he said after it happened? What kind of psychopath . . ."

"We can't assume he's guilty," I interrupt. "Not based on like . . . bad vibes. We need more than that."

"So let's get it," he says. "Let's make like Nancy Drew and follow whatever leads we've got. This—" He jabs at the photograph. "Your intuition about Josh. And our memories of the weekend. That's more than enough to start with."

Ah. There it is. I take a deep breath. "I won't be much help there, then. I don't really . . . remember that day." My words trail off in a mumble, like I'm five and being forced to admit to Mama that I threw every single piece of taugeh from my fried noodles into the rubbish bin, covering them carefully with discarded chocolate wrappers and orange peel instead of eating them the way I was supposed to.

He looks at me, his face all confusion. "What?"

I clear my throat. "I . . . don't remember anything. About that day."

"What are you talking about?"

It's a weird thing, to know so many more words than the average person and yet still have absolutely none of the right ones to explain myself. "Dissociative amnesia," Dr. Anusya calls it. "You've been through trauma, you see, and your brain is trying to protect you from having to relive that episode, from having to experience that pain again." She took her glasses off as she told me this, wiped the smudged lenses with the edge of her purple cardigan. Dr. Anusya likes vivid, saturated colors: bold teals, deep reds, splashes of marigold yellow.

"Oh," I replied. I was dressed in a gray sweatshirt and black jeans, a gray hijab, a pigeon chatting with a bird of paradise. "But I experience the pain anyway."

"Yes," she replied, setting her glasses back on her nose. "So think of how much worse this must be for your mind to be rejecting the possibility of revealing it to you."

I was examining my nails then, running a finger along their jagged edges; I'd taken to biting them, a habit my mother detested and was trying to break me out of. "Will the memories ever come back?" I asked.

"Do you want them to?" Dr. Anusya shot back.

I didn't have an answer.

I still don't.

So I just shrug instead and wait for Mark to speak again.

"You really don't remember anything? At all?"

"I remember bits of it," I say, focusing on the table, tracing each scratch etched into its surface with one finger.

"What do you mean?"

I wish he'd stop asking questions. "Like . . . really close-up snapshots of things that don't make sense without being able to see the whole thing."

"Oh." Mark sits back and stares up at the paneled ceiling for a long time. Above us, a fluorescent light flickers slightly before steadying itself, as if momentarily unsure of its own ability to shine. I brace myself, wondering what he'll ask next, which pieces of my trauma I'm going to have to recycle for his benefit. But when he speaks again, his voice is quiet. "Okay. So it was a Sunday."

I can feel the tension drain slowly from my shoulders. "The last day of the tournament," I say. "First game."

"Right. And Trina was going up against Josh. Our first suspect."

I think about my conversation with Josh and shiver in the chill of the air-conditioning. "None of that yet," I say. "We're just setting up the scene, okay? No speculation. Just facts."

"Okay, Detective Najwa."

"Like Poirot."

"I was thinking more along the lines of Pikachu." He winks at me. "He's cuter."

I can't help it; my lips betray me with a small smile. I

quickly put them to work talking instead. "So Trina was playing against Josh . . ."

"Right. I came straight to Trina's table after my game. I'd finished early. I lost . . ."

"Big surprise."

"Shush." He flashes me a quick smile and continues. "You and Yasmin were already there when I got there. You were waiting for her to finish so you could grab a snack or something. I remember Yasmin saying Trina had skipped breakfast. She was worried she'd be hungry, that she wouldn't have time to eat anything—you know how she is."

I nod slowly. "I think I remember," I say, but the memory is like an outline that hasn't been filled in, the merest ghost of a picture.

There's a slight pause. "I was kind of surprised you were there at all, to tell you the truth."

"What are you talking about?" I stare at him. "Why wouldn't I be?"

Mark shrugs. "You and Trina were in some kind of fight."

"A fight?" This was news to me. "Trina and I never fought." I realize I'm raising my voice, and I can feel my face grow hot. Why am I so outraged by this? Why does it feel so . . . so personal?

"Chill out, Najwa," Mark says, taken aback.

"What did we fight about?" I want to know, need to know, ache to know.

"How should I know? I didn't ask about that kind of stuff.

Not my circus, not my monkeys." He stretches, arms splayed into the air like he's hugging the world. I want to hit him. Can he not see how earth-shattering this is? Does he not understand?

"Oh. And uh. That Ben guy was there too. The Singaporean. Just leaning back and watching." Mark frowns slightly as he tries to remember.

"Okay. Who else?" I make myself ask the right questions, even though all I want to do is drag him back to the topic of this fight.

He moves a finger through the salt mound in front of him, scattering grains everywhere. "There was that Thai girl, what's her name . . . something to do with *Frozen*."

I squint at him. "Anna? Elsa? Olaf? The reindeer? Help me out here."

"Snow!" he yells out suddenly, snapping his fingers. "Her name is Snow! And she was playing against . . ." He stops abruptly then, as if he doesn't remember. But this time, I do.

"Against Puteri," I say.

"Right," he says. "Of course. Puteri. How'd you know?"

"Some things stick," I tell him. "Some things come back. It's not a complete blank, it's just that there are gaps I haven't filled in."

"Can't believe I didn't remember that," he says. His "oops, forgot my ex-girlfriend was there" act is SUPER convincing.

I rummage around in my tote for my notebook and pen. "So here's what that looks like," I say, sketching as I go, marking Trina with an X and using black circles for everyone else. "Here's Trina and Josh. Puteri and Snow. Yasmin and I are standing right here, watching. You're . . . where exactly?"

"Over here," he points. "Leaning against the wall. And Ben was over here by this pillar."

He points out the exact spots and I mark them down accordingly. "Are we missing anyone? I feel like we're missing someone. . . ."

Just then the disinterested waitress comes bearing our drinks and a platter of golden brown curly fries. "Nostraws," she says as she sets down our milkshakes, each piled high with whipped cream and crowned with a glistening red cherry. "Newpolicyfromthemanagement. Helpusdoourparttosavethe-environment."

I glance at the crates stacked up behind the counter. "You serve bottled water," I point out.

"Got it," Mark says quickly as her expression darkens. "Thanks."

The server turns on her heel and leaves. I'm still frowning down at my notes. "I just—" I stop.

"What?" Mark is mid-sip; there's a dab of whipped cream on his nose that causes a mighty internal debate over whether I should tell him about it.

"I can't shake the feeling that we're overlooking something."

Mark frowns as he wipes his face. "I've told you everything I remember."

I drum my fingers on the table. "That's just it, isn't it?

Everyone is going to remember things differently, because everyone pays attention to different things."

He looks at me. "So what are you suggesting?"

"I'm suggesting we talk to everyone who was there. Get their impressions of what happened that day. Try to build one complete picture from all their different pieces of it."

"But you're just going to get a dozen different stories and a dozen different murders." He flips a curly fry into his mouth. "Nobody will remember anything the same way."

"That's the point." I take a sip of my milkshake, which is starting to melt slightly, the whipped cream tower sitting sadly askew. "You can't rely on one source of information. If everyone's telling a different story, who would you believe?"

"The one telling me what I wanted to hear most."

It's disarmingly honest, and for a second, I am knocked off balance. "But we're not after that," I say eventually. "We're after the truth. Or at least, the closest we can get to it."

"Fair enough." He smooths back his hair and smiles. "Guess I'll just have to rely on my charm. Even if half of them hate my guts and the other half have already decided I killed my girlfriend."

"And where," I ask, "does that leave those of us without your charm or good looks?"

"Are you kidding me? You've got the perfect excuse!" He stirs his drink with the straw, and I watch as swirls of chocolate syrup bleed gently into the creamy vanilla. "You can tell them you're just trying to get your memory back. They'll all help you. How can they not after a story like that? They'd look like assholes otherwise."

I frown. "I don't know how I feel about using my messed-up brain as a cover for our amateur investigation."

"Might as well make it useful."

I throw a fry at him and he catches it neatly, grinning at me.

"Besides," he continues, "who said you aren't good-looking?"

"Shut up." I'm blushing and I hate it. "Anyway. I'll ask around, talk to whoever was there, use my brain as an excuse. I think you should look into this photo thing. See if you can find out what happened to last year's bulletin board, who took it down after the tournament. Someone might remember seeing something suspicious. And maybe we can take a closer look through these Instagram posts, too. I'm sure we'll figure out who's behind this. . . ."

"Sounds good," he says, hesitating for a brief instant. "Only, uh. I think you should let me talk to Puteri."

I raise my eyebrow at him. "Really? You think that's wise?"

"You think she'll talk to *you*?"

"Point taken."

"Maybe I'll talk to someone in security, too," he says, popping another fry into his mouth. "Get some idea what they may have seen, you know. That weekend."

"And what makes you think they'll talk to you?"

"People do, sometimes." He shrugs. "It's worth a shot."

"Fine." I sit back with a sigh. "I'll take on the rest. Report back with anything interesting or useful." I write it all down, everything we're each supposed to do, committing it to memory.

"What are you doing?"

I shoot him a look. "What does it look like, genius? I'm writing things down. Don't all great detectives keep notebooks? And anyway, I don't trust myself."

"I trust you," he says quietly.

"Yeah, well." I stare at my notes so I can avoid meeting his gaze. *REGICIDE. JANIFORM.* "Do you think we're going to like what we find?"

"Probably not." He looks at me and smiles, and this time I don't even try to hide it, I smile back. "But it's better than doing nothing. And it's better than doing it on my own."

And as we sit there, munching on greasy curly fries and sipping overly sweet milkshakes, I feel something inside me begin to unspool. And I hear a voice in my ear, a voice that sounds a lot like Trina's: *Oh, Najwa, what are you doing?*

CHAPTER TWELVE

QUAESITUM

twenty points

noun

that which is sought; the answer to a problem

We walk back to the hotel quickly, our steps brisk, my short legs working to match the stride of Mark's long ones. In the past year, I've often spent days drifting from sleep to sleep, my waking hours just a way to spend the time between blessed unconsciousness. Now, for the first time in a long time, I feel . . . awake. Every Scrabble player can rattle off lists of hooks—a letter that can be added to the front or the back of an existing word on the board to form another. ASPIRIN becomes ASPIRING; IRATE becomes PIRATE; FLAMING becomes FLAMINGO. I think of how I am the opposite way, how I am going from FUTILITY, as in utter pointlessness, to UTILITY, as in usefulness. Lose an F, gain a purpose.

"What are you thinking?" Mark asks.

I stop for a second. "I guess I'm still hung up on why," I say honestly. "Why someone would go through all this trouble."

"To kill Trina?" he asks. "Or to get into her Instagram account just to tell us they think she was killed?"

"Either. Both." I tuck a tiny strand of baby hair that's worked its way loose back under my hijab. "It's the same person we're looking for anyway, right? The only way someone could know this much about the murder is if they were the one who did it."

"You have a point. And really, it's not that hard to understand." He shrugs. "Trina was very, very easy to love, and also very, very easy to hate." Something about the way he says it makes my thoughts slam into each other like out-of-control bumper cars. "There was rarely any in-between. The highs were astronomical, the lows were abysses. And when you inspire those kinds of big, extreme reactions in people, well . . . you also inspire big, extreme actions sometimes."

We lapse into an uneasy silence as we walk, my mind mulling this over. Of course, I was aware of the hate—how could you not be? But my memories of Trina are filled only with love. Dr. Anusya and my mother both say I have to work to remember Trina the way she was, which was happy and full of life, and not the way I last saw her, which is extremely, irrevocably dead. Dr. Anusya says this is for my own mental well-being, so that I can think back on the past with fondness and love and not with anger or regret. My mother says this is so I stop being "so weird and morbid."

"People will talk, sayang," she tells me, smoothing my hair back from my forehead, always so eager to tidy me up and make me more presentable. "Buat malu nanti. We don't want that now, do we?"

I couldn't care less about people and what they talk about. But I know in their own ways, both Dr. Anusya and Mama are right.

So I remember.

In my head I erect a shrine and paper its walls with snapshots of my life with Trina: random dance parties in her bedroom, long conversations on notes slipped to each other in the middle of classes, video calls at two a.m. when we couldn't sleep, horror movie marathons even when we knew they'd give us nightmares, shared packs of M&Ms where she'd take all the blue ones and I'd take all the red ones. And everywhere, inevitably, there was Scrabble: Trina and I sipping cold boxed Ribena as we quiz each other from stacks of flash cards I'd made; Trina and I playing against each other and taking turns winning because we kept changing the terms of what winning meant, first best of three, then best of five, then best of ten, then best of thirty. Every memory laced with threads of love and laughter and togetherness.

And I remember this:

"Mark, this is my best friend, Trina." I had to raise my voice slightly to be heard over the din of the café where Trina sat waiting for us, flipping through a glossy magazine and sipping on iced coffee.

"Hi, Trina," Mark said, sitting down across from her, flashing her the same easy smile he had for everyone, his teeth white and gleaming. I'd warmed to him as soon as we'd played our first game against each other a few months ago, enjoyed his infectious laugh, that effortless charm. Trina, I thought, would like this boy. And I was right.

I used to tell Trina that she was like a cat in so many ways: lofty and high-maintenance, needy and demanding, doing whatever she wanted just because she felt like it, and always demanding head pats. There were other things I didn't mention: the way her eyes gleamed when they lit upon prey; the way she moved, sensuous and feline; and the way her voice often dropped to a husky purr when she laid her eyes on something that pleased her. The way it did then, when she replied: "So this is the famous Mark. You come with quite a reputation."

"I could say the same for you," he said, laughing.

"Oh?" She leaned forward, her hair brushing against his arm. "And what have you heard?"

Already I could feel their world shrinking down to two distinct points: him, her, and nobody else. To DIMINISH is to become less, and that was me, fading away to nothingness with each word they spoke.

"I'd rather keep that to myself," Mark said. He was leaning forward now too, mirroring her perfectly, their heads bent close together.

She bent close to his ear. "It's all lies," she whispered, just loud enough for him—and me—to hear.

"Oh?" He grinned, and as if in slow motion, I watched as

he used one finger to trace a path on the delicate inner skin of her arm, from her tattooed wrist all the way to her elbow, a touch so intimate I almost wanted to turn away, give them some privacy. There was a time when wooden Scrabble tiles had the letters engraved into their smooth surface, making it easy for unscrupulous players to feel for telltale angles and contours and pick the exact letters they wanted from within the bag without even looking. The practice was called brailling, and that's what it looked like Mark was doing: trying to gauge the real Trina, feel her out beneath that perfectly polished surface.

Trina and I drew shaky breaths at the exact same time, though I don't think she noticed mine. To DIMINISH is also to cause something to seem less impressive and valuable; it might as well be the title of the story of Trina and me.

"Will you tell me the truth, then?" Mark said, his voice soft and low, his eyes never leaving hers.

"Always," she said.

In 2008, Jesse Inman set the record for highest-scoring opening move, playing MUZJIKS during a game at the National Scrabble Championship for 128 points. You know what the odds are of having the tiles to play a word like MUZJIKS right out of the gate, on your first move of the entire game? They're 1 in 55,555,555. By contrast, I once read a magazine article that said the odds of finding The One, assuming that soul mates are set at birth, that they're roughly in the same age bracket, and that your love is recognizable at first sight, are only 1 in 10,000.

Given the sheer disparity of those numbers, Trina and Mark almost seemed inevitable.

"You okay?" Mark asks.

Easy to love, easy to hate. Maybe they're both just different sides of the same coin.

"I'm fine," I say. I'm glad I never told him my tell.

CHAPTER THIRTEEN

FLUNKY

sixteen points

noun

servile person

A re you sure you're okay?" I turn to see Mark watching me closely as the glass doors glide open to let us in and the bellhop mutters a polite "Good evening."

"Stop asking," I say. "You sound like my mom."

He looks aghast. "I thought we were friends now. That is incredibly insulting."

I grin. "I'm going to go find Yasmin and talk to her. What's your first move?"

"I'm going to mosey on over to some of last year's committee members and see if I can't figure out the story behind that photo," he says, jaw set, a determined look on his face.

"Okay. Text me when you have updates."

"You too, Pikachu."

I walk away before he can see my grin. I forgot how nice it can feel, to have a friend like this.

Now to find Yasmin. I whip out my phone and think about what I need to do.

Hey, you free?

I type carefully.

I could use some company . . . Things are just so hard right now.

There. I hit send and wait. I'm almost certain that Yasmin won't be able to resist the lure of someone to take care of.

Sure enough, the reply comes seconds later.

OMG of course!!!!! it screeches. Anything for you, lovely. Come hang out in my room and I'll make u some tea and we'll have a nice cozy chat <3<3<3 1105!!!

Right. Time to get my Sherlock on.

I sit on Yasmin's bed, watching her make me a cup of tea. She's in a batik kaftan, the kind my mother wears to lounge around the house. "Luckily you texted just then," she says as she works. "I was about to go to bed."

I check my phone. "It's only nine thirty," I say.

"I like to be well-rested," she says. "Especially for tournaments." Her movements are practiced, soothing; her sheets smell like vanilla, the way Yasmin herself often does. Trina used to say that Yasmin came out of the womb a grandma, wrapped in the scent of lavender and vanilla and Tiger Balm, dying to feed everybody. They grew up next door to each other, in neighboring semi-detached homes: two identical houses joined by a wall, two little girls joined at the hip all through primary school, before Trina's family eventually moved away. I was surprised when she'd started turning up at Scrabble tournaments too, but Trina had just shrugged. "She wants what I want," she said. "And she goes where I go." And so I just accepted that Trina and Yasmin were a package deal, the kind of two-for-one offer that makes my mother intensely skeptical. ("Why two for one? Why so cheap? Because they want to sell fast? What's wrong with the product? Got something to hide, is it?")

"Yeah, how's it been going for you?" I ask. "You seem to be taking all of this . . . much more seriously this year."

"I've been practicing," she says, gesturing around the room, and I take it all in: the sheaves of paper covered in word lists, the flash cards, the Scrabble set on the table where she's mapping out moves, the piles of dictionaries and reference books, their spines lined with creases.

"I can tell," I say, and I don't even try to hide how impressed I am. Not impressed enough to believe it'll work—there are too many sharks in the water to be taken down by a guppy like Yasmin. But something about all this effort is touching.

"It's for her," she says simply, and I believe her.

"Where's your roommate?" I ask her.

"Who knows?" She shrugs as she stirs a spoonful of sugar

QUEEN OF THE TILES

into my tea, then another. "We don't talk much. She's probably off with her own friends. Here you are, dear."

I sit up and accept the steaming cup, balancing it carefully on its saucer so it won't spill all over her bed. "Thank you." The first sip burns my tongue and scalds my throat, but I'm grateful for the warmth.

"No problem, sweetie." She smiles at me. "You look so pale, you poor thing. You just needed someone to take care of you a little."

"Like you always took care of Trina?"

Is it just me or does her smile freeze slightly at the edges? "Well. Some people need more looking after than others, alright," she murmurs, busying herself with tidying up the tea things.

Nice going, Najwa. I can practically see her closing herself off. Time to change course. "How's your Instagram hacking going? Any luck?"

She shakes her head with a small sigh. "Not yet. And I think I might have gotten a virus from some website that swore up and down that it could hack anybody's account. My laptop keeps freezing. . . ."

Oh, Yasmin. So trusting. So naive. "They all say things like that, Yasmin. They'll promise you anything as long as they can get your money."

I can see her getting physically worked up about this, her cheeks red, her breath huffy. "So bad!" she exclaims, and I almost want to laugh at her righteous indignation, the idea that you should expect scruples from people you're hiring to do something decidedly unscrupulous. "How can they do that to people?"

"Beats me." I shrug.

She sits down on the edge of the bed and offers me a packet of cream crackers. "You want some?" she asks. "I love these with tea, and you look like you could use some food."

I'm not really hungry, but I take one just for the comfort of having something to do. Yasmin takes one too, and we sit quietly for a while, nibbling on our biscuits, which make my mouth so dry that they stick in my throat, making me cough.

"Are you alright?" Yasmin says as I splutter.

"I'm fine," I croak, gulping down tea to wash the dregs of crackers down my throat. "Remember how much Trina hated these biscuits? She'd be all 'Why are you eating cardboard? These are *old people* biscuits.'"

Yasmin smiles. "God yes, she hated them! I tried to offer her some once when she was having an upset tummy, and she told me that they'd not only upset her tummy further, they'd actively offend it."

I can feel her relax, feel her start to let her guard down, and it's like a light bulb goes off in my head. *This is the trick, Najwa. This is how you get her talking.* "She could be so stubborn." I laugh. "Remember when she snuck an entire nasi lemak into the movies one time when we went to watch *Captain Marvel*? Even when we told her it was a bad idea! That they'd kick us out or something! Nope, she didn't even listen. Just took it right out of her bag, unwrapped it, and started eating, rice and sambal and all, right there in the middle of the movie, just because she felt like it."

"Of course I remember! And then that old man in front of us turned around and shot her this glare, and all she did was smile and ask him, 'Why, Uncle? You want some ke?'"

"Right! But she was always that way with nosy adults, anyway. One time we were out together and some lady tapped her on the shoulder while we were on the elevator and told her that her skirt was so short that it was offensive."

Yasmin snorts. "Oh, I'd have loved to see Trina's face for that one. What did she say?"

I grin. "She said, 'I was always told that the most polite thing to do was mind my own business, but since you've decided to mind mine, then I have to tell you that your breath is also very offensive, Auntie.'"

Yasmin gets the giggles and can't stop, and for a while all we can do is sit there and take turns laughing.

When we finally calm down, I look at her, a smile still lingering on the edges of her lips. "What do you miss most?" I ask. For once, I'm not buying time. I really want to know.

"Depends on the day," she says. "Her laugh, I think. What about you? What do you miss most?"

I think about this. Nobody has ever asked me this before. Most people act like my grief is something I need to get over, a blip to overcome so we can all get back to regularly scheduled programming. "I think I miss how it felt when we were together," I say, trying to find the right words. "The feeling of . . . completeness. Of belonging. I don't have that with a lot of people, so, um. It's hard. Not having it anymore."

Yasmin nods; I get the feeling she understands. And it surprises me how much it matters to me that she does, how validating that feels. I expected to go into this to get answers, not comfort, and yet here we are.

Focus, Najwa. I've laid it on thick enough. Time to zero in on what I need. "I guess that's why it feels so jarring to be here," I continue. "Without her. It feels like everywhere I turn, there's another memory waiting for me." Never mind that I can't quite figure out what those memories are; Yasmin doesn't need to know that.

"Dear, dear," she murmurs, reaching out to pat me consolingly on the hand.

I set my cup down and lean back, closing my eyes. "It's the worst when I play. I keep thinking about that last game. With her and Josh . . . and how weird Josh was acting . . ." I pause, waiting to see if she'll take the bait.

Yasmin frowns. "Was he acting weird? I didn't notice. You know Josh. He's . . . always the way that he is. He's so full of wanting to win that there's no room for anything else."

"Yes, like politeness," I supply. "A sense of humor. Basic human decency . . ."

She laughs again. "I suppose all of those things would apply. But at least it wasn't as bad as having both Mark *and* Ben there watching Trina play. Or at least that's what they were supposed to be doing. Mostly they were just watching each other. Like cats when they encroach on each other's territory, you know, hackles up, ready to pounce."

Yasmin gets up and pours herself another cup of tea. I wince as she slurps it down; eating and drinking noises always grate on my nerves. "That's right, I remember that," I say, lying like I've been doing it all my life. "It was so awkward."

"You know Ben was always a little bit in love with Trina—well, as so many of them were, I suppose, but he was more obvious about it." *Easy to love, easy to hate.* I nod and make "I'm listening" noises, and she keeps going. "And Mark, for all that they screamed and yelled at each other, he certainly didn't want anyone else to have her." Another noisy slurp, and I grit my teeth. "Nothing came of it, of course. You know how boys are, all bark, no bite. You remember? Trina told them she wasn't interested in watching them compare the size of their . . . you know . . . their thingies." She giggles. Yasmin can never bring herself to the words for . . . basically any part of male genitalia. Or any genitalia at all, really, a fact that used to be a constant source of amusement for Trina. Thingies, ding-dongs, "down there," Yasmin has a mighty arsenal of euphemisms and she isn't afraid to use them.

I force out a casual laugh. "Yeah, of course I remember!"

"'If I wanted to know, I'd compare them myself, and right now neither one of you is worth that kind of attention.'" Yasmin's impression of Trina's cool, sardonic tone is surprisingly effective. "Squashed all that macho hot air right out of them, had them deflated like balloons."

"As it should be," I murmur.

There's a pause. When Yasmin speaks again, her voice is low. "This is nice," she says softly. "Nobody ever talks about her with me, not like this. And here . . . it's like they just want to forget her. Or take her place." Her face darkens. "As if anybody could."

"I know," I say. "And she would have appreciated you standing up for her the way you did during dinner, and for working so hard to beat them all." I take a breath and go in for the kill. "That's the kind of thing a true friend would do."

"Of course." Yasmin raises her chin almost defiantly. "I took care of her then, and I'll keep taking care of her now."

Something about her words tweaks the ghost of a memory loose, pale and slight and just within my grasp. . . . "She wasn't feeling well that day, right? And you were . . ."

"I was trying to take care of her. Like I always do. Did," she says, quickly correcting herself. "Hard to remember her that way, all shaky and upset. She didn't even want to eat any breakfast. Not the hotel food, not even the food her roommate had. Whole room smelled of mutton curry when I went to get her that morning, but she couldn't even eat a bite, and you know how much she loved curry! Said all she'd do was throw it back up. She was so desperate to feel better she was even willing to eat one of Emily's medicines! Or at least I assume it was from Emily, who else could it be? But I did so worry about how poorly she was feeling. That's why I went back to the buffet after you and I were done with breakfast, remember? You went on into the hall without me, and I went back and wrapped a chocolate croissant up in tissues and brought it to the table with me. Just something light, something to settle her stomach . . ."

"Right," I say. Isn't that what you're supposed to do when you want to encourage someone to go on? Make encouraging noises? "And we were just standing there, watching, waiting for her to finish playing."

It seems to work. Yasmin takes a deep breath. "Anyway. I could tell she was still feeling pretty sick; you could see how pale she was, how she swayed in her seat sometimes, like she was losing control. And then she fell over . . ." She pauses, and I can see the tears start to gather in her eyes. I look away. I don't want her to cry, not now, not when my nerves feel so tender, so exposed. "I remember screaming for someone to call a doctor, call an ambulance, call somebody. I tried to get to her, but there were suddenly so many people around her and I got pushed out of the way. I just stood there, my mouth sort of hanging open, watching it all happen. And then I realized my hand felt sticky and I looked down and it was just covered in a mess of chocolate. I'd crushed the croissant in my hand without even realizing it. Crumbs all over me, all over the floor." She gulps. "I miss her, you know. So much."

My heart softens. Something Mark told me drifts through my head: *You're not the only one who lost her.* I let the minutes pass, give her some time to swallow her sobs, let her regain her composure. I think about how much losing Trina changed me, how I'm still trying to figure out this person I am now. I wonder if Yasmin has changed too. How could she not?

"Anyway, I know I only missed a little bit of the game," Yasmin says. "But I still wish I'd just been there the whole time. Like you, you know. It sounds silly, but for a long time I thought: What if I'd been there? What if I'd noticed something was wrong, something nobody else saw? Called for help? Would it have made a difference?" I swallow hard; I know these what-ifs too well. "I guess we'll never know."

Chris Martin's mournful wail suddenly rings out, making us both jump. *I'll always be waiting for you.* "It's my phone," I tell her, fishing it out of my pocket. Alina teases me endlessly about being the level of basic that calls for a Coldplay ringtone, but there's something about this song—one of our dad's favorites—that haunts me. "Wait a sec. Hey, Mark." As I listen to his voice, I see something flicker across Yasmin's face, a look I can't quite place. "Sure, see you downstairs in a bit," I say into the phone. "Bye."

"You're meeting Mark?" She's trying for casual, but Yasmin's never going to be up for an Oscar.

"Yeah," I say. "He wants to talk to me about something."

She takes another sip from her cup. I can almost see her choosing her words.

"Be careful," she says finally.

"Of what?"

"Of Mark. He's dangerous."

I want to laugh, until I realize she's being dead serious. "Mark? Dangerous? I know he's a little full of himself, but dangerous seems a little dramatic, Yasmin." I get up and go over to the mirror to fix my hijab, all crumpled and crooked from leaning against the pillows.

"Look at you, already preening for him." Her mouth is twisted in an expression of disgust. I can't believe what she's saying. I can't believe the cozy Yasmin of just five minutes ago is gone so completely. "That's the effect he has on all the girls, I suppose. But I would never have expected this from you of all people."

I feel the annoyance spark in my chest. "Expected what? God, Yasmin, I'm just trying to make sure my hair's covered and my hijab's neat. You're really overreacting here."

"Oh yes?" She crosses her arms and glares at me. "Did you know Trina was going to break up with him that weekend? For good?"

"What?" The thought had never crossed my mind. Trina and Mark broke up often, but them getting back together was as inevitable as the tides. Breathe in, breathe out, sunrise, sunset, break up, make up.

"That's right." I don't like the gleam in her eye, the pride in knowing something that I don't, at having Trina confide something in her that she hadn't trusted me with. I know Yasmin resented my friendship with Trina, but it wasn't often that she was this obvious about it.

"Trina was afraid of Mark," she tells me. "She was tired of the drama, the angry outbursts, the screaming matches. She wanted a clean break. He knew it. And so did you. Wasn't that part of the reason you guys had that fight in the first place?"

"That fight?" This is the second time I'm hearing about this mysterious fight between Trina and me, and I guess my surprise comes off as disbelief, because Yasmin's face hardens.

"I know. How unbelievable. Who would have guessed that you two, the dictionary definition of BFFs, destined to be together forever, soul mates even, bagai pinang dibelah dua, who would have thought you would ever disagree? But you did."

"I didn't mean that, I just . . ."

"Look, I don't know the specifics, okay? It's not like you guys filled me in." There is a trace of bitterness in her voice, an injured look that makes it hard to meet her gaze. "But you were in a fight, and it had to do with Mark. That's all I know."

I nod. I'm still trying not to show how much this has me reeling. "I have to go."

Yasmin grabs my wrist then, and I yelp at the strength of her grip. She leans forward so I have to meet her gaze, intense and piercing, so I have no choice, so I can't look away. When she speaks again, she emphasizes each word, as if to sear it into my brain: "Mark is dangerous. You hear me? Be careful."

Then she releases me and I stumble away, slamming the door behind me.

As I head downstairs to meet Mark, rubbing the red marks on my wrist, I think about the look in Yasmin's eyes, the fire in her words, this side of her I've never seen. Another face. *JANIFORM*, I think to myself, and just for a moment, I shiver.

CHAPTER FOURTEEN

UMBRAGE

twelve points

noun

displeasure or resentment

verb

shade

On my way down to the lobby, I reach for my phone and look through my favorite contacts for Alina's name. If anybody knows anything about a fight, it'll be Alina.

The phone rings once, then twice, then my little sister's face fills the screen; she always holds it way too close for video calls.

"Hi, Kakak!" she says cheerily. "What's up?"

"Hey," I say. "I have a question."

"Okay. Hold on." There's a clatter and the world on the other end of the screen tilts, then rights itself again as she leans it against something so she can see me while she ties her hair back. "I don't know if I have an answer, but you can ask."

"Were Trina and I fighting about something?"

"What? I mean, you fought sometimes, I guess, but . . ."

"That weekend specifically, though." I fiddle with the fringed end of my hijab. *Please, Alina, give me some answers.* "Did I mention anything?"

"Um . . ." I search her face for clues, but all I'm getting is confusion. "What are you talking about, Kakak?"

"Did I tell you anything about us arguing, or having some kind of disagreement? Or anything at all?"

She shakes her head and grabs the phone to bring it closer; her face is worried. "No. Kakak, are you okay?"

"I'm fine."

"No you're not." Alina is visibly distressed now. "You know what Dr. Anusya said. You've got to eat right, get enough sleep, all of that. You know how much worse it gets when you don't take care of yourself."

"I am."

"Stop lying to me." Even through a phone screen, I'm having trouble meeting her gaze. "What is this about?"

I swallow a sudden lump in my throat. "Nothing. I have to go." I hang up before she can say anything more.

I pull out my notebook once again, and I write it all down, all of it: everything Yasmin said about that day, and about Mark, and about the fight. When I'm done, my head feels like someone is squeezing it in a metal vise. So Trina and I were in a fight, yet somehow I didn't tell Alina anything about it; Alina, who knows all my secrets; Alina, who knows me better than anyone else. What was I keeping from her?

What was it about this fight that was so personal, so big, that I couldn't tell my sister about it?

I don't see Mark anywhere when I get to the lobby, so I lay claim to an empty corner, rubbing my wrist. The crowd has dwindled somewhat—it's almost ten-thirty p.m. now—though I do spot one half of the Tweedles, the one I call Dee, head bent, scribbling furiously. I'm grateful for the quiet, because the thoughts in my head are far too loud. I keep flipping through the pages of my notebook, reading and rereading, over and over and over again. These new revelations—about Mark, about Trina, about me—are almost too much for me to handle. Are they true? Was Trina afraid? Those little clues—her pale face, the sweating, how agitated she was—were they nerves, as Josh said, or symptoms of a stomach flu, or something else entirely? Mark himself had said that Trina was preoccupied that weekend. What if it was him she was scared of? Were we really in a fight? Is Mark the Janus here? Am I?

I close my eyes and try to steady my erratic breathing. *Calm down, Najwa. Trina was your best friend. You loved her. Mark loved her. Neither of you would ever have hurt her.*

The thought comes, unbidden, unwelcome: *Even if she hurt you.*

It is followed swiftly by a memory:

We were on my bed, curled up and facing each other so that our noses almost touched. The room was dark save for the soft blue glow of my childhood nightlight, a sleepy cloud that Trina insisted on plugging in every time she slept over. ("Why?" I'd asked her once, exasperation turning my voice into a groan. "Because I never had one," she'd said. "One like this?" I'd asked. "No," she'd said. "I mean, I never had a nightlight. At all." I'd thought of a tiny Trina, alone in utter darkness, and kept it out on the shelf for her ever since.)

"He kissed me today," Trina told me, a giggle catching at her voice, betraying her giddy excitement.

I felt my breath snag in my chest. "He did?" I tried to inject the appropriate level of excitement into my voice. "How did it happen?"

She snuggled closer, and I smelled the minty toothpaste scent of her breath. "It just happened," she said. "We'd just had this huge, delicious Indian lunch—biryani, tandoori, aloo gobi, baingan bharta, butter chicken, oh my god, we ordered so much food. And we were walking to the train station when we saw the train coming. So he grabs my hand and we start running and running and running to try and make it, and the food is sloshing around my stomach so much I think I might be sick. So I slow down and he asks me what's wrong, and I tell him. And he stops and looks at me and goes, 'Well, maybe this will calm it down.' And then he just leans in and goes for it!" She ended with a squeal, then quickly stuffed a corner of the blanket in her mouth to muffle it. It's a school night, and the only reason my parents reluctantly agreed to a sleepover was because we had a joint English project to work on—a mock newspaper, if I recall correctly—and because we swore up and down that we'd sleep on time. Early, even.

Spoiler alert: This was a lie.

"How was it?" I asked. I don't know why I did it. I guess sometimes you just want to push yourself to see how much of the ache you can take. Like prodding at a sore tooth with your tongue to see if it still hurts. You know full well that it does. You do it anyway.

Trina was silent for so long that I thought she might have fallen asleep. When she finally spoke, it was in a voice so soft I almost didn't hear it. "Amazing."

Yup. Still hurt.

I swallowed hard, trying to dislodge the inexplicable lump in my throat. "You really like him, huh." It's not a question.

"I really do." She traced a path along her full lips, as if the memory of his was seared into them. "I really, really do." Then, in tones of quiet panic, "Oh god, I hope I didn't have onion breath."

We stayed quiet after that, and it wasn't long before she fell asleep, long legs still intertwined in mine. I stared at her, taking in each of her familiar features as if she were a stranger: the long lashes that fanned out over the soft curve of her cheeks, the tangle of her hair spread over the pillow, the rhythmic rise and fall of her chest.

"Boo."

I jump so high I actually feel myself levitate for a second.

"Oh my god, Najwa, I'm so sorry, I didn't mean to scare you that much." Mark looms over me, concern written all over his face. "Are you okay? God, that was stupid, I'm sorry, I was just kidding around."

"It's okay," I manage to croak out. My heart is thundering like a racehorse down the track, but at least it's still beating; for a minute there I was fairly convinced it had stopped altogether. "Did you manage to talk to Emily?"

He shakes his head, sending his hair flying into his eyes. "Nope. She shut down the coffee idea and bolted. Told me she needed to rest up for her games tomorrow. 'I want to be in tip-top condition,'" he says. The pitch is off, but the accent is a dead ringer for Emily's posh tones. "'I've got a real shot at winning this whole thing and I shan't ruin it with poor decisions.' But! I did some digging, and I found something preeeeetty interesting."

"Spill," I say.

"Say pretty please."

I smile my sweetest smile. "Spill, or I'll put fire ants in your luggage."

Mark laughs. "Close enough." He leans close, and I catch a whiff of his cologne. "So. I was asking around about that commotion in the hall . . . You saw Josh's video, right? I wanted to know what happened. And apparently, it was a cheating scandal—that kid from Indonesia was shouting about how his opponent had palmed the blanks and demanding that they strip-search her to find them. It was a whole mess. . . ."

"Okay, but . . . what does this have to do with Trina?" Cheating isn't exactly common in tournament Scrabble, but it isn't unheard of, and this is far from the first scandal we've had during a competition.

"Guess who the alleged cheater was?" He leans back and crosses his arms, a wolfish grin spreading across his face.

"Who?"

"You know."

There is only one answer. "Emily?"

He nods. "Emily."

Of course. Everyone knows about Emily.

Emily is a masterful Scrabble player—or at least, she used to be. The first time I played Emily, she was deft and cool, measured and meticulous. Nothing rattled her. She played with confidence and conviction, hooking onto that word, taking advantage of open double- and triple-word scores, challenging my mistakes off the board, dropping bingos with the same devastating efficiency as some countries drop bombs.

It was my first tournament, and she beat me by 174 points.

"Good game," she said afterward, smiling prettily and lying through her teeth.

"Thanks," I replied, too in awe to say much more. She would go on to win the tournament, another notch on a belt so filled with notches that there was hardly any belt left.

Two years later, I sat down across from a very different Emily, and we began to play.

It was her first tournament in months after Trina had stood up in the middle of a packed hall and announced, in a voice as loud and clear as a bell: "My opponent is cheating, and I would like an investigation. Now." Slowly the events leading up to the incident became clear. You're supposed to lift the bag high above your head as you draw tiles, to make sure you can't see what you're about to get. Emily, Trina claimed, hadn't been doing that. Emily, Trina claimed, had been sneaking peeks into the bag to draw the best tiles for herself. Emily, Trina claimed, along with Emily's perfect match record, was a fraud.

The tournament director let it go, eventually. If you were Emily, you said it was because there was nothing to find you guilty of in the first place. If you were Trina, you said it was because they had no solid proof. Then you said it again, louder. You found a thousand tiny ways to say it, mostly in Emily's presence. And because you were Trina, people listened.

Two-years-later Emily wasn't calm and collected anymore; she was hesitant and anxious, radiating a nervous energy so potent she practically glowed. She bit her nails between turns, and she never stopped moving, from the constant tapping of her feet to the way her eyes darted left and right, up and down, never stopping for a second.

Maybe I should have been more sympathetic. Maybe I should have taken it easy on her. Instead I played MEAOW, placing each tile carefully on the board with a reassuring click. I watched her eyes flicker as she took it in, then looked away as she glanced up at me.

She let it go.

When, a few turns later, she tried to hook an S onto it to place SQUINT on the board, nestling the ten-point Q on a pale blue double-letter tile and turning MEAOW into MEAOWS, those eyes landed on me again, uncertain, beseeching.

I pretended not to see. Instead, I raised my voice. "Challenge!" I called out.

The tournament official who bustled over confirmed what we both knew: that the word was invalid. That it didn't exist in any Scrabble dictionary. That I'd played a phony despite knowing it was a phony for this exact purpose. Emily was forced to take SQUINT back and miss a turn, a turn that I used to block her path and pile up the points, extending my lead so she had no chance of beating me. Because I could have played anything from MEOW to MEOU to MIAOU to MIAOW to MIAUL and they would all have meant the sound that a cat makes, but MEAOW, despite all the other iterations, doesn't exist in official word list. Sometimes, when the tiles don't go your way, you have to resort to cunning instead. *It's a legit Scrabble strategy*, I told myself. I had nothing to feel guilty about. And yet I thought about the plea I'd seen in her eyes, and felt the guilt anyway.

"Good game," Emily said at the end, the plummy British tones laced ever so slightly with bitterness.

"Good game," I echoed. I'd won, after all.

The aftertaste of Emily's bitterness lingers, and I shake my head as if it'll help rid it of any stubborn traces. "I still don't understand what that has to do with whatever happened to Trina," I tell Mark.

He frowns. "Don't you see? That one accusation from Trina ruined her life—"

157

"Let's not get dramatic about it," I say. "It's just a game," I say, as if it isn't my whole world, as if it isn't the life raft I'm currently clinging to, the only thing keeping me from being swept away by my own darkness.

"Najwa, look around you." Mark opens his arms wide, as if to encompass the entire lobby and its tables filled with our peers discussing nothing but Scrabble. "For most of these kids, this game *is* life."

"Point taken," I say. "And Yasmin did say that Trina asked Emily for something to help with her nausea that morning . . ."

"You see?" Mark's tone is triumphant. "That has to be it. She must have given Trina something that . . . that . . ."

"That killed her?"

"Maybe."

"Be reasonable, Mark," I say. "So you're saying that Emily killed Trina to *change the subject?*"

"Look, I'm just saying—she gave Trina a pill, and a couple of hours later Trina ends up dead." Mark shrugs. "You've got to agree that the timing is suspect. And we want to make sure we cover all our angles, right? Leave no stone unturned, or whatever the expression is?"

There it is again, that pang of guilt. *You could have done something. You could have stood up to Trina. You could have stopped her from ruining Emily's life.* "So you think Emily went through all the other options at her disposal and thought, 'Huh, murder looks good, let's go with that'?"

"Maybe she never intended for her to die in the first place," he says defensively. "Maybe she just meant for her to get sick or something, and it all went too far. . . ."

I force myself to laugh. "You're being ridiculous. This is real life, Mark, not some Lifetime special."

He sits back and regards me, his expression confused. "I don't get it."

"What?"

"What was the point of agreeing to work together if you're just going to dismiss everything I say?"

I swallow, my throat suddenly dry. "I don't know," I say. "I'm not trying to dismiss anything. I'm just saying . . ."

"You're acting like everyone else," he says, his voice hard now, anger bubbling just beneath its smooth surface. "You're acting like I'm ridiculous. Like I'm some kind of bumbling fool."

"I don't . . ."

"You're laughing at me."

"I'm not," I bite back, my voice louder than I intended. "And the only thing funny about this is how you're grasping at the thinnest of straws to pin the blame for Trina's death on some random girl, when it took an Instagram post to get you to act like you cared about her dying at all."

He stares, openmouthed. "What are you talking about?"

I don't know why I say it. Maybe it's the frustration talking. Maybe it's this fight Trina and I had, and the fact that I can't remember anything about it needling at my insides. But the words come out before I can even stop myself, before I can even think: "Stop pretending that you care that she's dead when all I've heard and seen from you since it happened is when you're parading another one of your endless line of pretty distractions all around KL for the whole world to see."

"Dammit, Najwa." He bangs his fist down on the table so hard that the sharp crack echoes through the lobby and makes me jump. "You don't get to decide how I feel, or how I mourn, or how I choose to distract myself from those things," he says with so much force that each word lands like a slap. "You think your way of being sad is the only way? You are not the only person who lost her. I lost her too. And just because we experience that differently doesn't mean that my way is wrong, or that it doesn't mean anything."

My heart is lodged in my throat; I don't know how to respond. Yasmin's words ring in my head, over and over: *He's dangerous he's dangerous he's dangerous.* People sitting around us shoot us startled looks, and I'm reminded painfully, abruptly, of Mark's temper, and what it is like to be on the receiving end of it.

I stand and look at him directly, trying to keep my voice as even as I can. "We can talk again once you've calmed down," I say. Then I turn and walk away. When I look back, I see the same old dark look on his face, the one from the old days. *She loved you,* I think to myself. *She trusted you. That must mean something.*

I don't want to be afraid.

But I am.

CHAPTER FIFTEEN

LOGOMACHY

twenty points

noun

argument about words or the meaning of words

I f I had to pick a word to describe their relationship, I'd say Mark and Trina were a contranym, a word that is its own opposite. Maybe CLEAVE, which means both to hold firmly together and to break apart. Or WEATHER: to withstand, or to wear away, bit by bit. You never knew which it would be.

It was another classic Mark-and-Trina fight, a reality show–worthy slanging match in the most public place they could find: the Starbucks just down the road from the hotel. Mark had met us there, finding us reclined in the plush armchairs by the window, ogling passersby and sucking on iced fruit teas to escape the punishing Malaysian heat. His eyes immediately clocked Trina's outfit: tight pink top, short black shorts. Nothing particularly novel or offensive for Trina, and, if we're being honest, for plenty of the other girls out and about in similar clothes. It was a hot day, after all.

"Did you have to come out dressed like that?" he said, his brows furrowed.

Trina glanced at him, her eyes immediately hard and sparking dangerously. "What a pleasant way to say hello, my love," she purred, her voice like honey. "I can't wait to hear what the encore will be."

Mark brought his fist down on the table hard, and the sound was so loud and so sudden that for a second it seemed like it silenced everyone and everything around us. "People are staring at you," he spat.

"Now that's just not true," Trina said through that megawatt smile. "They're staring at you, lover. Because you're so handsome. And also because you're making a tremendous scene." She got up and began gathering her things. "Come on, Najjy, let's go."

"The only one making a scene around here is you." Mark took a step forward. "You're supposed to be my girlfriend, and that means not putting yourself on display for the whole world to see." And then he reached out and shoved her, so that she stumbled backward, her drink almost slipping from her fingers.

I shrank into my seat, gripping my iced peach jasmine sweet tea and wishing I was somewhere else—anywhere else. In 1982, Dr. Karl Khoshnaw set the record for the highest single-word score in Scrabble competition, playing CAZIQUES across two triple-word squares for a total score of 392. When Spanish explorers first reached the West Indies, they found tribes who described their chiefs as caziques; the conquistadors took that word and decided to apply it to *all* native chiefs. This always struck me as a bold, arrogant move: taking something that wasn't even yours to begin with, deciding what it meant, and then bending everyone else to your will. That was Mark: a conquistador, trying to impose his will on Trina, colonize her spirit and reap her charms for himself, bend her to his definition of what a girlfriend ought to be. A cazique is also a type of tropical bird, brilliant and colorful and free; you'd think Mark would know better than to try and put this one in a cage.

This time was no different. Trina trained her gaze directly at him, and when she spoke, it was cool and calm and brooked absolutely no disagreement. "My body isn't yours to control," she said evenly. "No part of me is. And if you touch me like that again, you're going to be very, very sorry. Come on, Naj. We're leaving." She grabbed her purse and stood waiting as I unfolded myself awkwardly, then took my arm, pointedly turning her back on Mark.

"Bye," I said, my voice barely a whisper, as we walked away. He never answered. When I looked back, he was still staring at us, his arms folded, his face dark and inscrutable.

If you'd asked me back then, I would have said Mark was passionate. That he was sensitive. That he was emotional. I would have used every word in my arsenal but dangerous. How could he be? I knew him so well. I knew *them* so well. This was the way it was with them, as changeable as monsoon weather. Their fights were raging thunderstorms, all bangs and crashes and flashes and roars, but in a minute the skies would clear and they would spend every spare minute entangled in each other so that it was hard to know where one ended and the other began, his fingers woven into her hair, her head resting on his shoulder, his lips by her ear, her eyes on his face.

And me? I stayed through it all, the loyal best friend, the eye of the cyclone. As the winds whipped and whirled around me and often made me lose my breath, I mopped up mascara-stained tears with dozens of tissues; I aided in the composition of dozens of texts both sent and unsent; I listened equally patiently to breathless whispers of devotion and long rants punctuated with showers of angry weeping; then I mopped those up too. I bore witness to the changeable temperatures, a dedicated meteorologist charting the climate of their love story. I weathered: I withstood, but almost without realizing it I also wore away, bit by bit. Maybe it was me that was the contranym all along.

I head outside, desperate for some fresh air to clear my head. As I walk out of the sliding glass doors, trying my hardest not to look back at Mark, my phone vibrates urgently. A text from Alina. Just two words:

Check Instagram.

It's suddenly hard to breathe.

There it is, that familiar circle ringing Trina's photo, signaling a brand-new Instagram Story. Just seven letters this time, a bingo: AMLEINT. The accompanying caption reads *Look again.* I frown, squinting at the tiles on the screen. Could it really be that easy this time? Even the greenest of Scrabble new-bies could look at those and see that they spell AILMENT.

I open my notebook, frowning as I write in the dim light of the streetlamps illuminating the sidewalk. I already knew Trina had been feeling unwell that weekend—Yasmin had said as much. But what did Trina being unwell have to do with REG-ICIDE or JANIFORM? Unless someone had done something to make her sick . . . My thoughts turn unbidden to Emily, the bag of medicines rattling around as she walked. Mark is so sure she had something to do with it. Could he be right after all? But why would she bring it all back up again? If you've gotten away with murder, why risk getting caught? Unless the Insta-gram messages are coming from someone else . . . I lean against the wall of the hotel, cooled now by the gentle night breeze, and try to focus. Breathe in, one, two, three, four, breathe out, one, two, three, four. Breathe in, one, two, three, four, breathe out, one, two, three, four. The waves recede. My heart slows its violent pounding. I try and pick through the tangled threads in my head, try to figure out which one to follow: Trina feeling sick, Emily's cheating, Josh's suspicious behavior, and through it all, the look on Mark's face, the way it contorted into a gro-tesque version of itself, anger coloring every contour. *CHOLER*, I think. Bad temper. Eleven points.

I'm still thinking about CHOLER, the satisfying curve of the C mirrored in the R, like the whole word is hugging itself, when I hear footsteps. As if I've called him out with nothing but the force of my thoughts, Josh has come out of the building and is standing on the curb, looking up and down the street as if he's expecting someone. What's he doing hanging around outside at—I check the time—eleven fifteen p.m.? I shrink back into the shadows, staying close to the wall, trying to make sure he doesn't see me. I don't know why, but it seems really, really important right now that I stay hidden. As I watch, he pulls out his phone and taps on the screen.

"Where are you?" I hear him bark. "Hurry up lah. I need to continue my training." Then he hangs up and I see him cross his arms, tapping one foot over and over on the ground. He coughs, and the harsh sound seems to cut a jagged path through the night air.

Who is he waiting for?

A car pulls up to the curb, deep blue and sleek. The passenger side window glides silently down and I see an arm emerge, clad in long green sleeves and holding a small brown paper bag. "Nah," a deep voice says from the car's dim recesses. "Here's what you asked for."

"Finally." Josh takes the bag and peers inside. "I've only been waiting for at least half an hour. . . ."

There's a disapproving sniff. "The world does not revolve around you," the voice says coldly. "Or, might I add, your little game."

"It's not just some game, it's . . ."

"Yes, well," the voice interrupts. "I suppose we all must have our hobbies. Are you sure you know what to do with that?"

Josh bristles. "Of course I do. I asked for it, didn't I?"

"Just making sure. Don't go taking too much, now."

"It's not my first time," Josh says. And then, in begrudging tones, he adds, "Thank you."

"You're welcome. Now we'll head home. Ma told us not to be out too long."

Josh keeps his gaze on the paper bag in his hands. When he speaks again, his voice is carefully neutral. "Did she ask how I was doing?"

"Silly Joshua," the voice says, bemused. "She assumes you're winning. Otherwise, what's the point?" Then the window glides slowly back up and the car drives off. The hand does not wave, and Josh only looks briefly at its retreating shape before he turns and walks back inside, grasping the brown paper bag as if he'll never let go. He never notices me standing there in the shadows, watching and wondering.

CHAPTER SIXTEEN

GLAIKIT
twelve points
adjective
foolish

walk slowly back inside, dragging my feet a little, not wanting to leave the cool air or the way all my worries seem much
smaller when faced with a wide-open night sky. Josh's words
ring in my head: *It's not my first time.* Am I imagining how sin-
ister that sounds, or does everything sound suspicious at this
time of night? *You're reaching, Najwa. Get some rest.* I still have
games tomorrow, after all, and even though it feels like I should
be concentrating on much bigger things—like, say, who might
have murdered the best friend I've ever had, or probably will
ever have—deep down, I still want to win, and I'm not sure
whether to be ashamed of that feeling, or delight in the fact
that I've come this far.

Alina: Checking in
Alina: What are you doing
Alina: Let me guess, moping and obsessing about words

instead of interacting with your peers in a healthy and age-appropriate manner

Me: Shut up

As I type out the message to Alina, head bent over my phone, I suddenly collide with someone who lets out a muffled "Ow!" I'd recognize that accent anywhere. Even Emily's exclamations sound posh.

"Sorry," I say. "That was my fault, I should have been looking where I was going."

"Hardly," she says, rubbing a sore spot where my shoulder inadvertently barged into her arm. "I wasn't exactly paying attention either."

I notice the word sheets in her hands. "Getting some last-minute studying done?"

"Yeah," she says, shrugging. "I'm doing pretty well, but I can't sleep. I decided some revision wouldn't hurt. And I can't do it upstairs since my roommate is dead to the world and it seemed rather rude to turn the light on."

"Of course," I say. Then, as if it just occurred to me: "Would it be okay if I sit with you for a while? I just . . . you know . . . everything's kind of getting to me and I don't want to be alone right now." *Perfect, Najwa, just the right notes of candid and vulnerable.* Trina would be proud.

Emily is immediately sympathetic. "Oh goodness, of course, Najwa. Come, let's sit." She leads me to a corner table with two overstuffed armchairs and we both settle ourselves in their depths. "Do you want to talk?" she says, her cold hand resting lightly on my arm. "Or do you just want to sit here quietly for a little bit? It's totally up to you, of course. Whichever is more helpful."

"You're so kind," I murmur. She preens ever so slightly. I get the feeling that Emily has a Yasmin-esque tendency to want to project goodness—it's not enough to do the nice thing, they must be acknowledged for it. Sure enough, for my compliment I'm rewarded with a smile and gentle pat on the shoulder. "I think I'd like to talk a little, unless that would bother you? I know you want to study. . . ."

"Not at all, not at all," she says, setting her papers on the table in front of us and plonking that huge bag onto the floor. She tucks her feet up under her on the chair and looks at me expectantly. "How have you been? What would you like to talk about?"

"Trina," I say simply, and Emily flinches—just a small flinch, but I notice nonetheless. I don't add *and whether or not you killed her*—at least not aloud—but that's exactly what I'm going to try and figure out.

"I don't know if I'm the best person for that," she says, and her smile this time is tighter, more controlled. "But if it would help to have someone listen, I'm all ears."

She loves being perceived as helpful, doesn't she? So let me use that in my favor. "Thank you so much. I know this isn't easy given your . . . history . . . but I just have nobody else to talk to, you know?"

Emily nods, and I continue. "It's so strange, being here without her. I guess I just feel a little lost. All day, I've just been reliving memories from that last weekend, everywhere I go. It almost feels like she's still here. There's been a couple of times where I've literally opened my mouth to tell her something, like she was right next to me. Is that even normal?" I pause to see how this is landing. Emily is gazing right at me, her eyes soft, radiating empathy. *Good job, Najwa.* "It's like she's haunting me. Not in a bad, Stephen King kind of way. She just . . . lingers."

"Yes, well." Emily coughs delicately. "The past has a way of doing that. Take it from me."

"Sorry," I say, my voice contrite. "I know that past makes her . . . not exactly your favorite person."

"Not at all," she says. "But that doesn't mean I can't understand how important she was to you, and how much losing her impacted you."

I squeeze her hand. "Thank you. It amazes me how gracious you are." She sits up just a little bit straighter at this, and I plunge on ahead. "After everything that happened, you still wanted to help her. I think that's amazing."

She frowns slightly. "Help her?"

"Oh yes," I say. "Yasmin told me you gave her something to help when she wasn't feeling well that weekend. I just thought that was so incredibly—"

"I didn't," she interrupts me. "Give Trina anything, I mean. Not that I wished her ill or anything, but, well . . . she didn't ask me for anything."

"She didn't?" Yasmin had seemed so sure. And if Trina hadn't gotten something from Emily, the tournament circuit's unofficial purveyor of pills, then who had she gotten it from? Was this the truth? Or was Emily just a better actress than I'd ever given her credit for?

Emily shrugs. "Like I said, I was never asked." She leans forward then, and when she speaks, it's slowly and clearly, so that I don't miss a single word. "And if she had, I'm not sure I would have." Then she settles back in her chair, smiling brightly as she gathers her sheets of paper together. "Now, if you're feeling better, let's take a look at some words, shall we? We want to be at our absolute best for tomorrow!"

"Sure." I swallow. I'd never been able to figure out Emily's tell before this. But the way her fingers dug into my leg just moments ago definitely sent a clear message.

This conversation is over.

Later, after Emily has left ("The brain needs rest, Najwa," she said, dropping a kiss that barely touched each cheek. "Make sure to rest yours."), I grab my phone to check the time and realize there's a new notification from TheTrinaProject.

The latest episode is up: *The Roommate.*

I take a deep breath. Then I press play.

I hear the footsteps before the picture fades into the screen, shoes walking along a carpeted floor—shiny red heels with pointy toes, high, fabulous, and absolutely out of place among the parade of sneakers and sandals it passes. Before the camera ever pans up to show us whose feet those shoes are on, I already know who it will be: Shuba, with their mane of dark curls, a silky teal top, tight inky-blue jeans that accentuate every ample curve. We follow them into the lift, watch them walk down the dim hallway, open their door, beckon us inside.

The door closes. THE ROOMMATE appears in capital letters on its smooth dark surface.

"Ya, I was Trina Low's roommate that weekend," Shuba says. They're seated in the one armchair the hotel provides in the room, hugging one knee to their chest, their feet now bare. The red heels lie abandoned on the floor just beside them. As they talk, they wave their hands, their gestures wending and graceful, light glinting off each perfectly painted fingernail. "It was whatever. It was fine. We weren't exactly staying up all night braiding each other's hair and talking about our crushes or anything. She was messier than I'd have liked, but she kept her mess to her side of the room, so I let it go."

"Did you talk to each other much that weekend? Since you were in such close contact all the time?" Tweedledee's voice asks just off-screen.

Shuba raises one immaculately shaped eyebrow. "You know what these tournaments are like, right? You spend all day either playing, talking, or thinking about the last game, or the next one. There's no room for anything else. When I get to the room at the end of the day, I want my bed. Not a heart-to-heart with some *influencer* I don't even really know." There is a light, sneering emphasis on "influencer."

"But you were in such close proximity that weekend. You must have seen a side of her most people don't get to see."

"Oh, sure. I got to see behind the scenes, as it were." Shuba sighs and traces invisible designs on the arm of their chair as they gather their thoughts. "But I mean . . . I still didn't *know* know her. I knew that Instagram version of her. The Queen of the Tiles. Perfect hair, perfect body, perfect boyfriend, perfect life. One brief peek behind the curtain doesn't tell you much about the Wizard of Oz except that he's a phony."

Perfect boyfriend. For a brief moment, the image of Mark's face contorted in rage flashes in my mind, and it takes me a while to shake it off and focus on what Shuba is saying.

". . . And she was really careful to maintain that façade. What I think a lot of people our age sometimes don't get is you only saw what she wanted you to see. Our social media presences are all just curated, manufactured images. Wikipedia entries instead of annotated biographies. You get what I'm saying?"

"I think so," Tweedledee says. "You never knew the real Trina."

"That version of Trina might have been just as real as any other." Shuba shrugs. "I'm just saying I didn't have the whole view. Just that one part. It's like saying you know Chris Evans because you watch all his movies. It's not enough to build a relationship on."

Tweedledee makes some understanding noises. "So tell us what it was like for you," Tweedledum chimes in from behind the camera. "You know. The day Trina died."

Shuba pushes a stray hair back behind one ear. "Not much to say lah," they say, frowning slightly as they try to recall what happened. "I woke up later than I was supposed to—spent a lot of time the night before going back over my games for the day, trying to figure out what mistakes I'd made, how to do better. I had a good win streak going, and then I'd lost my last game because I went overtime. Lost by just eight points okay." They grimace. "Bloody stupid, right? Anyway. I woke up and Trina was getting ready. Whole room smelled like my grandma's kitchen so I asked her why and she just pointed to this bag on the table. It was capati and mutton curry—still hot somemore! Told me I could have some if I wanted." They grin. "Apa lagi, I helped myself lah of course! It was good, too—almost as good as my grandma's."

"So she was willing to share, even though you weren't friends?" Tweedledum asks.

"You don't have to be friends with someone to do a nice thing."

"That's true." Tweedledee takes over. "What happened next?"

"Nothing." Shuba shrugs. "I ate while watching BBC news, and Trina headed out of the room early, like maybe forty-five minutes before the tournament was supposed to start for the day. Then I got ready and went downstairs."

"Why'd she leave so early?"

Shuba smiles, sweet and dangerous. "I didn't ask. Do I look like her parent to you?"

"Not at all," Tweedledum blusters. "Did you, uh, did you see her at all after that?"

This time, their grin is tinged with bitterness. "I didn't see much of anyone. I had the worst food poisoning ever. Before games, between games, sometimes even during games—all I remember is going to the toilet. Over and over and over. Really messed up my gameplay."

"So you didn't notice anything strange or different?"

"How could I? I was a bit preoccupied with trying not to literally shit myself." Shuba laughs, a raspy, surprisingly endearing sound. "Look, I know you want more from me. This doesn't make for great conspiracy theory fuel. But I'm not the one you're looking for. I'm just the person who ate something that had a violent disagreement with their stomach."

The minute they say the words, something inside me clicks.

I grab my notebook and begin flipping through the pages. AILMENT. AILMENT. AILMENT . . .

I sit up.

Something Shuba ate . . . made them sick . . .

AILMENT, I think. *Look again.* The tiles begin to move, rearranging themselves, clicking into place. . . .

And then, finally, I see it. Because it's not just AILMENT. It's ALIMENT: something that nourishes the body. Something that was meant to nourish Trina, meant to be good for her, something that made her sick instead.

It's not my first time.

Don't go taking too much, now.

Exactly what is in that little brown bag of Josh's? Yasmin said Trina had taken some medicine—what if the medicine was from *Josh*, and not Emily like she'd assumed? Doesn't that flush Mark's whole theory down the toilet? Josh, with his intense stare; Josh, with his knowing looks, Josh; who wanted nothing more than to win.

Everyone says Josh was just being himself. "That's just how he is." But which one of us really knows who Josh is?

On the screen in my hands, Shuba continues to talk. "There are people that feel real and solid and . . . whole. Trina wasn't one of those people. She felt hollow, and she was looking for something to make her whole. I think that's what the whole Instagram persona was about, and I think that's what winning was about for her." Shuba leans back and looks out of the window again. You can see the sunset just beyond their shoulder, the sky painted in slashes of orange and pink. "People will disagree. But that's what I think."

"What do you think would have made her feel whole?"

Shuba turns back to the camera and smiles. "Isn't that what we all want to know?"

Then it fades to black.

I stand up and brush off my jeans. I've strayed too far off course, gotten distracted by too many old feelings, followed too many false leads. Josh was the reason I started all of this to begin with; it's Josh I need to find, and Josh who has the answers I so desperately need.

CHAPTER SEVENTEEN

SIMULACRUM

sixteen points

noun

an image, a semblance

t takes me a while to find him; it may be late, but the hotel's various nooks and crannies are still occupied by a decent number of Scrabble scholars. Eventually I track him down in a corridor off the main hall where the tournament takes place. I can recognize him even from twenty paces: Josh Tan, sitting on the floor, leaning against the wall, grimacing at his laptop. I feel my chest tighten suddenly at the sight of his familiar profile, that burning gaze.

He's hiding something, and I'm going to make him tell me what it is.

He's so oblivious to everything going on around him that I'm practically on top of him before he notices my presence. "Oh," he says, pushing his glasses firmly up his nose. "You."

There have been warmer welcomes in the Arctic Circle.

"Yes, me," I say, sitting down on the floor next to him.

"I don't recall asking you to join me," he says.

"I don't recall caring," I say in my sweetest tones, and he scowls.

"What do you want, Najwa? I'm busy." I glance at his screen and see that he's got his Scrabble simulation program loaded up. Hardcore players—and let's face it, most of us here are as hardcore as they come—use it to log every move, re-create each game, see how they could have done better, changed the outcome, turned a loss into a win or a win into a massacre.

"I want to talk to you about something," I say, picking through the stack of papers on the floor beside him. There are half a dozen sheets covered in scribbles. We're all allowed some scratch paper to record words as they're played and keep track of tiles, so we can predict what kind of rack we'll draw next. Here they are, a record of Josh's wins and losses. That there are losses at all must irritate him spectacularly.

He snatches the papers out of my hands and scowls, clutching them to his chest as if they hold the secrets of creation. "How much of my time do you intend to waste?"

"Not much, if you cooperate." I take a deep breath. "What can you tell me about the day Trina died?"

He sighs. "Must I keep doing this? Why do people insist on having me rehash this rather unpleasant event?"

"So don't tell me the things you've already told everyone else." I cross my arms and force myself to look at him directly. "Tell me what you're not telling them instead."

Is it me or does he grow pale? "There's nothing to tell."

"Don't give me that. There's something . . ."

"No, there is not." He gets up quickly. "Now please excuse me. I have to attend to something." He walks off with urgent, mincing steps toward the restrooms.

"Wait, your stuff . . ."

"Keep an eye on it for me," he calls behind him. He's practically running now.

I'm confused—why would he just leave his laptop like this? But it does make for a great time to rifle through the tote bag he always carries with him. It's mostly empty now, but my breath catches as I spy a familiar brown paper bag. Looking around to make sure nobody's watching, I reach in carefully and grab its contents.

It's just a bottle of cough medicine.

It's so anticlimactic, I can feel my body go slack with disappointment. I really thought I'd had it. I really thought I was on the verge of some huge discovery. I really thought I was about to solve this whole thing and do Trina justice.

Deflated, I scan the label idly. *COUGH + CONGESTION,* it blares in all caps. Random phrases jump out at me. *MAXIMUM STRENGTH. 20ml every four hours. Not for children under 12. Dextromethorphan . . .*

Dextromethorphan?

Why does that sound so familiar?

A sound from farther down the hallway startles me and I try to put the bottle back, but my hands are shaking, and the entire bag falls out of my fumbling fingers, sending whatever's left inside—a couple of books, his wallet, a pack of gum—

tumbling to the floor. I hurry to pick it all up before Josh gets back.

I pick the books up and shove them into the bag, grab the container of gum from where it's rolled off, all the while looking toward the restrooms, sure he's going to come out any minute, see what I'm doing, tell me off for snooping.

Only the wallet is left. I bend over to pick it up. It's a dark brown leather bifold, so stuffed with receipts and notes and various other paraphernalia that it's worn at the seams, the fold scuffed and graying. I'm checking to make sure nothing has been dislodged in the fall when I spot the corner of something poking out of an inside pocket. A photograph. And it's only a tiny corner, but something about it—something about the streaks of pastel pink and teal and purple—sets off alarm bells.

That's hair. That's Trina's hair.

Carefully I work it out of its hiding place. It's folded, though not perfectly, and when I open it, I see from the way the paper is cracked and wrinkled that it's been folded this way for a long time. One side is jagged from where it's been ripped from its other half.

It's Trina staring back at me from the photo, Trina in a slinky, deep red dress, Trina laughing as she looks off to her left, to . . . to . . .

To Mark. Because this is the other half of the photo, the one that Mark got yesterday.

As if on cue, I hear a familiar ding, and my palms begin to sweat. Because I know what that is.

That's the sound of an Instagram DM.

He's coming for you.

Who? Josh? Josh is coming? I look around, heart racing wildly, the photo still in my trembling hands. I can't explain what it is that's scaring me so much—I've gotten so many of these DMs now, what difference does one more make? But this one is different. This one feels . . . ominous. *If Josh is the killer,* I think, sweat dripping down my forehead, *then who's the one warning me about him? Who's behind these messages? And how do they know?*

Quickly I stuff the photo back into the pocket where I found it. Then I walk away as fast as I can, not looking back, not even when I hear Josh's indignant voice from behind me—"Hey! You were supposed to watch my stuff! Had it been *stolen* there would have been *severe repercussions!*"

REPERCUSSION, I think. An unintended consequence. And I can't help but wonder how much of all of this Josh intended all along.

CHAPTER EIGHTEEN

DOLOUR

seven points

noun

grief or sorrow

A t one a.m., the lobby is almost entirely abandoned. I sit in one of the armchairs once again, furiously scribbling in my notebook. Why does Josh have Trina's photo in his wallet? Why would he slide the other half under Mark's door? I close my eyes, remembering the bold block letters scrawled across the back. *I KNOW.*

What does Josh Tan know?

"Hey." A low voice makes me whip around, heart racing, as if I'm the one about to be murdered. Mark is standing just behind me, his expression sheepish. He holds up a bag of chips—crinkle cut, sour cream and cheddar. Our kind, our brand. I almost want to laugh. After all that rage, after that public tantrum, he thinks I can be won over by some snacks and sentimentality? Pretty people really do live in a different world. "You want some?"

"No," I say. My mouth is dry, and the word comes out louder, harsher than I'd intended.

"Oh." His face falls and he slowly sits down beside me, dumping his backpack on the floor and ripping the bag of chips open. He puts one in his mouth, and it feels like it takes ages for him to swallow, each crunch deafening in the silence between us.

Mark clears his throat. "So," he begins. "I wanted to apologize for how I acted earlier."

"Ah." I cross my arms. "And by that you mean . . . ?"

"You know . . ." He waves one hand vaguely in the air. "The fighting, the yelling . . ."

I stare at him, not saying a word, and he squirms under my gaze. I'm determined not to make this easy for him. If he wants my forgiveness, he'll have to earn it.

He seems to understand. "Look, I get it. I deserve this. I'm sorry. It . . . it hasn't been an easy time for me."

"Or for me," I point out. "But you don't see me acting like a fool."

"That's true," he says. "But as we've determined, you're much smarter than I am." He offers me the bag. "Now, will you have a chip?"

"No."

He nods. "Okay," he says, his voice sad and low. "Okay."

For a while, the only sound that fills the air is the crunching of potato chips.

"Despite all evidence to the contrary," Mark says finally, "I do like to think I've changed, you know."

"What do you mean?"

"I mean . . ." He looks up at the ceiling as if the words he's looking for are somewhere to be found up there. "I mean I know what I was like before. When I was with . . . with Trina." He sighs. "I cared about that girl so much, but I don't think we were good for each other. And I think when I was with her it made all the worst parts of me come oozing out. Like toothpaste from a tube, you know. All that jealousy, all that anger . . ." He pauses. "Anyway. Not to make this about me. But I am trying. And I'm sorry I messed up earlier, that's all. I didn't mean for that old, ugly Mark to come back."

I think about the scene in Starbucks. Easy to love, easy to hate. A contranym.

Mark eyes me warily. "Are we . . . okay?" he asks.

I sigh. "No," I tell him, "but I guess we can be eventually, if you work hard enough at it." And he grins a giant puppy dog grin. This is the Mark I know, the Mark I trust, and although I resist, it's hard not to just let myself relax once again into the familiar contours of our friendship.

"Good, because I have something to show you." He wipes chip dust off his fingers with the hem of his T-shirt and grabs his backpack from where he's left it on the floor. He takes out a shiny silver laptop and opens it up. "Take a look at this."

"What is it?"

"CCTV footage from the corridor just outside Trina's room. From that morning."

"What?" I stare at him, wide-eyed, and he basks in my surprise. "How'd you even get that?"

"Bribed a security guard." He smiles. "Pays to be a rich douchebag sometimes."

"Your self-awareness is impressive."

"Yeah, well, so is my self-control," he says. "I've been dying to watch it ever since I got my hands on it like half an hour ago. But it didn't seem right to watch it without my partner in crime. Or more like partner in justice, I guess?"

He grins at me and I can't help it; I smile back. "Good work."

"Okay, let's see what we have here." He sets it on the table and we both lean in to get a better view; his shoulder accidentally brushes mine and he immediately pulls back. "Sorry," he says quietly.

"It's okay." The warmth of his touch leaves an imprint; I can still feel it.

Mark hits play.

For a while all we see is a grainy view of a dimly lit hotel corridor, the carpet in shades of pale green, patterned with geometric shapes; the twin rows of closed doors. Then we see him: the shadowy figure of a man, swinging what seems to be a plastic bag in one hand.

Beside me, Mark sucks in a breath.

The man pauses in front of a door toward the top left of the screen. He seems to waver there for a while. What is he thinking? What will he do? I find myself leaning forward, holding my breath.

Then the door opens.

Trina appears. You can tell it's her from the swish of her wavy hair, that familiar profile. She's still in the shorts she always sleeps in at these tournaments, her "lucky" pale purple shorts printed all over with cross-eyed corgis, the ones we picked out together from a bin at the pasar malam. It looks like she smiles. She doesn't seem afraid of him. They linger for a while in the doorway. She takes the plastic bag from him.

And then it happens. She leans forward. And they kiss.

It's a quick peck, not a full on make-out session or anything. But it's enough. It's enough to change everything.

I keep my eyes firmly focused on the screen. I don't dare look at Mark, not even when I hear his breath catch in his throat, not even when I see his fingers curl into fists on his knees. I think about his rage, the way his face darkens when the storm comes.

Trina disappears. The door closes. And the man walks off in the opposite direction of the camera. As he walks, a light glints off something hanging out of his back pocket, and I blink. *Oh.*

Mark closes his laptop gently. "Was that . . ." His voice trails off.

"I don't know," I say. "I don't know who that could be."

"Okay. I see. Okay." He nods, his eyes on his feet, his fingers laced tight, rocking slightly back and forth. "So I was right," he whispers to himself. "She was hiding something. I guess I just didn't think it would be . . . that. Or him."

"You know who that is?"

"Don't you know?" He laughs, a mirthless bark of a sound.

"It's that fucking Ben kid, isn't it? I'd recognize that walk any-where." Of course I know. And suddenly I wonder: *Is this what Josh knows too?*

Mark keeps flexing his hands, clenching and unclenching them into tight, hard fists. It makes me nervous. And it makes me wonder if Mark really has changed as much as he claims he has.

"Are you . . . What are you . . ." What I'm trying to say is, *Please don't do anything stupid.* But the words won't come out right. *He's dangerous,* Yasmin whispers in my head, and I wish she'd shut up right now. I wish I could help him. But I can't. DETRITUS means waste or debris, the kind Trina somehow still leaves behind her even in death; it comes from the Latin word *deterere,* which means "to wear away," which is what this whole weekend is doing to me, to Mark, to anyone who had the twin joy and misfortune of having been pulled into her orbit.

Eventually we run out of things to say. Eventually he stops clenching his hands. Eventually he leaves. Eventually on my own at last, I know what I have to do.

I have to talk to Ben. Alone. Before Mark gets to him.

CHAPTER NINETEEN

ENSORCEL

ten points

verb

enchant

spy Singapore Ben on the floor, his back against the wall, headphones on and tablet in hand.

"Hey, Ben," I say, tapping his shoulder. Turns out Singapore Ben isn't working on anything particularly Scrabble-centric; he's actually watching *10 Thing I Hate About You*. In fact, he's so engrossed in Julia Stiles reading her eponymous poem aloud in English class that he positively yelps at my touch, before turning a deep, dark red. I'm not sure which one he's more embarrassed about: the yelp, the blush, or the fact that I caught him tearing up to what some people might call a chick flick.

Not that I blame him. That movie's a classic.

"Hey, Naj," he says, feigning nonchalance as he quickly takes off his headphones. Only somehow he yanks them out of the jack. Music blares out into the lobby: *I waaaaant you to want me.* I didn't think it was possible, but Singapore Ben blushes even harder. I burst out laughing, and then he laughs too, and for a brief moment it's almost possible to pretend that everything is okay.

"Can I talk to you for a second?" I ask him.

He shrugs. "Sure, why not? What are the odds that I'll make an even bigger fool of myself?" He gestures for me to sit down beside him, and I do.

"I know what you did," I say, and he stares at me, puzzled. "What?"

"You brought her the food that morning, didn't you?" I don't bother saying her name. He knows who I'm talking about.

"Oh." He frowns. "How'd you know?"

I shrug. "I just do."

"Yeah," he says. "Yeah, I did." He runs a hand down his pale face. "She wasn't feeling well, you know. And I know she'd had a fight with that . . . that jerk the night before. I bet that just made it worse. So I went out early that morning and got her breakfast." He rubs his nose bashfully and I'm reminded suddenly of Alina. "Thought it would cheer her up. I ran all the way back because it was raining and I couldn't get a ride." As he tells this story, I picture Ben, hair plastered to his forehead, hands laden with plastic bags. And I feel a pang of sadness for him, his constant attempts to woo a girl who would never be his. I've been wracking my brain to think of what Ben's word is, and now I finally know: SCHLEMIEL, an awkward person whose endeavors usually fail.

"Capati and mutton curry," I say. He nods, and I feel a small tendril of pride unfurl in my chest. I remember. I *remember*.

"Her favorite. I remembered, you see? I always remembered stuff she liked. So even though I got tired from running, and I was totally soaked, I just kept going. I wanted her to have it while it was still warm." He grins suddenly. "Also because I needed to pee lah, to be completely honest. So I wasn't just powered by devotion. Luckily, Puteri was in the lobby so I could ask her to take care of my stuff for me while I went. . . ."

"Puteri?" I say, suddenly alert. "Puteri handled the food?"

"I mean . . . she held the bag for a couple of minutes, if that's what you mean."

I think about Puteri's face whenever she hears Trina's name, about how she calls Trina her nightmare.

Ben continues, oblivious to my churning thoughts. "I was glad I'd done it, anyway, because it did make her smile when I turned up at the door, although I'm not sure if it's because I was a sweaty mess or because of the food. She even—" He pauses here, and I see his cheeks flame all over again. "She even kissed me. Just the tiniest peck on the lips. But she said she'd eat it later because she had this terrible headache and was feeling so anxious, even though she said she couldn't figure out why. So I passed her this medicine my mother makes me take—"

"Medicine?" I interrupt. There are so many ALIMENTS now, I can't keep up. "What kind of medicine?"

Ben rummages around in his bag and emerges with a bottle that he hands to me. "Here. This one. My mother says it's good for anxiety."

St.-John's-wort, the label says. And suddenly, I remember.

A few weeks ago, I slipped back into what I called my

numb phase, where nothing seemed to matter and all I wanted to do was curl up in a ball in my room, shades drawn, and be still. My bones felt like they were lined with lead. I let myself melt into the bedsheets and shut out the world.

After almost a week of this, my mother had marched into my room and forced something into my hand, something smooth and cool to the touch. I squinted at it in the dark. *St.-John's-wort*, the bottle said.

"What is this?"

She threw back the curtains, forcing light into the room. "For your *problems*, dear," she said briskly. "To take care of these little *episodes* you've been having. Now please go and shower."

Later I looked it up. St.-John's-wort, I learned, is a natural treatment for depression, which I suppose was what this was that I'd been dealing with. I was skeptical at first—this felt like an Emily thing to do—but whether it was due to the pills or something else, I did begin to feel better. The trade-off, though, was a long list of medications that I had to be careful of taking while on St.-John's-wort, in case of harmful side effects.

Ben is still talking, and I struggle to focus. ". . . And I never told anyone because . . . well . . . you don't kiss girls with boyfriends, do you?" His face darkens. "Even if those boyfriends don't deserve them. Even if those boyfriends don't seem to care the same way . . ."

"Of course," I say. There's something about his gaze that unsettles me. "So she . . . she took the pills you gave her? The St.-John's-wort?"

"I don't know. She didn't take it right then. I told her she should probably eat first."

I nod. "It was . . . a nice thing you did for her," I say gently. "The food, the meds. I know she probably really appreciated that."

"Yeah, well, you know what they say about nice guys." He scowls at something in the distance, and I turn just in time to catch a glimpse of Mark's back as he walks out the door and into the streets of Johor. "I would've killed for that girl," he half whispers, and I feel a tremor of fear work its way up my spine.

I clear my throat. "Is there anything else you remember about that day?" I ask. "Anything about the other people who were standing around? I know there were a bunch of us there, waiting . . ."

"Let's see." He looks up, contemplating the swirly patterns engraved into the ceiling. "I had a game against this kid from Pahang that morning, this skinny kid with those big front teeth—never saw him before, so he was fresh meat. I was surprised by how good he was! Really took the game to me for those first few moves. He didn't actually stand a chance once I dropped my first bingo, though. GHERKIN." He grins at the memory. "Which makes sense because that move really put that kid in a . . . pickle."

"Can we maybe continue *without* the dad jokes?"

Ben laughs. "Okay, okay. So obviously I kick this poor fella's butt, and I'm done pretty fast, so I decide to see who else is still playing. Trina and Josh were one of the last tables still going at it. Puteri and Snow, too, just next to them."

"And was there anything weird about Josh?" I try not to let my voice give away my eagerness, my desperation to find out anything, anything at all about Josh Tan. "Anything strange about how he was acting?"

Ben laughs. "What's strange for Josh? He was just being himself, as far as I can tell. Insufferable as always. He hated that we were there, I can tell you that. Kept telling us to buzz off, that we were being too distracting."

Nothing new, then. I sigh.

"Funny now that you mention it," Ben continues thoughtfully. "There was one out of character moment for Josh. About halfway through the game. Trina was coughing a lot—she was looking kind of uncomfortable, you know—and Josh just grabs his bag and takes out this bottle and slides it across the table at her. Cough medicine. He didn't even say anything. I don't think he even looked at her. But I remember thinking, 'Oh, guess he has a heart after all.'"

"But you can't take cough medicine with St-John's-wort," I say automatically.

"What?" Ben looks at me, puzzled.

I blink. "Sorry, I'm not sure why I said that. Go on." Side effects. ALIMENT. I close my eyes. *Think, Najwa. Why can't you take cough medicine with St-John's-wort?*

Then my eyes fly open. *Because it has dextromethorphan.*

That's why it had sounded so familiar when I saw it on the label of Josh's cough medicine.

Something that nourishes you, making you sick instead . . .

"You okay?" Ben asks, and I open my eyes to see his brows furrowed with concern.

My tongue feels like lead in my mouth. "Fine," I say. "Was . . . was anyone else there when you got there?"

"Well . . ." He screws up his face as he thinks. "There was you, me, Yasmin, some other kids I don't know. We were all just watching the game. And then Mark walks up later, all swagger, like he expects everyone to be looking at him or whatever." Ben rolls his eyes. "Then he starts acting all territorial, as if nobody can be within ten meters of Trina without his permission. They were fighting! She didn't even want him there."

"She told you that?"

He shakes his head irritably. "She didn't have to. We all saw them going at it. And who wants to be around someone they're fighting with? Anyway, I ignore the guy shooting daggers at me and focus on watching the game. Trina wasn't playing too well. And I saw her hand shake a couple times when she was placing those tiles. . . ." He sighs and runs a hand down his face. "I wish I'd said something, the first time I noticed. Gotten some help. Maybe I could have saved her. I still think about that sometimes." He pauses. "You know, sometimes you see something, and it makes you so mad you're not sure what to do, so mad that when you do figure out what to do, it turns out to be the wrong thing after all. You know?"

I frown. "Wait, mad? Why would you be mad? What are you talking about?"

Ben is silent, picking at the strands of carpet near his feet.

"Ben. What did you see?"

He takes a deep breath. "I saw . . ."

"Bennyyyyyyy!"

Ben's face arranges itself into a resigned expression. "Hi, Ma," he says quietly.

"Benny! Why haven't you been answering your phone?" She drapes one arm around his shoulders and uses the other hand to give him a loving—but still fairly hard—poke in the ribs. Ben winces. "I've been trying and trying to contact you."

"Sorry, Ma," Ben says. "I was just talking to Najwa."

I give a half-hearted wave. "Hi, Auntie."

"Oh, hello, girl!" She turns the full force of her smile on me. It's clear she's been getting ready for bed; she's wearing a bat-wing top (or as Mama calls it, baju kelawar) with stretchy black yoga pants. "What are you still doing up? Got competition, you know, you really should go to bed."

"Can we just have a few more minutes, Auntie?" I say, desperate to get back to the conversation. "If we could just . . ."

"I just came to give Benny his medicine," she trills, cutting me off. "You forgot to take it just now!" she says, turning back to Ben and swatting his arm lightly. "Naughty boy!"

"Sorry," Ben says again, taking the bottle she proffers from the depths of her straw tote. "I'll take it now."

"Do you think we could . . ."

She ignores me. "Ya, you cannot forget, okay. Otherwise tomorrow you will regret." She smiles at me again. "Benny always has problems when he is stressed, you know. Tummy problems." She leans in closer. "He gets very backed up. And he cannot poop properly . . ."

"MA!"

"What?" Ben's mother puts on an injured expression.

"Nothing." He gathers up his things, his mouth a hard line. "Come on, let's go. See you, Najwa."

"Ben, can we maybe just finish what we were—"

"Ben has to rest now, dear," his mother says brightly before I can finish. "Tomorrow you two talk, okay. Too late already. Say good night, Benny darling."

"Good night," he says morosely.

I give up. "Good night," I say.

As they walk away, Ben's shoulders drooping more than ever, I can't stop thinking about our conversation. *Dextromethorphan,* I think. *St.-John's-wort.* What is it about that combination? I whip out my phone and start Googling until I find what I'm looking for.

Dextromethorphan. Taking St.-John's-wort with this cough suppressant might increase the risk of the accumulation of high levels of serotonin in your body.

High levels of serotonin? How could that be a problem? Serotonin is supposed to make you happy. *Serotonin syndrome,* the Internet tells me, *is when your body has too much of a chemical called serotonin, usually because of a medication or combination of medications. Serotonin syndrome symptoms often begin hours after you take a new medication that affects your serotonin levels . . .* I scan the list of symptoms, and my eyes feel like they're burning. Agitation, restlessness, confusion, heavy sweating, nausea, vomiting. She'd been ill, Yasmin said. She'd been nervous, Josh said.

In severe cases, serotonin syndrome can be life-threatening.

No, not nervous.

She'd been poisoned.

CHAPTER TWENTY

ABSTRUSE

ten points

adjective

not easy to understand

t's more than an hour later, but I know Josh will still be there, exactly where he was before, wrestling with words with that single-minded Josh Tan intensity.

Only he isn't there when I arrive. His things are, placed in an orderly fashion where he was sitting, each item lined up just so.

For someone who'd just been yelling at me about protecting his property, he certainly hasn't done much to conceal it.

I sit cross-legged among his possessions. There are so many thoughts in my head, so many that I want to scream.

Calm down, Najwa. Treat this like you'd treat a Scrabble board.

Okay. Okay. So here's what I know now, facts only: Josh keeps a photo of Trina in his wallet, the other half of which is in Mark's possession. Josh gave Trina cough medicine, medicine that interacts with a pill she may have already taken, and not in a good way. Josh could have seen Ben give Trina that pill.

No, Najwa, that's speculation.

Josh hated Trina.

Now that's a fact.

"What are you doing?" Josh's voice echoes through the otherwise quiet hallway.

"Waiting for you," I say.

He frowns. "Why? Our conversation has concluded. I have nothing more to add to my recollection of events."

"And yet you keep me coming back for more."

He sits down, angling his back decisively away from me. "Go away, Najwa. I have work to do."

"Funny you should mention that," I tell him. "So do I." And in one smooth motion, I leap to my feet, reach for his backpack, and grab his wallet.

"What are you doing?" He stares at me, aghast, angry. "Leave my things alone."

"No."

"This is stealing, you nitwit." He gets to his feet and starts approaching me, and I take a step back almost involuntarily. "Give it back."

"Not until I get an explanation."

"For WHAT?"

"For this." I reach into the wallet and slip the photo out of its hiding place. "What is this?" I ask him, holding it up, trying to make my voice strong, forceful. "And why do you have it in your wallet?"

There is a long pause. Is it just me, or does he look paler

than usual? "That is personal. You have no right to go through my private things."

"This is personal to me, too, actually," I tell him, jabbing the photo in his face. He tries to grab it from me, but I snatch it out of his reach. "Answer me, Josh. Why do you have this?"

"It's none of your business!"

"Trina is my business!" I'm so angry that I can see Josh wince as specks of spittle fly out of my mouth and hit his cheek. "I know you gave her cough medicine that day, Josh."

"You're faulting me for being *nice*?" He throws his hands up in the air, exasperated. "What is it with you people? I simply cannot win. Do one thing and you deem me too callous, do another and I am too caring. What is it you want from me?"

"Don't pull that caring act with me," I snap. "Did you know she'd just had St-John's-wort right before that?"

"I do not even know what—"

"Did you know what that would do?"

"Najwa, what are you even—"

"Did you know that it could kill her?"

He stares at me, and I can see the color visibly draining from his face. "What?"

"You can't mix St-John's-wort and dextromethorphan," I tell him. "But I bet you knew that all along."

"I . . . I don't understand," he stammers. "Did I . . . did I hurt Trina?"

"Stop pretending that you didn't know!"

"But I didn't!" He wrenches a hand through his hair, his

voice edged with a desperation that wasn't there before. "I didn't! I was just trying to help her."

"And why would I believe that? Why would Josh Tan help Trina Low when we all know exactly how you felt about her?"

Josh is silent for a long time. When he finally speaks again, it's through gritted teeth. "Did you? Did you really not know? Do you still not understand?" He avoids my gaze.

What does he mean?

Focus, Najwa. Try to think. Why does a person keep a photo in their wallet? To have it close. To look at. To . . . cherish?

And then I let out a breath.

Because of course I understand. There's only one reason to keep a photo of someone in your wallet, always close, always available, always there.

"What did you do with the other half?" I ask him.

"Threw it away," he says dourly. "Obviously. I had no use for it."

His eyes never blink. The truth, then, maybe one of the few truths I've heard all day. Only minutes ago, of all the things I was sure of in the world, Josh Tan hating Trina Low was one of them.

"During the game," I say, and I have to swallow to rid myself of the lump in my throat. "The medicine. . . ."

"It is a medicine I often take for my own cough. These tournaments are always stressors for my respiratory issues. And . . . she was unwell," he says quietly, not looking at me. "She needed it. If I knew it would hurt her . . . if I knew it would . . ." He gulps. The sentence hangs in the air, unfinished.

I nod. "Did she know?" I ask him quietly. "About . . . about you?"

He shakes his head. "Nobody did," he says. "Until now."

"I see," I say. And I do. Suddenly all the snide remarks, the barbs, the lingering gazes, even the willingness to do that interview with the Tweedles, the opportunity to talk about her to someone, somehow—all of it seems so clear. *Oh, Josh.* At least those of us who loved her in the open can grieve in the open, in all our different ways. To hide this seems like a special kind of purgatory.

I hand the photo and the wallet back to him and he quickly tucks it away where it belongs. We stand there for a while, not quite sure what to do, what to say next.

"Are you feeling okay?" I say, because he still looks so pale, so sweaty.

Josh's scowl deepens. "I have been hit with a particularly bad case of stomach troubles," he says stiffly. "It is greatly affecting my ability to play to the standards that I would usually hold for myself." He pauses. "Please leave me alone now," he says.

I don't think Josh has ever said "please" to me before. So I do what he asks, and I walk away.

This whole time . . . had Trina's death just been an accident? A horrible twist of fate that nobody could have predicted? Death at the hands of two different boys, who each loved her in their own ways? But if it was unintentional, why the posts?

As I head back toward the lifts, I take out my phone to check the time. The world has tilted on its axis, the competition is still happening, and I really should get to bed. Except just below, a notification has popped up, a notification that makes it impossible to rest, impossible to think of anything else.

trina.queenofthetiles has posted a new Instagram Story.

It's another clue—what else would it be? A short one this time, just four letters. AENG. I blink. This one is too difficult, not because there are no word combinations to be found here, but because there are too many. Is it AGEN, which means again? Is it GANE, to go? Is it GENA, which means cheek, or GEAN, which is a white-flowered tree? How am I supposed to know? How am I supposed to figure out which one makes sense?

Wearily I open my notebook again and write it down at the bottom of the list. *REGICIDE. JANIFORM. AILMENT/ALIMENT. AGEN/GANE/GEAN.* Next to the last one, I add two big question marks. Then I just stare at the words for a while.

All this time, I thought Josh was who I was looking for. But if he wasn't responsible, if *no one* was responsible . . . what has all of this been about? And who would go through all the trouble of making an accident seem like murder?

CHAPTER TWENTY-ONE

TRYST

eight points

noun

arrangement to meet

Whatever adrenaline has been pushing me on before this has given way to exhaustion. I'm more confused than ever; half an hour ago I anchored this entire investigation on Josh, and now that he's no longer at its center I find myself adrift once more. It's past two a.m. now, and I need sleep. I head back up to my room, past the thinning crowds of Scrabble players, pretending I don't see the stares, or the whispers that I leave in my wake. I wait for the usual anxiety to set in, wait to start spiraling, wait for the inevitable attack. It doesn't come. Instead, all I feel rise inside me is anger. I'm so tired of being at the center of all this attention that I never wanted and never asked for. *To hell with all of them. I'll beat them all tomorrow, and I'll find out what really happened to Trina, and who's behind those posts, and I'll shut them all up.* And the anger somehow surprises me and fuels me at the same time.

By the time I get to the room, I am more than ready to

lie down and lose myself to the sweet, sweet oblivion of sleep. I swipe my card in and out of the slot above the knob and push the door open expecting nothing but darkness and quiet. Instead, I hear urgent voices—"You have to tell her," one says, deep and insistent and familiar—and find myself staring straight into the stricken faces of Puteri and Mark.

"Tell me what?" That's what I say out loud. What I don't say is: *What are they doing? Why do they look so guilty?*

What I don't say, what I refuse to talk about, is the way my heart constricts seeing the two of them together, the way they instinctively seem to draw closer together, as if to protect each other.

I guess ours wasn't the only relationship Mark was mending this weekend.

Puteri crosses her arms and regards me with an expression I can only describe as SUPERCILIOUS: haughtily contemptuous, sixteen points. "And who says we're talking about you?"

"We can explain," Mark says hurriedly. He's radiating guilt from every crevice.

They're a "we" now? "That's good," I say slowly. "Why don't you start doing that?"

"I was just . . . uh." Mark flails for the right words. "I was just here to ask Puteri for her, you know, her side of the story. What she remembered about that day."

I cross my arms and say nothing, and he flounders. "I mean . . . I . . . She . . ."

Puteri smooths back a hair that has somehow escaped from her perfect ponytail. "What Mark means is that he suspected—

correctly, I might add—that I would be more inclined to talk to him in a private setting than in a crowded public space. Which, given the nature of this tournament and our peers, is literally almost everywhere else."

"And what did you learn?" I address my question to Mark directly, willing him to look me in the eye, willing him to repay the faith I'd placed in him. *Please, don't let me have been wrong to trust you.*

Mark wears the expression of a man stuck between the rock of his ex-girlfriend and the hard place of his dead girl-friend's best friend and liking none of his options. "Nothing interesting," he says finally. His nose twitches, and I feel my stomach drop. Bloody Mark and his bloody tell. "Nothing we didn't already know."

"What an insult," drawls Puteri, sitting down on her rumpled bed. "Frankly, I think I'm always interesting."

Puteri handled the bag of food, I suddenly remember. Puteri handled Trina's food right before she died, the food that made Shuba so sick they couldn't even compete. Puteri, who so hated Trina.

Did she do something?

Maybe it wasn't an accident after all?

Does Mark know about this?

And then, a beat later: *Are they in this together? Is that what this means?*

Mark ignores her. "So anyway, I think we should keep focusing on the clues we already have," he tells me, his eyes locked on mine, intense and almost . . . beseeching? "Maybe we should call it a night, y'know, regroup and discuss tomorrow. And hey, I know you don't think much of my Emily theory, but like, we should seriously talk about—"

"If anyone should be talking about anything," Puteri interrupts, "they should be talking about me, and how I'm going to win this whole damn thing while the rest of you play Scooby-Doo."

"Be quiet, Put." Mark turns back to me. "Shall we go somewhere and talk, Najwa? Just the two of us? Straighten out some things, get us both back on the same page . . ." His voice is gentle, coaxing. I want so badly to believe him, fall back into the friendship we've been rebuilding. *He's doing what he said he would do, Najwa. He's asking Puteri questions, trying to figure things out, just like you.*

So why does this feel like betrayal?

I'm about to reply when my phone buzzes urgently, then again, and again, and again. I fish it out of my pocket; it's Yasmin.

I FIGURED IT OUT!!!!!!

OMG NAJWA I'M FREAKING OUT

Can you meet me in the lobby in 5 mins

Hurry up!!!!!!!!!!!!!!!!!!!

"*Yasmin's* figured it out?" I whisper. "No way."

Coming.

I type quickly. Then I slip my phone back in my pocket and look up at Mark and Puteri, who are staring expectantly at me.

I draw a shaky breath, swallowing my hurt. "I have to go," I tell Mark. "We'll talk about this later."

"We definitely won't," Puteri mutters under her breath.

"And who says I was talking to you?" I toss over my shoulder as I walk out the door.

The lobby is silent now; only one or two stragglers remain. Everyone else has gone to bed. Yasmin is nowhere in sight.

Me: The suspense is killing me
Me: Where the hell is she??????
Alina: Kakak you need to sleep
Alina: What would Mama say?
Alina: Wait, what am I saying, that won't work
Alina: What would Dr. Anusya say?

I don't respond. I hate when Alina tries to play parent. Instead, I pace up and down in front of the lifts, wearing grooves into the carpet with every footstep. I bite the nail of my left pinkie, a habit I've had since I was a little girl, one I fall back on whenever nerves hit. Then I wipe my sweaty palms off against the sides of my jeans and reach for the notebook in my back pocket. I read my notes all over again, every single one, as if asking myself the same questions will somehow yield different answers. Five, ten, fifteen minutes pass. Each gentle ping from the lifts makes my heart race. The doors glide open and shut, but it's never Yasmin who emerges from behind them. In my head, the questions don't stop: *What is Mark hiding? Why is Puteri helping him? What did they want to tell me? What did Trina and I fight about? Was Trina's death an accident, or was it murder? If it was an accident, why would someone start posting on her Instagram? How long has Josh been in love with Trina? Does Ben know?* And most of all, over and over again: *Where the hell is Yasmin?*

As I pace back and forth, my phone buzzes gently. And my heart begins to pound painfully as soon as I see it, a Pavlovian kick in the chest: a new message, from trina.queenofthetiles.

Ready to give up yet, Najjy?

The worst part of the DMs is the way they adopt Trina's voice, use her special nickname for me, as though assuming her profile means they've assumed her entire identity and our whole relationship along with it. There's no point asking who it is or what it means—I know by now that I'm never going to get a response. But still, the message makes me antsy, and when almost forty-five minutes have passed and Yasmin still hasn't appeared or answered my messages, I head up to the eleventh floor to find her instead. There's a faint, insistent beeping coming from somewhere. I count off the rooms on either side as I make my way to her door—1101, 1102, 1103, 1104, 1105.

And then I find the cause of the beeping.

The door to room 1105 is slightly ajar and beeping loudly in protest. I push it gently and it swings open. "Yasmin?" I call out. "You there?"

The room is empty. And the brown leather bag she always carries around is still right there on the table.

That's weird, I think, trying to dampen the feeling of foreboding snaking its way around my chest. *Yasmin isn't the type to just up and leave without even closing the door behind her.*

I hover uncertainly for a while, wondering if I should stay and wait, or go out and find her. It doesn't seem right to sit in a room that isn't mine, so I go back outside, closing the door firmly behind me. I hang out in the corridor for a while, calling Yasmin over and over again.

She never picks up. But I keep trying anyway, because it gives me something to do besides feed the foreboding, stops me from thinking a million what-ifs.

Eventually, reluctantly, I start walking back toward the lifts, dragging my feet slightly, still hitting the little green button that says *Try Again?* every time my phone tells me the call has failed.

Another DM.

You're getting warmer.

My fingers trembling, I keep hitting the button.
Try again.
Try again.

Try again.

And then, just as I'm passing the stairwell marked EXIT, I hear a familiar sound: the tinny strains of "Build Me Up Buttercup," Yasmin's favorite song . . . and her ringtone.

I stop.

The song stops. "Call Failed," my phone says. "Try Again?"

I hit the button. And after a moment, I hear it again. *Why do you build me up, buttercup baby just to let me down?*

Yasmin? I follow the sound to the stairwell door, which is just slightly ajar. And in that sliver of space between door and wall, I see something I don't expect, something that lodges a knife of fear straight into my heart.

An arm, splayed out on the ground, fingers slightly curled.

I hurry over to the door and push it open, and there she is: Yasmin, sprawled unconscious on the floor, limbs akimbo, mouth slightly open, blood trickling from a gash on her forehead. The world spins, and there is a deafening roaring in my ears, and I think of Trina, head down on a Scrabble board thrown into chaos, eyes wide open, all the life drained out of them. As I try to remember how to breathe, their faces blink in and out, first one, then the other: Yasmin, then Trina, then Yasmin, then Trina . . .

Call for help, I think to myself, fumbling for my phone with frozen fingers. *Don't fall apart now, Najwa. Call for help.*

Somehow, I do. Somehow, I manage to find the words, croak them out, make myself understood. And then my legs give out, and I collapse on the floor next to Yasmin, and I wait, wait, wait, for us both to be rescued, and for all of this to be over.

CHAPTER TWENTY-TWO

SPLENETIC

thirteen points

adjective

spiteful or irritable

noun

spiteful or irritable person

I t feels like we lie there on the floor together forever until the hotel staff arrive, and longer still before an ambulance comes to take Yasmin away. For a while, everything is a blur, and my brain can only process things in snapshots, stills instead of the whole movie. Shot one: Someone places a blanket around me, and only then do I realize that I'm shivering. Shot two: two young men carefully placing Yasmin on a stretcher. "She's breathing, see? She'll be okay, don't worry." Shot three: an expanse of gray concrete. Questions that I'm barely capable of answering: *Yes, this is how I found her. No, I don't know what happened. Yes, she is my friend. No, I don't need a doctor.*

Too much of it is familiar. Sure, this time nobody died, but how many more times will I go somewhere to play a game I love, only to see my friends taken away from me to hospitals or to morgues? How many more times must I fear, or grieve, or cry? And through it all, there's a small, insistent voice right at the back of my head, a voice that says: *You say you want to remember, Najwa, so remember. Remember that rage. Remember the force of a blow to a table. Remember the look on his face.*

She slipped, I tell myself. She fell. She must have. An accident, and nothing more. And yet I can't stop thinking things I'd rather not be thinking. A KATZENJAMMER is a unicorn of a Scrabble word, a fifteen-letter behemoth that means a massive hangover, or distress, or a discordant clamor, and right now in my head it's somehow all three of those things at once.

I don't know where to go once the hotel is certain they're not about to have another dead body on their hands. So I open my notebook and write, in all capitals: *WHO HURT YASMIN? WHAT WAS IT SHE FIGURED OUT?* Then, because I still have no answers, I head back to the room I share with Puteri, bracing myself . . . although for what, I'm not even sure.

She's waiting for me when I open the door, alone this time, sitting on her bed, hands folded demurely in her lap. "Can we talk?" she asks politely, uncertainly. It's all so civil, as if we're telling each other about our day and that day doesn't include prodding into the death of a girl we both knew intimately, in our own ways, or the fall of another down a set of stairs in a way that doesn't seem like the unfortunate, clumsy incident the adults in charge are making it out to be.

"Given that I just dealt with seeing my friend get carted off in an ambulance," I say, "I'd really rather not."

She nods and looks down, lacing and unlacing her fingers. "So it wasn't an accident?"

I close my eyes briefly. "I highly doubt it. Not when she told me right before it happened that she knew who was behind the Instagram posts."

"What?!"

"Doesn't seem like a coincidence now, does it?"

Puteri lets out a long, wavering breath. "That's terrifying," she says quietly.

"Yeah," I say. "Yeah, it is."

"And it's not just that it happened to Yasmin. It's the idea that there's someone among us who's willing to keep hurting people like this." Her fingers never stop moving, nervous and fluttering, the most agitated I've ever seen her. "I didn't really think those posts were serious before this—just someone messing around with all our heads, some stupid prank. But this changes everything. This makes it *real*. And there could be more targets."

"Somehow," I tell her, "I doubt you'll be one of them."

She shoots me a look through narrowed eyes. "What do you mean?"

Images flicker through my head: Mark's face contorted in anger; Yasmin's, slack against a cold concrete floor. "Nothing." I sink wearily down on my bed and lie back on the plump pillows, headscarf and all. I can't be bothered to remove it; I don't know where this conversation is going and if I need to beat a hasty retreat out of this room, I'm not wasting time wrapping a hijab if I can help it. "Where's Mark?"

Somewhere behind Puteri's eyes, a door slams shut. She's suddenly guarded, suddenly wary. "He left."

"Want to tell me what you guys were talking about earlier?"

"He told you what we were talking about," she says, her voice calm, even. "*Remember?*"

Something about the way she says it makes me grit my teeth. Did Mark tell her about me? Did they laugh together over my busted brain? *Poor little Najwa, playing at detective over a day she can barely remember.*

"I remember," I say. "I remember a lot more than you think."

Puteri gazes at me, her eyes narrowed. "You think you know who did it," she says flatly, and it's a statement, not a question.

"Actually, right now I'm trying very hard not to think at all," I say. "I'm scared, and I'm exhausted, and tomorrow I have to play a bunch of games because in spite of everything that's happening, I still want to win because I'm not giving anyone the satisfaction of running me off. Not when I've made it this far. Not with what it took for me to get here. I'm not giving them that power over me."

There is a long silence.

Then Puteri clears her throat. "Look, not like we're pals or anything. But I did want to tell you what Mark and I were talking about."

I don't reply, and she continues anyway.

"Because I know it must have looked suspicious, given everything that's been going on."

I take a breath, but still don't respond. I don't know if I trust her. I definitely don't trust where this is going.

"Will you please just say something?" she snaps.

"I have nothing to add to the conversation."

"Fine. I'll just talk, and I guess it's up to you whether or not you want to listen." I hear rustling as she lies back on her own pillows and sighs. "Something happened that weekend that I didn't tell you about."

"You didn't tell me anything," I can't resist pointing out.

"I thought you have nothing to add to the conversation?" She takes a deep breath. "I put something in Trina's food."

I thought it would be more shocking to hear this out loud, make me feel something more than exhausted resignation. "I know," I say.

"You do?"

"I'd like to know why, though."

She tosses her head. "She was really pissing me off that weekend. And it's not what you think. It wasn't poison or anything. It was just some crushed up tablets from Emily's bag of marvelous medicines."

"So glad that's all it was," I mutter, massaging my temples. My KATZENJAMMER is still going strong; I'm not sure I'm cut out to be Poirot, or even Pikachu. "Just some tablets, given to someone who had no idea what they were or how it would affect them. No biggie."

"Relax," Puteri says. "It wasn't like I was trying to kill your beloved Trina or anything. It was just some vitamin C."

It's my turn to look confused. "Vitamin C? What were you trying to do, get back at her by making her healthy? 'Hate your guts, Trina, here's hoping you're adequately protected from the common cold!'"

She rolls her eyes. "I suppose you think that's funny. But the maximum dosage you're supposed to take of vitamin C in a day is like, two thousand milligrams. Any more than that and it does funny things to your digestive system. You get nauseated, you throw up, you get major diarrhea—"

"How do you even know that?" I interrupt.

She looks ever so slightly shamefaced. "I read about it in my mom's *Reader's Digest*." I want to laugh because *Reader's Digest* is another one of those things so many Malaysian parents subscribe to in the name of Providing Educational Content; apparently Puteri is one of the few people I know who actually read the thing and don't just use it to Test Their Word Power.

"Emily has these tablets that are, like, one thousand milligrams each," she continues, her fingers still constantly moving as she fiddles with them on her lap. *So this is Puteri's tell.* "I knew that, because she offered them to me once when I thought I was about to come down with a cold right before a tournament. She came in for breakfast when I was just about done, and she left her bag on her chair while she went to get food from the buffet. So I just snuck, like, four tablets out of her bag, put them on a napkin, and crushed them up with the bottom of my glass. I didn't even know when I was going to use them—or if I was going to use them at all. I was still in the lobby thinking about it when Ben came running in all hot and bothered. Asked me to hold the food because he had to use the toilet. And I remember being so surprised because he'd just had breakfast. I saw him in the café that morning, him and his mom. That's when he told me it was for Trina."

She pauses to take a breath. "So while he was gone I took my napkin of crushed vitamin C, and I opened the bag of curry—they'd tied it all up in a plastic bag—and I poured it all in. And then I tied the bag up again good and tight and I shook it a bunch of times to make sure it was all mixed up. And then Ben came back and I handed him the bag."

This is the most that Puteri's ever talked to me. I wish she'd kept silent. I wish I had.

"Anyway, when . . . *it* . . . happened, I wondered if I should feel guilty about doing what I did. If I'd maybe . . . maybe had something to do with it. I mean, it was only vitamin C! But still . . ." She pauses. "So I told Mark. And he started panicking, worrying about what would happen if people knew. And then later, what you'd think if you found out he—we—had been hiding this from you. 'It wouldn't look very good for you, Put. You have to tell her.'" Her impression of him is unsettlingly accurate. "I said I'd tell you myself. So here I am, telling you."

"None of this answers my question," I say. "Why?"

"I told you why."

"No, I mean why do it right then? Your breakup was old news. Mark had moved on. What was the point of doing it at all?"

Puteri shrugs. There's a discontented twist to her mouth, as if my question displeases her. "Why not?" she says. "She was annoying. She took what she wanted, and she never cared about anyone else, especially if they were in the way. Why wouldn't I want her to suffer? At least for a day or two," she quickly adds. "Don't get any ideas. There were plenty of times when I wanted Trina Low dead, but that didn't mean I was going to actually do anything about it."

She took what she wanted. I know she's talking about Mark, and I feel a sick squeezing deep in the pit of my stomach. "So this was about *him*. You did it because of him. Just like you're telling me now . . . because of him. To protect him."

"I did it because of Trina," she says coldly. "Because she was a bad person, and she deserved to feel some pain and discomfort, the kind she made other people feel. And I'm telling you now . . . well, because he wanted me to. But not to protect him!" she says sharply when I let out an involuntary snort. "Because . . . because he doesn't deserve this. He would never *kill* someone, or set out to cause all this drama with some Instagram posts. Why would he? He doesn't gain anything from any of this, and he doesn't deserve you thinking he's some kind of monster. He's not." She sighs. "You of all people should understand."

"What are you talking about?"

She quirks her lips then, a sad little smile. "All Trina did was latch on and take, take, take from the people who were stupid enough to love her. And you're still here, aren't you? Defending her, protecting her. When all she ever did was use you."

It feels as if I've been slapped. "Trina did not use me," I say. "Trina *needed* me."

Puteri laughs softly. "I've said those exact words to myself so many times. He *needs* me . . . and look where that got me." She sits back and regards me, head tilted to one side. "We're not so different that way, you and I."

I don't like the way the words feel as they scrape away at my nerves, the feelings they're exposing beneath. "I'm not sure I understand what you mean."

"I mean that feeling of being indispensable to someone, especially someone like Mark, or like Trina . . . it's addictive, isn't it? To be needed by people who seem like they have everything? Who seem like they shouldn't need anyone?"

I'm quiet, not because I don't agree, but because it's like Puteri has taken all the pegs I've placed into these neat little holes of my life and shaken them all up, and suddenly things are fitting a whole new way.

For all the years I've known Trina, I've made excuses for her. Other people simply didn't understand her, I told myself. I was special. I saw who she really was, understood how starved she was for attention as a child, how hard she worked to make up for it later on. I had a unique glimpse of the loneliness that moved restlessly below the façade of perfection. And every time Trina's drive to be seen, somehow, by anyone and every-one reached out and bit me, I forgave it, or shoved it aside, or rationalized it. *She needs you. She doesn't have anyone but you.*

Puteri watches me, and in her eyes, I see a sympathy that almost irritates me. "Some of us call that love," she says softly. "Took me a while to realize that this isn't what it's supposed to feel like."

How many things have I let go in the name of being needed? How many have I ignored? How many wounds, big and small, inflicted upon me and anyone else who happened to be in Trina's way? I look at Puteri, and it's as if I finally, finally see her for the first time. From where I'm standing, she looks a lot like me.

"I'm sorry," I say suddenly, and she frowns.

"For what?"

"For what she did to you." I sigh, rubbing my temples. "For the way she treated you. For everything."

Her face is impassive, but her voice is gentle. "It's not your place to apologize. You're not the one who did anything wrong."

"But I let it happen."

"You can't be held responsible for anyone's actions but your own." She shrugs. "Or at least that's what my therapist tells me."

I take a deep breath. I am suddenly tired beyond words. "Well, this has been a good talk," I say, pulling off my hijab, tossing it onto the floor next to my bed, and crawling under the covers, jeans and all. "But I'm going to bed. We can braid our hair and commiserate over our existential crises tomorrow."

But just as I close my eyes, I hear Puteri draw in a sharp breath.

"Not that we can't be BFFs tomorrow," she says, "but you should take a look at Instagram. Right now."

I guess the mysterygrammer doesn't want me to get any rest.

This time, the clue is a mere five letters. HECTA. *This is your final clue,* the caption reads. *Can you crack the code before it's too late?* And then on the bottom right, in smaller text: *Look again.* An echo of a previous caption. Our mysterygrammer is big on repetition, I guess.

TEACH, I think. *Or TACHE, a type of clasp or buckle. Or . . . or . . .*

CHEAT.

Emily, I think immediately, the obvious answer. Then, because to cheat on is also to be unfaithful, I think: *Mark.* And then, because a CHEAT is also an act of fraud or deception, I think of magicians, of sleight of hand, of the art of distracting an audience by causing an explosion in one corner, so that nobody notices what you're actually doing with your hands.

And then I sleep, and think of nothing more.

CHAPTER TWENTY-THREE

Sunday, November 27, 2022

LIPPITUDE
fourteen points
noun
state of having bleary eyes

I dream of Trina.

This is nothing new. I've dreamed of her often since she died, innocuous dreams where we do nothing but lie back in soft green grass, contemplating clouds in a blue, blue sky; sad dreams where she cries and cries and I can do nothing to help her; dreams from which I wake up angry that I'll never have that again, have her again, have us again.

This dream is different.

We sit on opposite sides of a Scrabble board, filled racks before us. The board spins and spins on its rotating base, so fast it makes me dizzy. Across from me, Trina watches without speaking.

The board stops.

"Your move, Najjy." Her voice is light, but her eyes are unbearably sad.

I look down at my rack. The tiles are arranged in alphabetical order. DEIOSUV.

I know it's easy. I know I should get this. Yet the letters won't move, won't rearrange themselves, won't reveal their secrets. My head feels like someone has stuffed it with cotton wool, absorbing every word I ever knew. "I can't think," I tell her. "I can't figure it out."

"You have to." She grips the table so hard I see her knuckles turn white. "For both of us. Concentrate, Najjy."

I stare at the rack until my eyes hurt, willing the word to appear.

"Hurry, Najjy."

I look up. Trina is starting to disappear; I can see the table through her fingers as they grip tightly to the edge.

"Stay," I say desperately. "Please stay."

"I can't, not until you figure it out."

I shuffle the tiles on the rack over and over again, my fingers trembling. I arrange them and rearrange them and arrange them again.

And then finally, I see.

I lay the letters down on the board, one by one. DEVIOUS. Skillfully using underhanded tactics to achieve a goal.

I stare at the faint outline of Trina. "Who?" I ask through my tears. "Who??"

But she doesn't say a word. She just opens her mouth and screams and screams and screams.

I sit up with a jolt, sweat dripping down my face, screams echoing in my ear.

The curtains have been drawn back; morning sunlight streams into the room, so bright that I have to squint to look around me.

Puteri isn't here. But on my bedside table, there's a takeaway cup, its contents still hot enough to send delicate wisps of steam wafting lazily into the air. It bears a note on a pale blue Post-it, in Puteri's neat, rounded handwriting: *Figured you could use some caffeine after last night. Don't worry, I didn't add anything to this one.*

I can't help it; I crack a smile.

I'm about to head into the bathroom when my phone vibrates, a loud clattering on the hard wood of the side table. *Maybe that's Puteri,* I think. Maybe this is what the start of a friendship looks like.

I pick up my phone.

It isn't her.

Close to giving up?
That's the Najjy we all know and love.

I type out a reply, the same one I've been typing for the past two days, over and over again, pressing so hard on each letter that for a second I think I may break the screen beneath my fingertips.

WHO ARE YOU

I'm about to hit send when I pause. I've asked this question over and over with no response. What kind of Scrabble player keeps using the same strategy when they know their opponent won't play along?

Okay, Najwa. Think like the player that you are.

Carefully I tap it out:

I can't figure it out

The reply comes back almost instantly:

Unsurprising, but you'll have to be more specific. There are so many things you're missing, after all.

What's your goal here? What is it that you stand to gain?

You're the expert, the message says. The would-be next Queen of the Tiles. We're in the endgame now, Najjy. And you know the principles of the endgame.

The endgame is when there are fewer than seven tiles left in the bag. Just a few moves left until the end. I close my eyes.

Of course I know the principles of the endgame. But how do they apply here?

I don't understand.

A pause. Then three dots, blinking slowly in and out as whoever it is on the other end types their response.

Don't give up, Najjy.

You're so close.

Here, have a very special hint. Just for you.

After these words, there's a gray rectangle, an image that hasn't loaded yet. It seems to take an age to appear. When it does, I find it hard to breathe.

A word clue. A private one. Just for me. Just three letters: ITD.

The letters swirl around in my head. TID means girl, but DIT means to stop something from happening.

It's me. I'm the girl who has to put a stop to this whole thing.

I hold my phone in one hand and use the other to pull my notebook from my back pocket and flip through its pages.

REGICIDE

JANIFORM

AILMENT/ALIMENT

AGEN/GANE/GEAN (??)

CHEAT

TID/DIT

That swooshing sound again and again.

Do you see now, Najjy?

Remember: They hide among us.

There are no more messages, and I sit there tapping my

feet and staring at the clues. What does it mean? How is this all connected? I run a finger down the words, mentally listing the definitions for each one: the killing of a monarch, two-faced, sickness and something that nourishes the body, again . . .

Again.

I think about the definition of AGEN, and how it's a mere two words: "see again."

See again. Really see.

I stare at the list, looking by now so much like one of the sheets I'd use to track Scrabble games. This is Scrabble, isn't it? These weren't just words given to us randomly; they were presented to us on a board. And what are words on a board to most of us here?

Point-amassing units. Nothing more.

I grab my pen, calculate the points of each word in my head and note them down: REGICIDE (12), JANIFORM (20), ALIMENT (9), AGEN (5), CHEAT (10).

Can you crack the code before it's too late?

Code? What code?

12, 20, 9, 5, 10. The numbers jump out at me as if they're ringed in neon.

Slowly, I write down the alphabet all across the bottom of the page: A, B, C, and under each one I write the corresponding number, from A, one, all the way until Z, twenty-six:

12 - L

20 - T

9 - I

5 - E

10 - J

The letters swirl and move into place. J. I. L. T. E.

There's a letter missing. I think back to the one word in my DMs, the one just for me. DIT (4). With trembling fingers, I write down the last letter and sit back.

My head spins as I stare at the word on the page. JILTED. Rejected or abandoned, especially a lover. I remember the way Puteri defended Mark so vehemently, the way she called Trina her nightmare. I remember Ben's dejected face. I remember Mark's anger, so terrifying in its potency. He's dangerous, and Trina was afraid. Isn't that what Yasmin said?

Another swoosh. Another message. *Do you see now?*

Mark, I think. *She was going to break up with Mark.* And then I think, *Or Puteri, who was abandoned for Trina.* And then again, almost immediately, thinking of heads bent close, of hands drifting protectively to slim waists, of the way Puteri was so quick to leap to his defense last night, *Or both of them.* But the more I think about it, the more I hone in on just one name, just one possible solution that fits every clue. *Mark,* I tell myself, feeling a strange sinking in my chest, that camaraderie I felt before gone far too soon. *It's Mark.* It's the obvious answer. He was there when Yasmin texted me. He knew she had something big to tell me, something that could have been about him. He could have gotten to her first, pushed her down those stairs with those strong athlete's hands. *He's dangerous. Stay away from him.* CHEAT, JILTED, JANIFORM, it's all forming a blurry picture, one that I can't seem to bring into focus.

Or maybe I just don't want to.

CHAPTER TWENTY-FOUR

GLAMOUR

ten points

noun

alluring charm or fascination

verb

bewitch

The feeling sticks. My body feels like it's on the brink of fight or flight, and none of my usual techniques for calming myself work. I'm wound so tight I feel like if someone were to touch me I'd combust.

It's still early once I make it downstairs, and there's no way I'm going to be able to manage breakfast, so I walk toward the main hall and watch staff put the finishing touches on today's setup. I'm filled with a nervous, fizzy energy that won't allow me to stay still; I tap my fingers against my thighs, shift my weight from one foot to the other, fiddle with the ends of my hijab. Yet there's something about the rows of empty boards gleaming under the lights that's almost soothing. And even with everything that's happened, everything that's still happening, even with all the thoughts and theories racing through my head, I realize as I stand there surveying this battlefield that I want this. I want to win. I want to be the Queen, and not just because of Trina, and not to prove anything to anyone else, but because . . . because I'm that good. And I deserve it.

Do you? A pang of guilt shoots through me. *JANIFORM,* a little voice inside me hisses. *You betray her memory. You're no better than the rest of them.*

But I am, I think, trying not to let the poisonous barbs take root, trying to kill the ants before they kill me. *I loved her.*

Love wears a lot of different masks.

Seconds later, still wrestling with my ants, I hear footsteps, and people begin to stream past me into the hall, ready to start the day. I brace myself against the wall and watch them all, scanning their faces, like, if I just look hard enough, I can see behind their masks and find the one who threatens this world for all of us. My fingers drum urgent tattoos against my legs, and my brain will not stay quiet. *No better than the rest of them.*

I feel a hand clasp my elbow and almost jump out of my skin when I turn around and see Yasmin, a bandage covering the gash on her forehead, a sunny grin spreading across her face.

"Good luck, Najwa!" she says, squeezing my arm. "Didn't I tell you? Nobody is going to stop us from getting to this final. For Trina."

"Yasmin, how . . . I . . ." But before I can string a coherent sentence together, she's gone, leaving a trail of unanswered questions behind her. What's she doing here? Is she even okay to play right now? What happened? Does she know? Does she remember?

Ding. It's not even a surprise anymore when I look down at my screen and see a new message come in. Trina always did know when to shake things up, after all.

I tap on the notification.

Endgame, Najjy. Let the tiles fall where they may.

I sit and wait for ages for my first opponent; when they fail to turn up on time, I tell the tournament director, a silver-haired woman with a Meryl Streep in *The Devil Wears Prada* haircut and a raspy smoker's voice, and she starts the timer. "You know the rules," she tells me. "If she turns up and there's less than fifteen minutes on the clock, she can choose whether to play or to forfeit, and you'll be recorded as the winner, with a one hundred–point spread. If she turns up and time's already up, she doesn't get that choice." I nod and she leaves. In the time that I'm forced to wait I scroll through YouTube for TheTrinaProject's latest upload.

The title of today's episode is *The Boyfriend*, and my head begins to swim all over again.

Words appear, stark white on black. *Mark Thomas refused to be interviewed for this episode,* they say. *So we tried our best to build a picture of Mark based on what others could tell us. After all, aren't we all just an amalgamation of others' perceptions?*

We cut to a shot of a crowd streaming in and out of a hall

where a tournament is clearly being held. "Do you know Mark Thomas?" I hear Tweedledee's voice ask.

A girl nods earnestly on-screen, all frizzy hair and braces. "Yes," she says. "Of course."

"Ya," says another girl, who wrinkles her nose as she answers. "He beat me by seventeen points once. I was drawing some bad racks, but I didn't expect him to be that good either." She smiles, suddenly, ruefully. "Guess I underestimated the guy."

Cut to a guy in glasses and a Manchester United jersey, who laughs. "Doesn't everybody?" he says. "Who *doesn't* know Mark Thomas?"

A girl in a headscarf frowns slightly as she answers: "He came with his own mythos, almost. The jock who gave up his athletic career to hang out with the word nerds. Like a tagline for a teen movie, right?"

Suddenly Mark is on my screen—a younger Mark, a Mark without the anger, the tense energy of the Mark I know now. Today's Mark is a closed fist; this Mark is a warm handshake. He smiles that easy, wide smile, big-eyed, shiny, mugging straight to the camera. "Yeah, uh, my name is Mark Thomas. This is my first Scrabble tournament."

"How do you think you're going to do?" the anonymous interviewer asks, and he laughs.

"Hopefully, well enough. I'm just trying not to embarrass myself."

"We hear you used to be a swimmer," the interviewer says,

and the screen fills with pictures of Mark in the pool, his swim cap and goggles making him look like some giant water bug. "What made you switch to Scrabble instead?"

Mark shrugs. "I like words," he says. "And I needed a change of scenery."

"And are you enjoying the people you've met so far?"

That laugh again, so light, so familiar. "There have been some interesting characters," he says. "And some memorable ones. I look forward to getting to know more of them, and better too."

The screen pans through a quick series of stills, taken, I gather, from social media—Trina and Mark eating ice cream, Trina and Mark kissing in front of the giant Christmas tree they put up every year at KLCC, Trina and Mark playing video games, Trina and Mark smiling at each other across a Scrabble board. A sea of images of Trina and Mark, filling up the screen one by one by one. The last one is from her Instagram account—I shiver when I see the familiar profile picture. It's a picture of Mark in front of a birthday cake, his face lit up by both his grin and the candle flames. It comes with a caption that the Tweedles helpfully zoom in on. *Happy birthday, beloved,* it reads. *Thank you for being born. For being you. For choosing me, and for us. Gonna spend the rest of the year showing you my gratitude, until the next birthday, and the one after, and as many more beyond that as we can manage. Love, your T.*

The pictures fade.

"Do you know Mark Thomas?" Tweedledee's voice asks again.

Three girls giggle, huddled together over the mic. "Wasn't he Trina Low's boyfriend?"

Cut to a guy hunched over his laptop, who looks up and says, "You mean the guy Trina was hanging out with?"

"The power couple!" another girl says, her red lipstick smearing at the edges. "True love's dream!"

Her companion, a boy with bleached blond hair, laughs. "Yeah, some people get all the luck."

"Luck?" the girl says.

"I mean . . . he was dating *Trina Low*."

"I don't know how lucky that was," the girl says. She pauses to take a sip from a takeaway cup, the straw stained red from her lips. "They fought a lot."

"How do you know?" Tweedledee asks.

"E-ve-ry-one knew," the boy says, rolling his eyes. "It's not like they hid it. They'd start yelling at each other at, like, Starbucks, or McDonald's, or in the middle of a hotel lobby."

"I saw her try to punch him once," the girl supplies helpfully.

"You're exaggerating, darling." The boy sniffs. "But still. They knew we were watching and they did it anyway. Maybe they wanted us to see it all."

The screen goes black. Words appear slowly, letter by letter.

Do you know Mark Thomas?

CHEAT, I think. *To act dishonestly to gain profit or advantage.* I think about Mark and Puteri together in the room, his guilt-stricken face. At first, I was convinced it was guilt at being caught with Puteri; then I thought it was because they were both hiding something. Now I'm almost certain the guilt was all Mark's, and Puteri was just a convenient cover.

Do you know Mark Thomas?

Do I?

Time ticks down minute by minute as I sit and watch everyone else around me wrestle with words while I think about Mark, searching the hall for his face. *Could he really be the one to hurt Trina? To hurt Yasmin?*

To hurt me?

No answers appear, and my opponent never comes.

"Looks like you win," the tournament director says when I let her know. "Congrats! A nice, easy round for you."

"Thanks," I say through gritted teeth. I know this is a good thing; I want to be done with my games as quickly as possible, so I can find Yasmin, or Mark, or both. But the win needles me. I don't tell her that I don't want nice and easy. I don't tell her that I detest winning by default, with none of the thrill of playing the perfect word, of shepherding my rival into opening up the spot I need, of hearing "challenge!" on a play I'm certain is good. I don't tell her I don't just want the little *W* by my name. I don't tell her that somehow, in spite of everything, maybe *because* of everything, I still want to play. I want to earn it. I want to prove myself.

Before I can process this, my next opponent appears. "Hi!" he says as he takes his place across the board. "My name's Nabil."

I nod. "Najwa," I say, and then "Shall we begin?"

The game starts, and I take all that frustration—from not being able to move, from not knowing any of the answers, from fighting my way through this fog of mystery and lost memories—and dispense of him so handily it almost feels cruel. I play BOZOS (men, especially stupid ones). I play OBEAH (to cast a spell on). I play IDOL (object of obsessive devotion). And to top it all off, when he uses my Z in BOZOS to play ZOO, I play through it to form WATERZOOI, a type of Flemish stew. To STEW means to cook slowly in a closed pot; my opponent looks like he's *been* stewed by the time I'm done with him. I may still be filled with jitters, but I channel them all into the game. I am unstoppable. And the idea that Scrabble is still there for me, grounding me through everything that's going on, is comforting. It takes me a second to realize that I'm not even thinking about doing this for Trina anymore—I'm doing this for me now, and I feel not one twinge of guilt about it.

It's a revelation.

My next opponent arrives ten minutes late, flustered and sweaty, and tries to tell me some long-winded story about being locked in a bathroom, unable to get out. "I don't know what happened," she says as she arranges tiles on her rack with a shaking hand. "It was so frightening." I nod and make sympathetic sounds as I make my first move: VAUNTIE. V on the double letter for eight points, nine, ten, eleven, twelve, thirteen, fourteen, double that for twenty-eight, add fifty points for the bingo . . . "Seventy-eight," I say, writing it down.

My opponent stares at the board, then at me. "Is that even a word?" she whispers.

I shrug. "You can challenge if you like," I say, knowing full well that it is, and that it means proud.

She waits for a bit and then, just as I thought she would, she shakes her head and concentrates on her own rack. As she plays, she has a habit of fiddling with a strand of hair and jiggling her feet. Her timidity is her downfall; I win by more than two hundred points. *I will be Queen,* I tell myself, *I will be Queen.* And it's hard not to believe it.

And so the day goes on, and I win game after game, and in between my victories, I search. I search for Yasmin; I search for Mark; I elbow my way through the crowds of people in the hall, frantic and anxious, searching for clues I don't even know how to recognize. And as I search, I listen to the chatter of the kids around me, still so focused on their games. Names float to the top of the usual sea of chatter, some expected—Josh, Shuba—some, less so. "Yasmin is doing so well," I hear one kid whisper. "I didn't realize she was this good."

Someone switches on the microphone and there's a screech of feedback that makes me wince and silences everyone in the hall. "We will now take a one-hour lunch break," the announcer says. "Please be back and ready for your next games at one forty-five p.m. That's one forty-five p.m. ya. Thank you, enjoy your lunch."

Lunch. *Find Yasmin,* I think. *You need to find Yasmin.* I let myself be pushed along by the stream of people heading toward the main doors, still frantically looking for Yasmin, so busy searching that I ram my hip right into the corner of a table and wince in pain. "Sorry," I murmur to the player seated there, but she doesn't say anything back. She doesn't even seem to notice. It's Emily, and she isn't playing anymore; instead, she's arguing intently with her opponent. "The game is over," she says. "And I won fair and square."

"Are you sure about that?" the boy sitting across from her shoots back. "Because we all know the stories . . ."

Emily stands and grabs her things, every line on her face radiating anger. "Look, if you had a problem, you were free to challenge any of my words during the game," she says tightly. "But it's over now, and I won, no matter what you say. And you can take your snide little remarks and . . . and . . . and shove them."

She turns quickly toward the exit, almost barging into my shoulder as she brushes past, but never stops or looks back. And as she walks away, I hear her mutter under her breath: "I'm sick of being this community's punching bag."

I've won all my games so far. I'm that much closer to becoming the Queen of the Tiles. I should be exhilarated, and a part of me is. But I can't shake the fear, the feeling that something's wrong, that there's something I'm not seeing, some word that hasn't quite swum into focus yet, and that if I don't find it, my whole world is going to come crumbling down.

I look in the bathrooms. I look in the lobby. I walk the corridors, I call her phone, I send a dozen messages that are never answered. Over and over again, I ask:

Have you seen Yasmin? Do you know where Yasmin is?

But she is nowhere to be found, and I can feel panic start to rise, eclipsing everything else. Where is she?

Eventually, after I've exhausted all my other options, I head outside. Yasmin's never been an outdoorsy person, but maybe, just maybe, she came out here looking for some fresh air. But when I look around me, all I see is manicured lawns and neatly trimmed bushes, with no Yasmin in sight.

"Hey." Ben sits half-hidden on a bench just behind a frangipani tree, the ground beneath scattered with brilliant crimson blossoms. He almost makes me jump right out of my own skin.

"Hey," I say back.

His smile is warm and welcoming. "You look like you could use a break. Want to sit down?" I hesitate, but he seems so sweet and concerned, and it's hard to say no. He swats stray flowers and leaves from the bench to make room for me, and I perch gingerly on the hard wooden slats. "How's your day going so far?"

"Okay," I say.

"That great, huh?" He laughs. "You look stressed. Had some tough racks in there?"

I think about the clues and shiver. "You could say that."

"Me too," he says, nodding sympathetically. "Some really great competition in there this year. But it feels good to be back here, after all . . . after everything that went on last time, you know? I know I joke around a lot, play the fool and everything.

But I mean it. It's nice to be here." He smiles. "I miss all these buggers when I'm not around them."

"All of them?" I say, sensing an opening. "Even Mark?"

The smile falters. "Maybe not everyone," he mutters.

"The other night," I say, watching him closely. "Before your mother turned up, you were talking about something. Something that you saw that weekend. Can you tell me what that was?"

I can tell by the way he sucks a breath in through his teeth and looks away that he hadn't expected this, hadn't expected to ever talk about this again.

"Come on, Ben," I say. "Tell me."

"I don't know if it's important. . . ."

"It was important enough before."

It's a long time before he speaks again, and when he does, I barely hear him.

"What?"

"I said I saw them kiss," he says, loud and clear, though he still won't look me in the eye.

"Mark and Puteri?" My heart pounds and pounds, even though I tried to tell myself I knew it all along. Even though I tried to warn myself. *You knew this, Najwa. You knew.*

He nods. "I needed to get something from my mom's car and it didn't seem to make sense to take the lifts when it was just one floor down, so I decided I was going to take the stairs, and I opened the door to the stairwell, and . . ." His voice trails off.

I knew it, I think to myself, *I knew it,* but I still find myself fighting the urge to cry. "Did you tell anyone else?" I ask. I think about the photograph. I KNOW. *Who knows? You, Ben? Was it you? If Mark lied about this, has he been lying about every-thing else, too, all this time? Did he know Trina was going to break up with him? Was this his revenge?*

"No," he says. "Or if I did, I don't remember. To be honest, I . . . I try very hard not to think about it."

A strategy I understand all too well. "Okay. Well, thank you. And uh . . . good luck today."

"You too," he says. As I head back inside, I pass Ben's mother looking around frantically for him, and tell her that I think I saw him heading to his room for some rest.

I figure it's the least I can do.

CHAPTER TWENTY-FIVE

EXIGENCY

twenty-one points

noun

urgent demand or need

D o you know Mark Thomas?

The phrase echoes in my head over and over again as I walk toward my next table, my legs barely holding my weight. *Do you know Mark Thomas?* Maybe once upon a time, before all of this, before he became one half of Trina-and-Mark and nothing more. Can I say I know him now? Do I want to?

It's hard to believe, but when I reach my seat, my opponent looks worse than I do. "Hi," I say, quickly followed by "Are you okay?" She's flushed and slightly sweaty, but she just nods.

"I'm fine!" she says in tones of faux gaiety, pushing back a stray hair that has somehow escaped from her ponytail and sliding a barrette in place to keep it under control. "Better than ever, really! Are you ready to play?"

"Sure," I say. I'm wary, but I'm ready.

"It's my first tournament," she says. When she smiles, she

shows all her braces-covered teeth and some gum for good measure. "I can't believe I'm doing as well as I am! I've got a real shot at top five!"

"How exciting for you," I murmur. "Shall we begin?"

She nods, her ponytail bobbing up and down, and we begin.

Her name is Nora. I know this because she tells me so, several times, not allowing me to forget. Nora is from Melaka. Nora has been playing Scrabble since she was seven. Nora also happens to be a fidgeter. She taps and she jiggles, she scratches and she smooths, she picks and she pouts. Much of this is due to habit—she can no more control the movements than I can control the weather—but part of it, I realize as we get further and further into the game, is due to something else entirely. I've just played AERUGO—the green film on copper, brass, or bronze, and a good way to dump that inconvenient letter U— when I look up to see my opponent looking fairly green herself, her arm straight up in the air, her eyes scanning the room. For a split second, I wonder if she's issuing a challenge. Instead, she calls out, "Director!"

The tournament director weaves her way through tables and makes it to us, in which time Nora has probably lost five kilos from all the tapping her right foot is doing. "What is it?" she barks at us.

"Restroom," Nora says.

"Must you? Really?" Nora nods, and the TD sighs. "Alright. Play your turn, then go. But remember, your opponent gets to play her turn and start your timer again as soon as she's done. So don't waste any time."

Nora nods again, hurriedly places her word on the board (MARK through a floating A, and I am filled with an inexplicable sense of foreboding), records her points (ten; there are no premium tiles—a waste, I think, of the five-point K and the three-point M, but I suppose she was desperate), hits the timer, and then bolts out of the room so fast I can practically see the dust clouds kicked up by her feet, cartoon-style.

I glance at the TD, who shakes her head. "Newbies," she mutters under her breath. Then she looks at me. "You know what to do," she says before walking off.

I have zero vowels on my rack, but a quick scan of the board shows me the space I need. I play through a floating H to place PHPHT, an expression of irritation or reluctance. This is the kind of move non-Scrabble players hate you for. I hit the timer and wait.

Nora returns moments later, flustered, still wiping her damp hands on her jeans. "I'm here, I'm here." She twitters and flutters like a bird. I say nothing while I wait for her next move.

Three plays later, the TD is back by our table, responding to Nora's frantic hand waving. "Again?" she says, one eyebrow arched.

Nora nods. She knows what to do this time; she's already made her move and it's my turn.

"Alright, go ahead."

By the third time Nora raises her hand, it's to forfeit the

game. Her face is pale by now, and sweaty, and strained. "I'm so sorry," she whispers. "It must have been something I ate."

"That's okay," I say. "I'm sorry too. And I hope you feel better soon." It's not a fun way to win, but it's an even worse way to lose.

As she walks away, I turn my attention to the board and begin the process of arranging the tiles for the next players. *It must have been something I ate.*

Just like Shuba, I think, and my heart begins to pound.

Something I ate. . . .

AILMENT, I think. An illness. ALIMENT, something that nourishes the body.

AGEN. Again.

And then I see. I finally see.

It's all happening. All of it. AILMENT, ALIMENT, the sick opponent, forced to forfeit because of something she ate. JANIFORM, referring to Mark and his betrayal of Trina, of me, with Puteri. AGEN. Again. All over again. CHEAT. A trick, a magician creating an explosion, so nobody notices what he's doing with his hands.

All this time, were these words clues to what happened in the past . . . or what was about to happen, right here, right now?

Someone brushes against my shoulder as they hurry past. "Sorry," they throw back over their shoulder. "Come on," they say, turning back to their friend. "Hurry up. They've posted the list for the final games."

In a daze, I get up and make my feet walk to the bulletin board, which is surrounded by other players. I look up and my mouth drops.

FINAL: NAJWA B. VS. YASMIN L.

She did it, I think, almost proudly. *Yasmin did it.*

And then I think: *REGICIDE. AGEN.* And a fear reaches out an icy finger to trace a line of goose bumps up and down my arms.

Can you crack the code before it's too late?

It's too late.

One of us will be the Queen of the Tiles.

One of us is in danger.

CHAPTER TWENTY-SIX

CONFUTE

twelve points

verb

prove wrong

Tweedledee's hand accidentally brushes against my left boob as she does her best to hook a mic onto my shirt.

"Sorry, sorry," she mutters, blushing furiously.

"It's fine," I tell her. I've spent a lot of time using the word "fine" this weekend; maybe eventually it will be true.

Right now, it's a lie. It's not fine. I am not fine. Nothing is fine. There might be a murder about to happen, the perpetrator might be the boy I've always thought of as perfect, the victim of that murder might be me, and because the world doesn't deal in might-bes, I can't figure out what I'm supposed to do about it.

The silence is too fertile; within it, my thoughts bloom until they take over my whole head and I feel like it may burst. "Can we hurry this up?" I say, my knees jiggling up and down. I can't seem to stop moving. "I have some things to take care of."

"Hold on ya, hold on," Tweedledum murmurs as he checks

the camera. "No need so impatient, we're working on it . . ."

"I thought you guys were just filming for your documentary thing," I say. "I didn't know you did this, too."

"Oh." Tweedledee smiles as she threads the mic cable beneath my hijab just so. "Ya, we're actually the social media team this year. We'll be interviewing both finalists and putting up the snippets on the tournament social media accounts."

"Right." My fingers tap-tap-tap incessantly against my knees. "How long is this going to take?"

Tweedledum pokes his head out from behind the light he's fiddling with. "About ten, fifteen minutes max lah," he says. "Is that okay? Your game isn't for another, like, half an hour."

"It's fine," I say again. To be FINE is to be very good, but a FINE is also a payment imposed as a penalty. Trina's the one who died, but it feels like I'm the one paying the price, over and over and over again.

Alina: I feel like you should be happier about making the finals

Alina: After a FULL YEAR out of the game

Alina: So why aren't you celebrating??

Me: Something feels wrong

"So Yasmin was a surprise, huh?" Tweedledee steps back, finally pleased with the placement of the mic. "I didn't think she was that good."

"She isn't," I say without thinking, then hastily correct

myself. "I mean . . . she must have worked hard to improve over the past year."

"Well, it paid off." One of the lights flickers off, and Tweedledum groans. "Can you fix it?"

"Ya, ya, hang on."

"Give us five minutes," Tweedledee smiles at me. "I'm sure he'll sort it out."

She leaves me alone—finally—and I try to take deep breaths and think. There is a loud clang, followed by a string of muttered expletives from Tweedledum.

Tweedledee rolls her eyes as she sits at her laptop. "Just going over some footage," she says by way of explanation when she sees me looking.

"Hello, can you please help me instead of messing around with the footage ah?" Tweedledum says, and his partner rolls her eyes.

"Okay lah, I'm coming," she says, and they both set to work on a mess of lights and cables. The laptop continues to run, and I automatically focus on the screen, taking in nothing, my mind a blur of racing thoughts. For a while it's just an image of a chair exactly like the one I'm sitting on right now, a generic hotel banquet chair with its metal frame and barely cushioned back. There is laughter just off-screen and Yasmin enters the picture, taking her seat, smoothing her skirt, talking animatedly to someone I can't see—one of the Tweedles, I assume. Her interview was just before mine; I suppose the Tweedles need to edit it quickly so they can upload it before the final. People mill around in the background as Yasmin sits there, hands folded in her lap, waiting patiently to begin. I realize I've never really seen Yasmin this way, silent and still. The contours of her face are suddenly both familiar and alien to me.

"Hello." A voice forces me out of my thoughts. It's Emily, and she's smiling brightly at me. "I just wanted to congratulate you on making the finals. And after a year away, too! What a comeback. You must be so excited."

"Uh-huh," I say. My tongue feels like it's covered in glue.

Emily's face creases in concern. "Are you okay?" she asks. "You look a bit . . . ill."

"Just need some water or something," I manage. "I feel a headache coming on."

"That won't do at all." She rummages around in that big bag of hers, and I think I may be sick. "Would you like me to give you something? Even just some ibuprofen? I have it here somewhere . . . At least I think I do." She scowls, her pale face all twisted for a brief second. "People keep taking my stuff again. I'm already almost out of vitamin C, and I'm sure that bottle was at least half full when I got here. . . ."

"That's okay," I say quickly. "I'm sure it'll be fine. I probably haven't been drinking enough."

"Oh, I know what that's like," she says, patting my arm sympathetically. "I always forget to stay hydrated at events like this. But you should, you know! You've got a big game coming up."

"Yeah," I say. "I do, don't I?"

"You'll do great!" she says. "Oh, and I also wanted to apologize."

"For what?"

"For not turning up." Embarrassment tugs at the edges of her smile. "We were supposed to play together, remember? That first game?"

"Oh, right." I hadn't even looked up my no-show opponent's name.

"Yes, I had the most terrible tummy bug," she says, patting her midriff, and I just stare at her as the horror of what she's saying begins to sink in. More stomach issues? First Josh, then Nora, and now Emily, too? I could have brushed two incidents off, but three? Three isn't a coincidence anymore. Three happens on purpose. "Ours wasn't the only game I missed, I'm afraid. Rotten luck, really. I'll just have to make it up somehow next year." She glances at her watch. "Well, it's almost time. Good luck!" she says, giving me a hug as I sit there, stiff and awkward and anxious. "I'll be watching!"

"Great," I say. And then, as she starts to walk away, "Emily—"

"Yes?" She turns to face me, and I wonder if I'm imagining the nervous look on her face.

AILMENT. ALIMENT. I remember how I tested Josh, tried to make sure my thoughts were going in the right direction. If the clues are meant to be a sign of things to come and not just things that happened before, there's a chance those stomach troubles people have been having aren't a coincidence.

"This is going to sound strange, but . . . did you . . . did you eat or drink around Shuba today?"

Emily's face is one big question mark. "No," she says slowly. "I saw them for a little bit earlier today, but that was all." She thinks a little bit, then snaps her fingers. "I did take a bottle of water from Mark, though. My own was empty and I was absolutely parched. He'd only drunk a teensy bit of his, and he didn't want anymore, so he let me have it. Rather nice of him, I thought. I did wipe the lip off really well beforehand, though, because, you know. *Germs.*" She grimaces. "Does that help at all?"

I swallow hard. "Yes, actually, it really does. Have you seen him around at all since then?"

She frowns. "He's probably in the hall somewhere. Does he know you're looking for him?"

I hope not, I think as I walk away. *I really hope not.*

CHAPTER TWENTY-SEVEN

ANAGNORISIS

twelve points

noun

the point in a play, novel, etc., in which a principal character recognizes or discovers another character's true identity or the true nature of their own circumstances

We sit across from each other, Yasmin and I, the empty board between us. Tweedledum is setting up a camera to capture all our moves; the game will be streamed online for anyone who wants to watch it. People wander around us, and somewhere in the sea of faces a camera flash goes off, blinding me for a second.

I try to breathe, try to remember my rituals, try to ground myself in this moment, spreading my fingertips to try and feel the board, the chair, the rack, all of it. *You want this, Najwa. You deserve this.* But every line I tether slowly unravels itself. By the time I am finished, I have lost them all, all over again. *This game is yours,* I tell myself. *But REGICIDE,* I reply. *The murder of a monarch. The Queen of the Tiles. This game is yours—but do you really want it to be?* I scan the crowd for Mark, as I've been doing over and over again all day, and my anxiety makes it seem like every face is his.

Yasmin reaches her hand out to grab my own restless, tapping one. "I'm really glad we're the ones who made it to the final, sweetie," she says. Her smile is wide, euphoric. It's not the spotlight; Yasmin is glowing. This may be the happiest I've seen her in a long, long time. I think: *What if she's in danger right now?* and the thought is like a punch to the gut.

"Me too," I say, because Yasmin expects a response, and because I don't know what to do with this silence. How do I warn her? What if there's nothing to warn her about? Who will believe me, the girl who went a little bit crazy after her best friend died? "How are you feeling?"

"Absolutely wonderful," she says.

"And that—" I gesture to the bandage on her head. "That doesn't hurt?"

"This?" She touches it. "No, not at all! Silly of me to slip and fall like that, wasn't it? Almost ruined my own chances . . ."

"You slipped?" I stare at her incredulously. "Are you sure? Are you absolutely certain?"

Her smile wavers, lost, uncertain. "I'm sure I must have. How else could I have . . ."

"Someone could have pushed you."

"Oh." Yasmin's eyes go wide with fear. "Oh. That would explain . . . but that can't be right, can it? Because why would anybody do that?"

I hesitate. Something about ruining this moment for her seems so wrong, but I need answers and only Yasmin has them. "Before . . . everything . . . happened," I begin, "you were going to tell me something. Do you remember? You said you'd figured it out. You insisted I come and meet you. And then . . ."

"Of course I do." She nods and leans in close. "And what I found out was . . ."

"Ladies and gentlemen," a voice booms over the PA system, and I grit my teeth. "We are about to start ya. The match for first and second place will be at table one. And the match for third and fourth place will take place at table two. Fifth and sixth place, table three. Seventh and eighth, table four. And finally, ninth and tenth, at table five. Players, are you ready?"

There are a handful of scattered responses, varying in enthusiasm from limp to strident. ("YES," Josh says firmly at table three, his face like thunder.)

"Very well," says the announcer. "Ready, set . . . play!"

The room fills with the light clattering of tiles being moved around a bag. I turn back to Yasmin. "So you were saying—?" I begin, but she frowns at me slightly.

"It's time to play, Najwa."

I sigh and offer Yasmin the first draw before taking my own and setting the bag down, willing my hands to stop shaking. I don't want her to see how scared I am; I hope she can't.

"D," Yasmin says.

I open my palm, revealing the tile nestled there. "J."

She smiles. "I go first."

"Yup."

We draw our tiles, I hit the timer, and we begin.

There are games you go into knowing you will win. The act of playing, then, becomes secondary because you already know the outcome. It's just down to the tiles to figure this out and work themselves out in your favor.

Then there are games where you can't seem to find your footing, where your win is going to depend on cunning, on gritting your teeth and clawing your way back, letter by letter, word by word, bleeding a little across the board with every turn.

This game is the latter. From the start, I can't seem to focus. Like Nora, I become a fidgeter; my right foot will not stop tapping. My thoughts will not leave me alone. The ants keep biting. I look for Mark in every face. I cannot relax.

Yasmin doesn't seem to notice. She lays down her first move: PROVE, P on the double letter. "Twenty-six," she says.

I scan the board, then use the P to place PLOTZ, getting rid of that troublesome Z and helping myself to the double-word score. "Thirty-two," I say.

Yasmin nods. "Nice one."

The game falls into an uneasy rhythm. I don't. I keep trying to talk to Yasmin, but she keeps shushing me—"No chatter, sweetie, ni bukan kopitiam!"—focused as she is on the game. Time and again, I try to ask questions, get her to tell me what she knows, warn her about my own fears; time and again, she rebuffs me. "The game," she keeps telling me. "We have to play the game." And I suppose if you've worked this hard to get this far, like Yasmin has, you wouldn't let a little thing like possible murder stop you. *Whatever she knows, I reason with myself, it can't be that bad, if she isn't as scared as you think she should be.*

And yet, still, I can feel the ants crawling all over my brain, making their way down to my fingertips, easing me into mistakes I don't usually make. I rush and play SALINED, which doesn't exist, when I should have waited until SNAILED revealed itself to me; Yasmin challenges it off the board and uses the extra move to build a slim lead. I open a triple-word lane when I know Yasmin has the Q; she uses it to play UMIAQ, an Inuit word for a type of canoe. "Forty-eight," she says once she's placed every tile. It's particularly impressive because most people think of Us coming after Qs . . . not the Q coming at the end of a word.

I'd always thought of Yasmin as part of the Scrabble scenery. And I know how hard she's worked, how much she's improved—she wouldn't be sitting across from me right now otherwise. But even through my haze of fear and anxiety, the surprising realization slowly seeps through: Yasmin is also *good*.

Very good.

When did that happen?

There's little time to ponder; the game continues. I draw

a series of bad racks—too many Is, a double N that I can't find the space to shake off—and have to waste another turn to trade tiles, and in the meantime Yasmin uses a blank in place of the I to play VIRTUES on a triple-word score. Her lead keeps climbing, and I can't tell if this prickling fear I feel biting at the edge of my mind is the fear of losing, or the fear of one of us getting hurt. *REGICIDE,* my brain chants over and over again. *REGICIDE, REGICIDE, REGICIDE.* It's so loud that I don't see a hot spot I should be blocking, and Yasmin uses the DEN already on the board to play IRRIDENTA, a region historically tied to one country, but ruled by another. It derives from an Italian word, *irredento,* which means "unredeemed." Kind of like me in this game. There are only three tiles left in the bag. To redeem is to make up for; there is no making up for this point deficit. I am going to lose. And I am going to lose to Yasmin.

"Hey, Najwa," she says softly, and I look up, surprised. *What happened to no chatter?*

"What?"

"What are the principles of the endgame?"

The world begins to spin. I swallow, hard. "You . . . you were the one who . . ."

"I'm just asking," she says, smiling sweetly.

"I . . ." Is she serious? Or is she the one? The mystery-grammer who's been messaging me this whole time?

"Well?"

Play along, Najwa. Maybe she really wants to know. Maybe

she's forgotten. "There are a few," I say. Around us, the crowd begins to murmur, confused by our coffeehousing. "You try to trap your opponent with awkward tiles. You play to maximize your spread. You never forget to keep tracking. You try and play through your opponent's eyes, figure out what they'll do if you do this, or this, or this. And you . . ."

"And you try to look for setup plays," Yasmin supplies.

"That's right," I say. "You've been studying." I'm trying so hard to figure out where this is going.

"I have," she says quietly. "And I'm sorry."

"Why?" I say, puzzled. "You drew better racks. It's just how the game goes sometimes."

"Not for that," she says. "For the setup."

And she raises her hand and calls out loud, so loud that the room echoes with the words: "Tournament director. Tournament director, please. My opponent is cheating."

Of all the things I'd expected, this wasn't it. It feels like someone has taken a fistful of tiles and rammed them down my throat so that for a moment, all I can do is choke. "What?" I finally manage. The entire room is looking at us now; I'm keenly aware of the stares and whispers, the way the cameras are trained on our every move. The TD bustles over, looking annoyed.

"What is it?" she says curtly. "We're about to be done here, there's a lot we need to—"

"My opponent," Yasmin says loudly. "She's cheating. I saw her palm the tiles."

"That is absolutely ridiculous," I say. I can feel my face turning red, the heat creeping up to the tips of my ears. "I have been playing this game for far longer than you, Yasmin, and I have never cheated in my life. I have never needed to," I can't resist adding.

"Until now," Yasmin says snidely. "Just check her pockets, I bet she's hidden them somewhere."

"Enough." The TD raises her hand to stop us and lets out a deep sigh. "Najwa, just empty your pockets, please."

"But . . ."

"The faster you do it, the faster we can all get back to the games."

I can feel the other players shuffling restlessly, all the attention diverted to us instead of the boards still in play. "Fine," I mumble. "Let's get this over with." I start taking out the contents of my pockets. First my jeans, which have a stick of gum, two folded squares of tissues, my phone, and a fifty-cent coin; then my cardigan, which I know has nothing in its two large pockets.

Or should have nothing.

Except when my hand fishes around inside the left-hand pocket, it closes around two little squares, smooth to the touch, familiar and foreboding all at once.

"Well?" the TD says, a note of impatience coloring her voice.

There's no way to stop this from happening.

I open my hand. The two tiles sit in the center of my palm, pale and unassuming: a blank and an S.

The TD's face is a mask of shock. So, I assume, is mine.

Yasmin, on the other hand, just smiles and smiles.

"That's just how the game goes sometimes," she says softly.

CHAPTER TWENTY-EIGHT

NADIR

six points

noun

point in the sky opposite the zenith

t was *her*?"

Puteri and Mark are sitting side by side on her bed, looking at me with twin expressions of worry and disbelief. The worry is mostly because I've done nothing but lie here on my back, on my bed, staring up at the ceiling, for what seems like hours now, trying to untangle all the threads of this mystery, trying to see where it was that I went so wrong. The disbelief stems from the fact that, as Mark keeps saying repeatedly in shocked tones: "It was Yasmin? *Yasmin??*" Somewhere beneath my despair, my rage at not figuring any of this out sooner, and yes, the hurt to my pride at being outfoxed by Yasmin, it's gratifying to know that I'm not the only one who didn't see this coming.

"But the question is, *what* exactly did she do?" Puteri says, drumming her fingers against her thighs. "Was she just behind the Instagram posts? Or did she actually kill Trina?"

"She has to be the murderer, right?" Mark asks. "How else could she know everything she knows?"

"It just doesn't make any sense." I sit up and slam a fist into one of the pillows, letting it sink deep into the softness. "Why would she murder Trina? She loved her. And why would she do this to me? Just to win a game?"

"I mean . . ." Mark shrugs. "Have you seen the kids at this tournament? I'm just saying, it's not outside the realm of possibility. . . ."

"But why frame me?" No matter how I rearrange the pieces, I can't quite find the solution, and the sheer frustration is setting my teeth on edge. "She was already winning. She didn't need to take everything away from me."

"Unless," Puteri says softly, "that was the whole point."

"What do you mean?" Mark turns to Puteri, his brows furrowed.

"She means they're going to tell me I'm banned." It's hard to get the words out. I think about life without Scrabble at its center and shiver. Without this world, what am I?

"Would they seriously ban you for this?" Mark is incredulous.

"Of course they would. That's what happens when you cheat." I swallow hard. "Remember Allan Simmons?"

"Who?"

"Allan Simmons." I sigh. "He was the British champion in 2008. In 2017 they said he was peeking at the tiles he was drawing from the bag. You know. Trying to make sure he chose the best ones, discarding the ones he didn't want. He got banned for three years."

"But you didn't do anything," Mark says. "You were set up!"

"He said that too."

"Right. They don't know that she was set up," Puteri says quietly. "It's her word against two tiles literally in her pocket. Why would they believe some story about a setup?"

"They wouldn't." I punch the pillow again, hard. "That's the problem."

"So how do you plan to . . ."

A timid knock on the door interrupts her, and Puteri sighs as she goes to answer it. "You? What do you want?"

"I'm here to see Najwa."

"I doubt she wants to see you."

I sit up. "Let her in," I say. "I'm the one who called her here."

Emily walks inside, carefully avoiding eye contact.

"What's she doing here?" Mark asks me, bewildered. "Why would you want to see Emily?"

"Because Emily's the one who framed me," I say calmly. "Isn't that right, Emily?"

She shuffles her feet, stalling before she finally answers. "You know it is."

Puteri sucks in a sharp breath. "You have some nerve. . . ."

I ignore her. "Why did you do it?" I ask. "What did I ever do to you?"

She takes a deep breath and lifts her head, forcing herself to look straight at me, tear-stained, shamefaced. "Yasmin told me to," she says simply.

"Yasmin?" Mark squints at her. "Why?"

"Because." Emily draws in a shaky breath. "Because she found out I was cheating, and she was threatening to tell the organizers. And I panicked, because neither my Scrabble career nor my mental health could have survived another scandal like the last one. . . ."

"But you decided sacrificing mine was absolutely fine." I can't keep the venom out of my voice. It hurts to think about everything I'm about to lose, everything that's about to be taken away from me.

"She said all I had to do was slip the tiles in your pocket, and maybe say something about Mark if the opportunity came up—" Mark clicks his tongue at the sound of his name. "She said she'd never talk about this again." She gulps. "I didn't have a choice."

"You did," Puteri says coolly. "You just chose the wrong bloody thing."

Emily hangs her head. "I'm sorry," she says again.

"Get out," I say. I'm spent.

She leaves, and Puteri closes the door with a firm click behind her. Then she turns to look at me. "So you weren't going to tell us you'd figured that part out?"

"There was only one possibility," I say. "Emily's the only person who came close enough to plant those tiles on me. And then it's just a matter of working backward. Why would she do that? Because she wanted me to be accused of cheating. Why would she want that? Because she was the one cheating herself. She actually had something to lose."

Mark shakes his head. "How do you always manage to weed out the cheaters?"

"It's a skill." I force myself to look at both of them. "Take you two, for example."

Puteri blinks. "Wait. What are you . . . ?"

At exactly the same time, Mark blurts out, "How'd you know??"

She rolls her eyes. "There he goes again, Mr. Subtle," she mutters under her breath. Then she turns her gaze on me. "It wasn't what you think. It was just one kiss. One time. And then when everything happened, it was just too strange, too wrong, to think about anything else. So we stayed away from each other until, well . . ."

"Until this weekend," Mark says. He takes Puteri's hand in his, but she removes it from his grasp, patting him gently as if she doesn't want to hurt him.

"Don't get me wrong," she tells me, as Mark tries to hide his disappointment. "We're not together or anything. But we've been . . . talking things over."

"Right," Mark says quickly. "We've been sort of . . . getting to know each other again." I wait to feel that flash of pain, that feeling of having something taken away from me. But I don't. Recalling a feeling, I'm starting to realize, doesn't mean living with its ghost always. "She was a blip," Mark continues, lacing and unlacing his fingers as he speaks, not looking at me. "Trina, I mean. I was dazzled for a while—I mean, who wouldn't be when you're chosen by Trina Low, you know? It's like getting too close to the sun. You can't see anything else. It's beautiful, until it hurts. It's warm, until it burns. When I could see again, I realized that I'd made the wrong choice. That I should have stayed with Puteri all along. But, well . . . imagine telling Trina Low she was a mistake."

"So what was this weekend about, then?" I ask him.

"I mean . . ." He spreads his hands out helplessly and looks at me directly for the first time in a while. "I wanted the truth. That part was real. And I wanted to get back to being your friend again. That part was also real. But it was hard to face you and think about telling you that your best friend, the person who meant the most to you in the whole world, just didn't mean as much to me as you thought. Or as I thought," he adds. "That was a surprise to me too. And the guilt was a lot to take in. I, uh . . . probably didn't handle that very well."

"No kidding," Puteri mutters.

I feel the knot in my chest begin to undo itself. One question answered.

Puteri clears her throat. "Not to break up this Jejak Kasih moment," she says, "but what are we going to do now? We now know very clearly that Yasmin has an agenda against Najwa and played her like a rack of prime tiles. The question now is: Was she just the Instagram poster? Was she also Trina's murderer?

And whichever she is, whether it's one or both, how do we prove it?"

I think about the smile on Yasmin's face. *That's just how the game goes sometimes.* "The Instagram thing, for sure," I say. "It wasn't just some prank, either. She very deliberately set out to destroy my world."

Puteri stands above me, her arms folded, her expression grim. "Then you'll need to figure it all out," she says. "If you loved Trina, you need to find out what happened and why she did it." She glances at Mark and her expression softens. "For closure," she says softly. "So we can move on. All of us."

That word again. I close my eyes and take a deep breath.

An idea forms.

Slowly I swing my legs over the edge of the bed, sit up, and fix my slipping headscarf.

"Okay," I say quietly. "Here's what we're going to do."

It's time to put this past year to rest.

CHAPTER TWENTY-NINE

CODA

seven points

noun

final part of a musical composition

> Alina: Good luck Kakak
>
> Alina: I love you
>
> Alina: . . . but if you bring up the fact that I sent you that, I will deny it forever

When the door opens that evening, there is no loud creak, no dramatic entrance. Instead, Yasmin simply walks in, closes it softly behind her, and comes to sit down across from me.

There is nobody else in the room. Only the two of us, one board, a hundred tiles, and a million questions.

"Are you ready to play?" I ask her, an echo of one of those DMs that seem like they happened so long ago.

She just nods.

The invitation was a simple one. Just a text message.

So you've gotten rid of me, it said. But that doesn't mean

you won. Let's see who really deserves to be the new Queen of the Tiles. Just you and me, my room, no audience, no cameras. Only Scrabble, and the satisfaction of beating someone fair and square.

And then I waited, and waited, and waited. And now here she is. I had a hunch she wouldn't be able to resist.

I offer her the bag, and she rummages around before drawing the first tile. Her shoulders sag slightly. "P," she says, tossing it onto the board.

I draw my tile. "C."

She clicks her tongue while I make my draw, the sound unnervingly loud and harsh in the quiet evening stillness. It doesn't take long to make my first move: GHARRY, a horse-drawn carriage, for thirty-four points.

"No timer?" she asks, and I shake my head.

"Let's just let the tiles run their course."

Yasmin frowns as she shuffles her tiles, then responds by playing through my G with EGLOMISE, bingoing out for sixty-four points. EGLOMISE means gilding, putting a thin layer of gold on something, the way we're trying to cover up the elephant in the room with this veneer of civility and Scrabble.

No more.

"Why did you do it?" I ask quietly as I survey my rack. Two Os, two As, M, V, and N.

"Do what?" Yasmin says, arching an eyebrow at me. "I've

done a lot this weekend, you're going to have to be more spe-cific." She smiles.

I place NOMA right up against the last three letters of EGLOMISE, forming IN, SO, and EM and taking advantage of both a double letter and triple word. Thirty points. "Why not start with me?"

"Ah." She doesn't even pause as she places SALTIERS on the board, the first S nestled under the final E in EGLOMISE, the final S a blank tile. Another bingo. Two in a row? What are the odds of that? Someone like Josh would probably be able to tell me. "Seventy points," she says, and I detect more than a hint of satisfaction in the way she says it.

"Well?" I say as I survey my rack. I know we have more important things to focus on, but I can't help it—I want to beat her. I want to beat her so badly my hands are shaking.

"I wanted you to lose," she said simply. "But not just the one game. I wanted you to lose everything. Everything you cared about. This game, this community, these friendships. I wanted you to lose it all."

"But why?" My voice trembles, and I will it to stop. I hook COWPEA onto the S to form COWPEAS, take the thirty points, and hate myself for my weaknesses.

"Because." Yasmin places D, A, and F through the first E in EGLOMISE to make DEAF, overlapping with GHARRY to make AH and FA. It's only twenty-six points, but she's two bingos ahead; what does she care? "Because you took what mattered most from me. It was only fitting that I should take what matters most from you."

"I never took anything from you." I fight to keep the rage out of my voice. "What are you talking about?"

She looks at me then, her eyes clear. "Trina," she says. "You took Trina from me. And I missed her. Even before she died. I have spent so much time missing Trina Low. There was a time, once, when we were never apart, never, not for a single day. And then she went to this new school and changed! Literally, just changed every single thing about herself! And she started to shut me out, more and more."

I blink back tears and place FAVOUR on the board, using the floating R in GHARRY. Twenty-four points. I'm still so behind, in everything. "And how was that my fault?"

Yasmin carefully plays OUPHE over a triple-word score, using the C and O in COWPEAS to form CH and OE. Thirty-nine points. An OUPHE is a stupid person; I feel like she's trying to tell me something. "She'd never have gotten into this Scrabble thing without you." Yasmin sniffs, and it's a noise full of disdain. "Without you egging her on, she'd never have turned herself into the . . . the *monster* that was the Queen of the Tiles."

"So that was why you killed her?" I'm having trouble getting the words out. It's hard to think of Yasmin—fluffy, servile, people-pleasing Yasmin—committing murder.

Her laugh is sharp, and bright, and completely mirthless. "Nobody killed her lah! She died suddenly. Even the police said, remember? Sudden cardiac arrest, unknown causes. No foul play suspected. That's just how it happens sometimes.

People just die." She shakes her head in. "Honestly. Murder. What do you think this is, an episode of *Riverdale*? You people are so gullible."

So all this time I've been trying to find a killer that never even existed? "How did you . . . Why would you even . . ." I don't even know where to start. It's too much. It's too much to take in.

"Oh, HOW was easy," Yasmin says, waving her hands dismissively as if the question doesn't even merit her attention. "Trina accidentally misplaced her phone at my house one time"—she mimes big, exaggerated air quotes around "accidentally misplaced"—"and I took the opportunity to install some nice, discreet spyware that let me have access to what she was up to all the time. As for everything else . . . People simply haven't been playing their best, have you noticed? It's as if . . . oh, I don't know . . . as if the idea of murder makes an excellent distraction."

"And the . . . ?" I gesture to the gash on her head, now covered by a Band-Aid.

"That might have been the easiest thing of all," she says. "All I had to do was throw myself off the stairs. It wasn't hard. Once I make up my mind to do something, I follow through. That's the difference between you and me, Najwa."

I remember my conversation with Alina before I left for the tournament, before this weekend turned my world upside down. A lifetime ago. *Let go. Surrender yourself to gravity.* "You're despicable," I say.

"I'm brilliant," she says with a toss of her curls. "Just admit it. Of course, to get both of us to the finals, I had to do a little . . . finessing."

"Which means you cheated," I say flatly.

"Such a harsh word. I just moved things along." She shrugs. "Jammed the lock on some girl's bathroom door. Used Puteri's neat little vitamin C trick on someone else. And Emily, well, she turned out to be the perfect helping hand, just when I needed it." Yasmin allows herself a slow smile, the smile of a cat who has just caught a mouse and eagerly anticipates a feast. "You aren't the star player you think you are, Najwa. You didn't really deserve that spot. You were only there because I wanted you there. Did you find my little clue?"

"Clue?"

"JANIFORM? *They hide among us?*" She smiles at me. "Surely you must see it now."

I close my eyes. The letters move, rearranging themselves, clicking into place. . . . "MIN," I whisper. "And NAJ. They're both hiding in JANIFORM."

Yasmin claps. "Brava! You see? Wasn't that clever? I was telling you all along how it would be. Just you and me, with all of our faces, to see who would inherit Trina's title." She nods toward the board. "Now make your move."

I stare at my tiles for a long time before placing ROBATA through an open A. Only after I've made the play do I realize my mistake—instead of using the double letter spot for my B, I've gone with R instead. I grit my teeth. *Get it together, Naywa.*

"A grill, right?" Yasmin says. "ROBATA? For Japanese food."

"How did you know that?"

Her eyes are hard as flints and sparking just the same. "You all underestimate me, don't you? Oh, *Yasmin* couldn't possibly be the one to come up with all of this. *Yasmin* couldn't possibly know so many words. Not like Najwa does." Her voice is high and mocking. "You want to know the truth? The fight with Trina wasn't yours. It was mine. We were at the hotel for the tournament, and I just wanted to hang out with her, you know? I didn't get to see her very much otherwise, after she switched schools . . . She said it was time for me to stop following her around and get a life of my own. She said she was tired of me. That I was suffocating her. Meanwhile you were right there, always, hanging on to her coattails, making puppy dog eyes at her boyfriend when you thought nobody was looking. But she didn't have a problem with *that*." Yasmin blinks back tears. "I said best friends shouldn't talk to each other like this. We should be able to communicate, you know? And she said . . . she said . . ." She swallows hard. "She said 'Yasmin, we are not best friends. We haven't been best friends for a long time.' And we were kind of hidden away in a corner and I guess Mark or someone overheard that and thought it was about you. Because it's always, always about *you*."

"JILTED," I say softly. "You were JILTED."

"Yes. Yes, I was." She draws herself up, squaring her shoulders, sticking out her chin. "Not that you'd ever understand what that felt like."

"I'm sorry," I say, and I mean it. "I'm sorry Trina made you feel that way."

"You think this was just Trina's fault?" Yasmin stares at me, wide-eyed and incredulous. "You still don't see it, do you?"

"See what?"

"How long are you going to hide in Trina's shadow, Najwa?" she spits out. "How long are you going to pretend you weren't part of this too? Pushing me out when you could just have let me in, laughing at me when you could have just included me in the joke. She would have listened to you if you'd told her to stop. She always listened to you." Yasmin stops and rubs the back of one hand roughly across her eyes. "What would have possibly been so bad about being three instead of two?"

There's a lump in my throat so big I can't even speak around it to answer her. Guilt pulses in the base of my stomach like a beacon. *It's true, I think. It's true. I could have stopped this. I could have done something.*

"That Mark, he was just as bad. I knew he was cheating on her. The photo was perfect, right? I found it crumpled up near a rubbish bin after the tournament and thought: I can use this. . . . And I did. I KNOW. I showed you all. I put in the work, didn't I? I laid the trap so well, you never saw it coming. I wanted to beat you, and I did. And I'm going to do it again." She plays KNAR on a triple-word score. "Twenty-four points. You don't stand a chance."

"You're probably right," I say, gulping hard. "But why go through all this trouble? Losing Trina was already the worst thing that could happen to me. Why are you even doing all this? What's the point NOW, one whole year after she died?"

She leans forward to pat my cheek gently. "Because, lovely, I've never been one to let an opportunity pass me by. Trina died, and that was sad. Truly! I was sad about it for a long, long time. Some days, I still am. I'm not sure I'll ever stop being sad. But it also felt like a gift, a final apology from Trina for sidelining me for so long. Especially when I found out you were going to start playing again, and I finally had my chance to beat you. I couldn't just let that go to waste, could I?"

And that's when I finally, finally see. That's when I understand. Just as it had been for me and Mark and Trina, so had it been for Yasmin and Trina and me. Because of course, when there is SYZYGY—when three celestial bodies are perfectly in tune and aligned in the vastness of the cosmos—you know what happens? One must block the light of another. That's just how it goes.

"Don't you have anything to say to me?" Yasmin is taunting me now, trying to get a response out of me. "The great Najwa, always able to find the perfect word. Tell me, are you finally out of them now, *Najjy*?"

It's the tone that does it, the sneering emphasis on Trina's nickname for me. "I do have one more, Min."

"Don't call me that," she mutters. "Only she called me that."

"Do you want to know what it is?" I continue, ignoring her. "ZYZZYVA."

"Excuse me?" She's puzzled now, unsure where this is going.

"It's the last word, the absolute last word you can find in the official Scrabble dictionary—hell, in any dictionary."

Yasmin sighs noisily. "Are we really doing this now? Nobody cares, Najwa."

I go on as if she hasn't even spoken. "The thing is, it's an impossible word. You'd need to have the Z, both Ys, both blanks, and a V to play it. It's ridiculous."

"You're ridiculous."

"Do you know what it means, Min?" I don't wait for her to answer, though I can see her twitch at the use of the nickname. "A ZYZZYVA is a type of tropical weevil first discovered in Brazil. Thing is, the name itself isn't associated with any Latin or Brazilian name, so some people say that the dude who discovered it just named it that way to make sure it was the last thing you saw in guides and manuals. Can you imagine?" I manage a laugh, a small, strangled sound in the darkness. "A tiny bug no bigger than an ant, insignificant in so many ways except in where it appears in a sea of words."

"Is there a point to this lecture?" She's impatient now, distracted.

"The point," I say quietly, "is that you're a ZYZZYVA. Your only significance came from your position—which was always trailing after Trina. Although I'm pretty sure that's about to change."

"What?" Yasmin's look of confusion only deepens as I stand and rap on the wall of the room next door.

"Got everything you need?" I call out.

A second later the door opens, and in walk Mark, Puteri, and the Tweedles, Tweedledum holding a laptop in his arms, Tweedledee wielding a microphone and a pleased expression. "Got it!" she crows. "We've never had *so many people* watch one of our streams, what a *fantastic* season finale for us, better than we could have ever dreamed. . . ."

"Did the cameras work okay?" I ask, and Tweedledum nods.

"Perfect," he says. "Not the angle I would have gone with, but, well, beggars can't be choosers and all that . . ."

"What," Yasmin says, enunciating each word. "Is. Going. On."

"Oh." I smile winningly at her. "Meet Shanker and Diana. They run a fast-growing YouTube channel, and they've been working on a documentary about Trina. And as it turns out, you're the unexpected star of the show!" I lean down to pat her on the shoulder. "Congratulations!"

She stares at me, openmouthed. "You mean . . . I . . . I just . . ."

"You just confessed to cheating and manipulating the game to thousands of people watching live on YouTube," Puteri supplies helpfully.

"Bet the organizers will love that," Diana says, winking at me, and I tell myself that I will never forget their names again.

Yasmin sags into her chair. I've never seen someone look so deflated. "What happens now?" she asks quietly.

Outside, I hear heavy footsteps approaching us in the

corridor, and a smart rap at the door. Then "Open up!" in the familiar rasp of the TD.

I look down at Yasmin. "Consequences," I say. "That's just how the game goes sometimes."

And then the adults are taking her away, and they're telling me I need to go and answer some questions, and as everyone is talking, as the Tweedles give me delighted thumbs-up, as I see Mark and Puteri embrace each other, there's only one word in my head. Only three letters, a mere four points. It means the last part, to kill or to die, to terminate, to cease. It means, finally, a conclusion.

This is the END.

AFTERWORD

sixteen points

noun

epilogue or postscript in a book, etc.

still don't get it," Mark says.

"Hardly a surprise, darling, coming from you," Puteri drawls as she spreads pink gloss on her lips and checks her reflection in a small handheld mirror. "But what don't you get, exactly? Given your storied history of incompetence, you're going to have to be more specific."

The three of us are sitting side by side on the lobby's stuffed leather armchairs, waiting for our parents to turn up and take us home. We've spent the rest of the day answering question after question from adults who seemed flabbergasted that we solved this whole thing without them. Puteri has made it clear she'll never forgive me for making her waste her time like this. But that's okay. I'm starting to understand Puteri, starting to understand there's more to people than you can ever really see, and that once you start seeing more of them, their words can change. Language is a living, evolving thing, after all.

"JANIFORM." He leans back and props his feet on the coffee table in front of us. The lace on one of his sneakers is untied, and the longer I look at it, the more it irritates me. "What does it even mean?"

"Now you've done it," Puteri mutters, but it's too late. This is my time to shine.

"It comes from Janus," I explain, "And Janus was an ancient Roman god with two faces, looking opposite ways. So JANIFORM literally means two-faced—a backstabber. Which we thought meant someone who betrayed Trina, but as it turns out, was how Yasmin felt about me and Trina. But you know what's funny—"

"Is it really?" Puteri interjects. "Or is it just funny to you?"

"What's *funny*," I continue, ignoring her and turning my attention fully to Mark, "is that Janus is literally the god of beginnings and endings. So it figures that JANIFORM is where we'd find our answer. Our ending."

"I can't believe Yasmin did all of this," Mark says, shaking his head. "And all to get back at you! That's intense."

Yasmin, the Mary Poppins of friends. Yasmin, who was always prepared for anything. "Trina inspired intensity in a lot of different people, and in a lot of different ways. I think the three of us . . . well, we're probably the best examples of that, don't you?"

"I guess." He fiddles around in the pocket of his backpack until he finds the pack of gum he's looking for and pops a piece in his mouth. "So," he says, chewing noisily, and I wince.

"What about all the pooping problems people were having? Those people you were supposed to play against, and me, and Josh, and Emily . . ."

"Yasmin was only responsible for some of those. Emily's was made up," I say. "Just something else Yasmin told her to do. Josh . . . well, let's just say Puteri wasn't the only one getting tips from *Reader's Digest*."

She arches a single, perfect eyebrow at me. "I beg your pardon?"

"Shuba was sneaking vitamin C out of Emily's bag too," I tell her. "After all, they really, *really* wanted to be the next Que . . . er . . . Monarch of the Tiles."

"And me?" Mark rubs his belly. "I've been having problems all weekend too."

I grin. "This one's just a guess, but . . . Ben has laxatives, and I don't think he minds sharing. Especially with people who annoy him. Deeply."

Mark lets out a string of expletives, and Puteri snickers.

"Honestly, you were one of my main suspects all weekend," I tell him, and he frowns.

"Me? Why?" I stare pointedly at him and he rubs his head sheepishly. "Okay, okay, I'm not oblivious. I get that I was an asshole in the past. And that I had some pretty bad anger issues . . ."

Puteri snorts, and I stifle a grin. "You might say that, yes."

"I know, okay? I wasn't a good person when I was with Trina, but when you're in that kind of situation . . ." He sighs.

"It's hard to see that without getting some distance from it, is all." He glances sidelong at me. "I'm sorry. And I'll do my best to make up for it."

"And I'll do my best to make him," Puteri adds cheerily.

Mark turns to her, eyebrows raised. "Does that mean you're going to say yes to me after all?"

"Say yes to what?" I look at Puteri, then at Mark, then back again. "What's going on?"

"I asked Puteri to be my girlfriend again," he says. "But she's keeping me hanging."

"You, my friend," Puteri says calmly, "are a work in much need of progress. And I need to know you're going to put in the effort required to change. Then, and only then, will I even consider getting into any kind of relationship with you again."

"Wise choice," I say, and Mark groans.

"Why would you encourage this?"

"You need to earn her trust," I point out. "And mine, to be honest."

"I know, I know." He subsides with a sigh. "I promise to keep trying, and please continue to call me out on my bullshit. Deal?"

"Deal." It's strange to feel this light, to smile this much. "Any other questions?"

"Just one." Mark pops a piece of gum in his mouth and shoots me a knowing look. "You have feelings for me, huh? Puppy dog eyes and all?"

Puteri rolls her eyes. "Insufferable," she mutters under her breath—though loud enough for us to hear.

I have to laugh. "Had," I say. "Past tense."

"Less points on a rack," he points out.

"But more accuracy in meaning."

"Nobody cares about meaning in Scrabble."

"I do."

Mark's phone beeps, and he takes a quick glance before standing up and grabbing his backpack. "I have to go. My dad's here." He envelops us both in huge hugs, one after the other, kisses Puteri on the forehead, then heads out the door. "I'll call you later, babe. Peace out."

"He's the only person I know who can say that unironically." Puteri shakes her head and smooths out her top, rumpled from Mark's show of affection. "What do you think is going to happen to her?"

"Yasmin?" She nods. "I don't know," I say honestly. "She got hit with that five-year ban for cheating. But besides that . . . everything else she did wasn't really a crime, was it? Posting some stuff on Instagram. She never really physically hurt anybody but herself. The grown-ups will just brush it off, call it a prank."

"And Emily?"

"Two years," I say. "She won't be allowed to play for two years."

"The amount of planning this all took . . ." Puteri shakes her head. In spite of herself, she almost looks impressed.

"Imagine where she'd be if she'd just . . . taken all that effort and put it into playing Scrabble." I smile weakly. "Anyway. My guess is Yasmin will just . . . disappear. Go somewhere else, start fresh."

"Stay off social media," Puteri adds. "If you think about it, this may be the best thing for her. Get away from all things Trina-related for a while. Like a detox. Maybe it'll get the poison out of her system."

I don't reply. I'm thinking about my last conversation with Yasmin, before they took her away to wait for her parents somewhere quiet, away from prying eyes and hungry ears. "Was it worth it, in the end?" I asked her.

"I don't know," she said simply. "I haven't figured it out yet." And somehow it made me sadder still, because somewhere in Yasmin I recognized shades of myself, the old Najwa, to whom Trina's opinion was the only thing that mattered. I remember my conversation with Puteri and think: *Love shouldn't feel like this.*

"I wish this had all turned out differently," I told her, and it seemed like such a paltry, sentimental thing to say, but I meant it. *I wish I had seen you, really seen you, Yasmin. I wish I could have stopped this.*

"It doesn't matter," she replied. "I won. You'll never be the Queen now. Even if you win, you'll always think back to this, and how I beat you. *I'll always have beaten you.*"

But was it worth it? I thought as they escorted her away. What does it mean to be Queen? Why does it matter? Maybe none of us deserved the crown after all. Maybe at the end of the day, it was always meant to be Trina's, another reminder that even in death, her shadow is long and inescapable.

Puteri sighs noisily, dragging me out of my memories. "I'll

probably regret asking, but: What are you thinking?"

"I'm thinking about braconids."

"I knew it. I knew I'd regret this."

I brace my elbows against the arms of my seat and steeple my fingers together. "Do you know what BRACONID means?"

Puteri shoots me a look. "Seriously, Najwa?"

"Okay, fine, silly question." I take a breath. "In 2016, Brett Smitheram beat Mark Nyman to win the World Scrabble Championships. He described Mark as being one of his Scrabble idols when he was growing up. They were friends. Can you imagine what that's like, watching a friend eclipse you, reach these amazing new heights, leaving you behind?" I pause to gather my thoughts and take in the expression of understanding dawning on Puteri's face. "Anyway, Brett won the game with the word BRACONID, a type of parasitic wasp that leeches on another creature and prospers at their expense."

"And Trina was the braconid in this situation?"

I shrug. "I guess that's what Yasmin thought."

Puteri reaches up to tuck a stray hair behind her ear. "Do you think Trina knew how Yasmin felt?"

"Maybe." I gaze out the window at the cars lining the driveway, waiting to take all those kids home. "But the braconids of the world don't always think about how their victims may feel."

"Don't tell me you feel sorry for her now. After everything she did to you! Everything she tried to do!"

I sigh. "I can't help it. There's something pathetic about the whole thing."

She's quiet for a moment, picking at the hem of her pale green T-shirt. "What happens now?"

"To who? You? Me? Mark?"

Even Puteri's shrug is graceful. "All of the above."

"I don't know," I answer honestly. "We do what we've always done. We take the racks we're dealt, and we keep making the next move."

A familiar car pulls up. The back window opens and I see Alina's face peering out, her eyes wide and searching, the smile that spreads all over it when she spots me.

"I gotta go," I say, standing up and gathering my things.

Puteri looks as unsure as I feel. How does one say good-bye in a situation like this? After the things we've said, the things we've done, the things we've been through? She settles for a casual "See you around," and I nod back.

"See you," I say.

As I walk away, my phone dings, and I scramble to get it out of my pocket.

It's an Instagram notification, and for a second my heart stops.

PU3.lilin wants to add you as a friend, it says. Puteri's familiar face looks up at me from the little circle by her username.

I smile. It only takes me a second to hit accept. I'll need to find a new word for her, but we've got time for that.

Then the glass doors slide open, and I'm swept up in the biggest, most comforting hug in the world.

"Did you get everything you need out of this?" Alina whispers in my ear.

"I think so," I say, smiling at her. "Now let's go." And we head toward the car, ready for the long journey home.

ACKNOWLEDGMENTS

My lifelong love of words has its roots in the books I was always surrounded with as a child, even before I ever learned to make out what the letters meant. For that, I must thank my parents, who always treated reading as a pleasure and privilege, not a duty or chore, and passed this on to us as we grew up.

Special shout-out to my brother, whose many weekend tournaments I often tagged along to watch, and who probably influenced my own decision to join the school Scrabble team, and to my two sisters, so they won't feel left out.

Many heartfelt thanks to my agent, Victoria Marini, who continues to champion my words even as she tells me to lay off on manifesting new projects online—one day I'll listen, I promise.

Deeba Zargarpur, editor, friend, and the one person besides my agent who has read every single one of my works prepublication—this book wouldn't be what it is without you. Thank you for shepherding me through the many, many rewrites and revisions. I'm so glad we finally made it. My gratitude also to the team at S&S who helped take my words and created this thing of beauty you hold in your hands: Dainese Santos, Sarah Creech, Hilary Zarycky, Emily Ritter, Katrina Groover, Chava Wolin, Shivani Anirood, Kendra Levin, Justin Chanda, Anne Zafian. And of course, to the brilliant Leonardo Santamaria, for this amazing cover illustration and bringing Najwa to life.

I truly appreciate Rozlan Mohd Noor for answering my many questions about police investigations despite never having met me, and Gina Yap for connecting us; Martin Teo for providing so much information about the local Scrabble scene; and Mayture Yap for her guidance on grief counseling and therapy.

Thank you to Molly, Becca, Mizah, Jaymee, May, Pat, Tariq, and so many other author friends who provided the support, advice, listening ears, friendship, nudges, and screams into the void I needed to make it through. If you don't see your name listed, please forgive me—I have been working on this book for four years and seven drafts, and am now half-dead.

And finally—as always—thank you to Malik and Maryam and Umar, just because. I love you.